W9-BZY-124

Ralph Compton: Return to Gila Bend

Carlton Stowers

THORNDIKE PRESS
A part of Gale, a Cengage Company

The Gunfighter Series
Thorndike Press, a part of Gale, a Cengage Company.

This is a work of fiction. Names, characters, places, and incidents either are the product of the author's imagination or are used fictitiously, and any resemblance to actual persons, living or dead, business establishments, events, or locales is entirely coincidental.

Thorndike Press® Large Print Western.
The text of this Large Print edition is unabridged.
Other aspects of the book may vary from the original edition.
Set in 16 pt. Plantin.

**LIBRARY OF CONGRESS CIP DATA ON FILE.
CATALOGUING IN PUBLICATION FOR THIS BOOK
IS AVAILABLE FROM THE LIBRARY OF CONGRESS.**

ISBN-13: 978-1-4328-8294-5 (hardcover alk. paper)

Published in 2021 by arrangement with Berkley, an imprint of Penguin Publishing Group, a division of Penguin Random House, LLC

Printed in Mexico
Print Number: 02 Print Year: 2021

Ralph Compton: Return to Gila Bend

THE IMMORTAL COWBOY

This is respectfully dedicated to the "American Cowboy." His was the saga sparked by the turmoil that followed the Civil War, and the passing of more than a century has by no means diminished the flame.

True, the old days and the old ways are but treasured memories, and the old trails have grown dim with the ravages of time, but the spirit of the cowboy lives on.

In my travels — to Texas, Oklahoma, Kansas, Nebraska, Colorado, Wyoming, New Mexico, and Arizona — I always find something that reminds me of the Old West. While I am walking these plains and mountains for the first time, there is this feeling that a part of me is eternal, that I have known these old trails before. I believe it is the undying spirit of the frontier calling me, through the mind's eye, to step back into time. What is the appeal of the Old West of the American frontier?

It has been epitomized by some as the dark and bloody period in American history. Its heroes — Crockett, Bowie, Hickok, Earp — have been reviled and criticized. Yet the Old West lives on, larger than life.

It has become a symbol of freedom, when there was always another mountain to climb and another river to cross; when a dispute between two men was settled not with expensive lawyers, but with fists, knives, or guns. Barbaric? Maybe. But some things never change. When the cowboy rode into the pages of American history, he left behind a legacy that lives within the hearts of us all.

— *Ralph Compton*

Prologue

During the time Lewis Taylor spent in the Texas State Prison, it had more than its share of infamous inmates.

There was Billy Wayne Alton, who was apparently as crazy as an outhouse rat when he chopped his family into pieces with the same ax he'd used to cut firewood just an hour or so earlier. He killed his grandma and grandpa, his parents, his wife, and a cousin who was visiting at the time. His bloody massacre finished, Alton put a couple of logs on the fire and went to bed without even washing the blood from his hands. He was still sleeping when the sheriff arrived.

A judge later ruled that he shouldn't be hanged because of some kind of brain damage he had suffered as a child. Instead, he was given a life sentence and spent twenty-four hours a day alone in his cell, carrying on lengthy conversations with his invisible dog, Max.

The McClellan brothers earned their fame robbing banks. When marshals arrested all four of them — Doc, Willie, Horace, and Cy — they were stunned at how the thieves flaunted their criminal success. Embedded in the concrete floors of their upscale ranch house were thousands of silver dollars. They all claimed they had no idea how the coins got there.

There were more cattle rustlers than you could shake a stick at, several men who had set fire to or dynamited everything from barns to barrooms, one who had a brief but lucrative career selling farms and ranchland he didn't own, and Mexican kidnappers who held the ten-year-old daughter of a wealthy cattleman hostage for forty-five days.

The most famous prisoner, however, was Kiowa war chief Satanta, the first Indian convicted of murder and sentenced to life in a Huntsville cell, eating gruel and spoiled meat and only dreaming of one more buffalo hunt or raid on a white man's settlement. It wasn't a life the proud Satanta could foresee for himself. So he faked an illness that earned him a visit to the prison's second-floor infirmary. Once there, he bolted to a window and launched himself through the glass to the prison yard below. He died on impact, breaking up a game of stickball that was in progress.

That event, which was written about in newspapers as far away as New York City, occurred on the same day Lewis Taylor was released back into the free world.

Taylor was not among the famous inmates. Neither was he guilty of the crime that had caused him to be there. As he had tried to explain to a judge who kept dozing off, he was in the San Antonio saloon celebrating his twentieth birthday when a fight broke out between drunken cowhands from two rival ranches.

It had quickly become a blur of cursing, breaking bottles, flailing fists, and wild gunshots. Taylor could only remember a chair hitting him in the back, knocking the wind out of him, and forcing him to his knees. His next recollection was of a boot to his face, breaking his nose and causing a deep gash just below one ear before he passed out.

When he regained consciousness, there was a Peacemaker in his right hand and a sheriff's deputy standing over him, saying he was under arrest. The bartender, he later learned, had been shot and seriously wounded.

The judge's eyes were closed, and he was snoring softly when Taylor pleaded that he'd never even owned a handgun, certainly not one as nice as that Peacemaker.

Nonetheless, he was convicted of attempted murder and sentenced to five years' hard labor.

Part One

Chapter One

Just a short walk from the Texas State Prison's front door was Dynamite Billy Wayne's Freedom Store, where released inmates, eager to resume a new life, could spend their paltry chain gang earnings and any cash they might have had in their pockets when taken into custody on anything from new clothing to one of the horses or mules waiting in a nearby corral. Himself a former inmate, Billy liked to brag to folks he was in the prison's inaugural class, a man who earned his living blowing open bank safes before becoming Texas State inmate no. 19. Now he ran a thriving business in which he bartered for every dime his customers had in their pockets. No one, he insisted, should return home without a new pair of britches, a clean shirt, and a decent-looking hat. If they could afford it, he also had boots in all sizes. In back, his wife offered haircuts and shaves.

If, after emerging from his changing tent in their new finery, they still had money to spend, he led them to the corral. If not, he gave them directions to the nearest town.

By the time Lewis was properly outfitted and groomed, he had just enough money left to buy a swaybacked mare that he hoped still had enough life in her to get him home to Gila Bend. He would have to ride bareback since his budget didn't allow for even a used saddle. The owner threw in a length of rope that could be fashioned into a harness.

Before leaving, Billy Wayne offered him a token good for one free beer at the Cowman's Bar, a gesture of kindness he extended to all paying customers. Lewis, wary of ever setting foot in a saloon again, declined.

Wayne reached into his vest pocket and pulled out a different-colored token. "Seeing as how you ain't inclined to imbibe, which I must say I admire, take this one down to Minnie's Café, and she'll serve you a free bowl of cornmeal mush that'll stick to your ribs better than anything you've had in a coon's age. For her sweet tea or lemonade, you'll be required to pay."

The mush was good and the glass of lemonade took the last few cents of his prison bankroll.

Lewis Taylor was dead broke, free, and ready to head home.

As he slowly made his way southward, feeling the warm breezes on his face, watching white, puffy clouds float past, Taylor felt new energy surging through his body. It was, however, the stars at night that provided him his greatest sense of being a free man.

Aware of his horse's age and limitations, he resisted the constant urge to hurry her along. Instead, they stopped often to drink from streams and springs and rest in the welcome shade of sprawling oak trees. When Taylor's stomach would begin to grumble, he found sweet wild grapes to satisfy his hunger.

Then, at night, he would lie in the grass, arms folded beneath his head, and stare at the night sky while his horse grazed nearby. He would fall asleep counting the stars that twinkled their welcome to freedom. He'd never seen anything more beautiful.

On the third day, he named his horse Dolly. "Can't carry on a proper conversation without you having a name," he said. "First thing we'll do once we get to the farm is see that you have your fill of oats, a good brushing, and plenty of rest."

It was late in the afternoon of that same day that he saw the lazy curl of chimney smoke in the distance.

"Let's go see if we can make us some new friends," Lewis said as he turned Dolly.

As he approached the small cabin, a hen and her chicks scurried from his path. A dog, roused from his nap, stood on the front porch, barking. He was soon joined by a bald, stoop-shouldered old man dressed in overalls and pointing a shotgun. "State your business," he called out.

"Name's Lewis Taylor, and I'm headed south, to home. Been traveling for a few days. I saw your farm here and was wondering if you might have chores a fellow could do in exchange for a meal."

The shotgun was still pointed in his direction when a woman appeared on the porch and began gently petting the dog, urging him to stop barking.

"I'm known as Preacher Goolsby, and this is my wife, Nina. I'll thank you to remain on your horse until we've done a bit more talking. You carrying a firearm or any other kind of weapon?"

"No, sir."

Goolsby turned to his wife. "I've seen his type before," he said. "You can tell it in his eyes and by the fact he's wearing store-bought clothes. That and the fact no self-respecting traveler would be riding bareback on a horse as broke down as that one appears to be."

He turned to Taylor. "Just got out of prison, I'm guessing."

"Yes, sir."

"You here to knock us in the head and steal our belongings?"

"No, sir."

"Let him get down and stretch his legs," Nina said. "He seems a young man who's repented his sins."

Her husband stared at Lewis for several seconds. "Would that be the case?"

"I did no crime, and I mean you folks no harm."

Goolsby slowly lowered the shotgun. "Come on up and sit on the porch. My wife will fetch you something to wet your whistle while we have us a talk." He tried with little success to hide the fact he was pleased to have company. "You're coming from up at Huntsville, right? Back in the day when I was traveling all over, preaching the Word, I once visited the convicts there. Wasn't a one of them interested in salvation. All they wanted was to get out and return to their evil ways."

"All I'm wanting," Lewis said, "is to get home to Gila Bend, Texas, and resume living my life."

Goolsby stopped short of asking why he'd been in prison. "Let's us take your horse out to the barn and get her fed and watered."

The farm seemed to be on its last leg. As they made the short walk, Taylor could see fences that needed mending, a garden that obviously hadn't been weeded in some time, and the last rays of sunlight streaming into the barn from holes in the roof.

The preacher read his mind. "I'm getting too dang old to properly tend the place," he said. "I had help from my boy before he went off to fight in the war. Got himself killed just a week before the surrender. You serve the Confederacy?"

"Yes. Some of my friends died. Guess I was lucky."

By the time Nina called them to supper, they'd still not discussed any work he could do to earn the meal. She'd fried chicken and boiled collard greens. A loaf of bread, still hot, sat in the center of the small kitchen table.

"You can sleep in the barn tonight," Goolsby said later as his wife cleared the dishes. "If you were serious about earning your keep, maybe you can stay on for a few days. Think about it, and we can discuss it further in the morning.

"Meanwhile, we have us Bible reading every evening before we go to bed, and you're welcome to join in."

"I appreciate the offer," Taylor said, "but I'm feeling a bit tired and would like to get on out to the barn, if you don't mind." He tipped his hat to Mrs. Goolsby. "That was a mighty tasty supper, ma'am."

She smiled. "God bless you, young man. Sleep well."

He had already done the milking and was mucking out one of the stalls when Goolsby entered the barn. He was limping and holding two large cups. "Getting harder to get up and going every day," he said. "Since you already done my milking, you've earned yourself some coffee. If you're wanting milk in it, I'm sure my old cow will gladly oblige."

Taylor put away his rake and sat on a bench with Preacher. "I thought on it last night, and here's an offer I'd like to make, if you're interested," Goolsby said. "Me and the wife have been considering putting the place up for sale, but obviously it needs some work before it might interest a buyer.

"You've probably got ants in your pants,

wanting to get home as quick as possible. I can understand that. But if you would be willing to stay on for a few days, working on the fences, patching the roof, things of that nature, I can offer you a modest wage, a place to sleep, and three meals a day. Having already sampled Nina's cooking, I expect you'll consider that the most attractive part of my offer."

Lewis smiled. Getting home was all he had thought about since walking out the prison gate. But the idea of earning a few dollars by working outdoors with no guard standing nearby, constantly cursing him, was appealing.

He extended his hand and accepted Goolsby's offer.

The "few days" stretched into a week, then two, as he worked sunup to sundown, digging postholes, stretching barbed wire, patching the roof of the barn, and clearing weeds from Mrs. Goolsby's garden. He trimmed dead limbs from her blooming pear trees and helped her sturdy the legs on her table and chairs, cleaned the ashes from her stove, and cut firewood.

Each morning, as soon as he'd done the milking, he would release Dolly into the pasture, where she spent the day lazily grazing alongside Goolsby's two mules.

"You're getting some color back in your cheeks," Nina said one morning as he finished breakfast. "You've done fine work for Mr. Goolsby, which I greatly appreciate, but I expect it's near time you get on with your journey. Home's waiting."

"I've been thinking the same thing," Taylor said. That evening, he told Preacher that he'd be leaving the following day.

"Before we start our Bible reading," Goolsby said, "I'd like you to accompany me out to the barn for a minute."

Carrying a lantern, he led Lewis to the door of the small tack room. "Door sticks," he said, "so I'll need you to muscle it open for me."

As Preacher's lantern lit the small area, Lewis saw a saddle astride a sawhorse. "You'll need to soap it good since it hasn't been used in some time," Goolsby said. "It belonged to my boy, God bless his soul. I'd like for you to have it. There's a blanket and halter in here somewhere. And saddlebags . . ."

"I can't . . ."

"Hush up. Of course you can. You should know passing it along was my wife's idea. Like she told me the other day, it wouldn't be right for you to make your return home riding bareback."

As he spoke, Preacher was bent over, rummaging through a dust-coated footlocker. Finally, he stood, holding a pair of boots. "You look to be about the same size as my boy," he said. "Try these on."

As his visitor slipped on the boots, Goolsby said, "My son, he would be about same age as you now." Even in the semi-darkness, the sadness in his eyes was visible.

Late into the night, Lewis carefully rubbed soap onto the leather, wiped it away, then repeated the process.

By daybreak he had saddled Dolly, done his final milking, and was ready to be on his way. Nina had filled his saddlebags with corn bread, cakes, and sandwiches. "I also put some matches in a little pouch for campfires," she said, "and Mr. Goolsby found you a canteen, which I filled with hot coffee."

Preacher handed him a twenty-dollar gold piece. "Wish it could be more," he said. "You done fine work and were good company."

Lewis shook his hand and hugged Nina.

"If you're ever back this way," Goolsby said, "it's not likely we'll be here. If we have success selling, we'll probably be moving to one of those boardinghouses filled with old folks. Maybe I can even do a little preaching there if anybody's still got their hearing and good sense."

Nina's eyes teared. "We're gonna miss you, young man," she said. "God be with you. And travel safe. If there's ever anything we can do for you, just let us know."

The spire of the Blessed Redeemer Church appeared in the distance, signaling that Gila Bend was only a short ride away. Lewis resisted the urge to nudge Dolly into a lope, instead using the final stage of his journey to contemplate what awaited him. Five years was a long time to be away, and he struggled to even see his father's face in his mind, to recall the landscape of the farm and the town, to remember the names of some of those he'd once called friends.

The only clear image he had, the one that had kept him company in his absence, was of a girl in a gingham dress, her golden hair flowing across her shoulders, her blue eyes sparkling, and her gentle laughter like sweet music. No amount of hard labor, unfair treatment, or time could make one forget a girl like Darla Winslow.

When he reached the entrance to the farm, he stopped to familiarize himself with the place where he'd grown up. The house and barn looked well kept, and the pens were sturdy. Tall stalks of corn waved from the field, and the live oak under which his mother had been buried when he was only a child had grown considerably. Nearby a rooster crowed and a dog barked.

As he sat, letting the familiar sights and smells return, the dog slowly came in his direction, cautiously at first, then at a run. Whisper, the German shepherd Lewis had raised from a pup, was glad to see him.

He was the only one.

Axel Taylor didn't bother to get up from his chair as Lewis made his way onto the porch. "Wasn't expecting company today," he said before taking a final sip of his coffee. His hair was white, so was the stubble of beard that did little to hide the wrinkles on his face. No doubt up since sunrise, he already looked tired.

"Good to see you, Pa."

There was a long silence before a reply. "I see they finally let you out." He looked toward Dolly, who was nibbling on a nearby patch of grass. "Where'd you get that sorry excuse for a horse? You ought to take her down to the barn and see she gets fed. That or put her out of her misery."

Whisper's tail lazily wagged as Lewis scratched behind his ears. "Place looks good. On the way home, I was thinking about all the things I could do to give you a hand now that I'm back," Lewis said, "but you seem to have everything in fine shape."

"Don't need much help," Axel replied. "When I do, I call on one of the Menendez boys and pay them for daywork."

The stern look on his father's face had not changed since he'd seen his son ride into the yard. The frigid reaction to his arrival puzzled Lewis. "Something wrong, Pa?"

The response came painfully slow and measured, as if rehearsed time and time again over the lost years.

"I've been dreading this day for the longest," the elder Taylor said. "The honest-to-God truth, boy, is you ain't welcome here."

Chapter Two

His father's blunt statement, lacking further explanation or discussion, stunned Lewis. The last time they had spoken was a few days before the trial, and Axel Taylor had been supportive and believed Lewis when he had insisted he was innocent. Prior to his incarceration, their relationship had been good. As a single father, Axel had been strict but loving, proud of his boy's work ethic, proud of his excelling in reading and writing in school, proud of him when he had joined the Confederacy, and proud when he spoke of how one day the family farm would be passed along to his son.

And now there was a cold, hard edge to his voice when he said, "You can bed down in the barn for the night, but I'll thank you to be on your way come morning." It was the worst pain Lewis had felt since the day he was marched to his prison cell.

"I'm done talking," his father said when

Lewis asked for some reason, something that would help him understand the stunning dismissal. Axel simply turned and walked into the house, closing the door behind him, leaving his only kin speechless and alone.

That night, sleep evaded Lewis. The cool breeze that always came on spring nights did little to ease the knot in his stomach and the overwhelming sadness that gripped him. Lying in the darkness, with the only sound Dolly's occasional movement, he felt it slowly turn to anger, then to concern for what he would do when the new day arrived.

Sometime during the night, Whisper entered the barn and quietly lay beside him, resting his head on Lewis's chest.

As the sky turned from black to gray, he heard faint movement outside. He got to his feet, brushed straw from his clothes, and set about saddling his horse. In the rafters, pigeons began cooing softly.

Walking Dolly from the barn, he saw a bandanna on the ground in the doorway. It was wrapped around a half dozen biscuits and an envelope. Inside were fifty dollars and a note that read, "Start-up money I been saving for you."

Axel Taylor was nowhere in sight.

■ ■ ■ ■

Gila Bend had changed considerably since Lewis had last been there. With nothing to do and nowhere specific to go, he'd ridden into town to see if he might find a friendly face. The few people he did pass seemed to view him as a panhandling stranger. They put their heads down and kept walking.

Several of the main street's businesses he remembered from times past were shuttered and closed. The feedstore had moved to a new location, the mercantile apparently had a new owner, and a fire had put the little women's dress shop out of business. The combination saloon and café, conveniently located next to the jail, had a new name over the entrance. It was now called the Captain's Bar and Good Eats.

Only the bank and the livery at the end of town looked the same. With time on his hands, Lewis pointed Dolly in the direction of an elderly man standing at an anvil, pounding away at a bent wagon axle. He tried to recall the blacksmith's name but it wouldn't come to him. Neither did the blacksmith seem to recognize Taylor.

"Been traveling and was hoping to get new shoes for my horse," he said. "Thought this early of a morning I might catch you before you got too busy."

The blacksmith eyed Dolly with no hint of admiration. "I'd be lying if I didn't say you're likely wasting your money," he said, "but I got the time if that's what you're wanting. I'll even give her a good brushing, which she appears needing, free of charge." He took the reins and rubbed the horse's nose. "Name's Ezra Zale. Folks call me Ezzie. You just passing through?"

"Seems so," Lewis said as he dismounted.

"You're welcome to sit in the shade and wait, or they're serving breakfast down at the café. Still a bit early for strong drink, though."

Taylor had no appetite, but coffee sounded good.

The café was full of customers talking in muted voices of second spring plantings, the need for rain, and new calves and lambs that had been recently born. There was none of the boisterous laughter one would expect from early-morning coffee drinkers. Lewis didn't see a single familiar face as he made his way to a vacant table in the back corner of the room.

The waitress took his order without ever raising her head to look him in the eye.

Lost in troubling thoughts, he was staring into his coffee cup when he became aware of a figure standing over him.

"Lewis? Lewis Taylor, that you?"

He looked up into the freckled face of his old friend Luke Bradley. "That's me," he said, smiling for the first time since he'd arrived.

"Good to see you. How long you been home?" Bradley took a chair across from him. "My God, how long's it been?"

"I been back a day . . . and, as I'm sure you know, it's been five years."

Bradley blushed and was thankful that the waitress returned to ask if he wanted a bowl of grits and biscuits with his eggs. She refilled Lewis's cup, then again hurried away.

The two men had known each other since boyhood, sitting next to each other in class, attending Sunday school together, and fishing and skinny-dipping on weekends. They had smoked their first cigarette together as ten-year-olds, sharing the delicious sin in a tree house they had built in the woods behind the Bradley place. As they got older, they hunted for rabbit and squirrels, had long talks about girls, and discussed what they would achieve in adulthood. Luke saw himself as a famous writer one day, maybe living in New York. Lewis would be satisfied to stay in Gila Bend, being a farmer like his dad.

For a time, they had lost track of each other while they both fought for the South. Then there were those five years when Lewis was serving time.

"Tell me about what you're up to these days," Taylor said in an attempt to avoid discussion of anything about himself.

"You recall back in high school when I had a part-time job helping old man Reynolds down at the paper? He passed. Throat cancer. With help from Dad and the bank, I bought the *Sentinel.* You're now looking at the owner and editor, chronicler of everything important that goes on in town, from births to weddings to church socials. My biggest scoops so far have been the stories I wrote on the ladies' shop burning down and the birth of a goat with two heads out on the Caussey farm last spring. Oh, and there was the Fourth of July picnic when the Benton brothers got into a drunken fight and wrecked the bandstand and turned over Miss Chalmers's canned goods table."

Lewis smiled. "And you and Sue Ellen?"

Bradley grinned and told him he had married the girl he'd begun courting in sixth grade. "Got me a two-year-old son we call Little Luke."

Though Lewis was focused on their conversation, Bradley noticed that the tables near them had cleared, some with plates and coffee cups not yet emptied. "If you've got some time, maybe you would like to walk over to my office and see what a weekly newspaper's all about. Big news is probably already pouring in."

The *Sentinel* office wasn't much, just a small two-room building hidden away on a side street. It was badly in need of paint, and the sign above the entrance — GILA BEND WEEKLY SENTINEL, LUKE BRADLEY, OWNER & EDITOR — was barely hanging. The room where Bradley worked was piled with the debris of news gathering — books, mail, stacks of paper, a stained coffee cup, and the same typewriter the previous owner had used. In the back was the hand-cranked press that spat out the ten-page newspaper every Thursday evening.

The place was airless and smelled of ink and old coffee grounds. There was no sign that Bradley was getting rich.

He pointed Lewis to a chair piled with old editions of the paper as he went to a small filing cabinet. Pulling out a bottle of whiskey and two Mason jars, he said, "It's a bit early, but I think it's necessary to have us a toast to your return." He poured into the jars, then lifted one. "Welcome home, Lewis Taylor."

They sat, sipping their drinks, before Luke broke the silence. "Lewis, never for a minute did I ever believe you to be guilty of that shooting over in San Antonio. It just wasn't in your nature. If I remember right, you used to feel bad even when we shot squirrels out at your farm.

"I'm sorry for what's been done to your reputation and the years you had taken away."

Lewis nodded. "I appreciate that. Just wish some other folks felt the same."

"So tell me your plans."

"Got none at the moment. Speaking with Pa yesterday, he made it clear he's done with me. He invited me to take my leave almost before I could get off my horse. Said he gets what help he needs from the Menendez boys these days."

Luke shook his head and fell silent for a moment. "You got a place to stay?"

"Haven't thought that far ahead."

Bradley didn't ask about money, assuming his friend had little, if any. "For the time being," he said, "I've got an idea that might suit your needs. Out back, I've got a storage shed that's full of useless junk, mostly what Mr. Reynolds left behind. With a little cleaning, it could be made into a place where you could hang your hat and rest your head. You're welcome to it.

"Then, once you're settled, we can start asking around to see who might need some work done."

"I wouldn't feel right about . . ."

"Let's call you my night watchman. You keep an eye on the place and in exchange you get free board. Just temporary until you get yourself settled."

With no other option available, Taylor reluctantly agreed. "Just for a while," he said. "I appreciate it."

"Hey, seeing you back in town has brightened my day," Luke said as his friend rose to leave.

"My horse is being tended to down at the livery," he said. "I'd better go see about her. Then, if it's convenient, I'll give your shed a look and see what I can do about cleaning it up."

Bradley stood as Lewis put on his hat. "One thing you haven't asked about," he said. "Darla. She got married a while back, Lewis."

Taylor's stomach again tightened, and he stared at the floor. His mind suddenly filled with quick memories of picnics and barn dances, of quiet evenings sitting in her porch swing, the moonlight reflecting in her eyes. And he could hear her musical laughter.

Finally, he nodded but said nothing as he left Luke's office.

Old man Reynolds had been a pack rat. Amidst all the trash and keepsakes from his lifelong career were a cot he'd once used when working late nights at the *Sentinel,* a small storage chest, and a lantern that needed only a new wick to be returned to working order.

After negotiating an arrangement with the livery owner, Ezzie, to muck stalls and feed his livestock, he had agreed to board Dolly temporarily. By late afternoon, Taylor had used the broom, soapy water, and cleaning rags provided to him by Luke to clean the shed.

It wasn't fancy, but it sure beat a prison cell.

It was nearing sundown when Sue Ellen Bradley arrived. She was carrying a quilt and a pillow under one arm and a basket filled with fruit and sandwiches in the other. She put them down and threw her arms around Lewis's neck. "I see you haven't put on weight like some newspaper editor I know," she said. They both laughed.

She inspected his cleanup job and gave her approval. They talked for a while, covering much the same ground he and her husband had earlier in the day.

"I hear Darla got married," he finally said, the words coming from his mouth dry and forced.

Sue Ellen nodded. "To a man named Archer Ringewald. Captain Archer Ringewald, if you please."

"I hope she's happy."

"Don't see how she could be, living with that man."

"You don't like him?"

"Nobody does, believe me." Turning to go, she invited Taylor over for supper one night soon. "You need to meet Little Luke," she said as she walked away.

For a moment, she stopped and looked back at him. "You know, she waited for you, Lewis. For the longest time . . . and never heard so much as a word from you."

Taylor was puzzled by what she said. He had written Darla on numerous occasions.

CHAPTER THREE

As evening approached, Lewis was restless, tired but still with no urge to sleep. He ate one of Sue Ellen's sandwiches, then decided a walk might help clear his head of the things that had occurred during the past couple of days.

The *Sentinel* office was closed and dark; Luke by now was at home with his wife and son. Lewis glanced at the sign over the door and reminded himself to put it back on its hinges tomorrow. As he made his way toward the main street, the only lights he saw came from the saloon. Out front, only two horses stood patiently at the hitching rail. As he neared, he heard no clinking of glasses, no loud laughter or arguing over whose poker hand was the winner. He could remember a time when rowdy behavior and a full house of thirsty cowboys and farm-hands were a nightly tradition.

As he walked past the doorway, he saw

Ezzie Zale standing on the sidewalk, lighting his pipe. He nodded in Lewis's direction.

"Thought I'd come down and check on my horse before calling it a night," Taylor said.

Ezzie puffed until a ring of smoke circled above his head. "I'll walk with you. I just came for my nightly shot of whiskey before settling in. Helps a man my age to sleep."

Lewis peeked inside. There were only a half dozen customers he could see, all silently slumped over their drinks. "Looks like a pretty slow night," he said.

"Always is these days," the blacksmith said, "except on Saturday nights when the Ringewald hands come to town. I'd advise you to stay clear of the place then." As they slowly walked toward the livery, he offered no further explanation.

Even in the semidarkness, Taylor could see the sheen of Dolly's coat. She briefly lifted her head as if to greet her owner.

"Seen her better days, ain't she?" Zale said.

"I figure a lot of us have."

"I'm sorry for my remarks about your horse earlier today. Man's got no right to pass that kind of judgment. You treat her kindly and don't ride her too hard, she'll serve you well for some time to come. That's how it is with us old folks, man and beast." Swinging his lantern away from the stall, he said, "Let's let her get some rest. Tomorrow she'll be raring for some exercise in her new shoes."

When they reached the doorway of the barn, Ezzie stopped. "I got to thinking after we spoke earlier," he said, "and it finally came to me. I thought you had a familiar look when I first saw you. You're Axel Taylor's boy, ain't you?"

"Yes, I am. Name's Lewis."

Zale extended his hand and nodded. "I remember you when you was just a pup. You boys running all over town, cutting up and having your fun."

"Long time ago," Lewis said. He paused for a moment, then said, "What was it you meant back at the saloon?"

"Just that things change. The town ain't like it was before you left," Ezzie said. "The place you likely recall was lively and full of happy, friendly folks. These days, it's got a real sadness about it."

"Why's that?"

"Stay around long enough and you'll see." The old man abruptly changed the conversation. "I'll expect you here early morning to tend your chores," he said before turning away.

As Lewis walked back to the *Sentinel,* he pondered what Ezzie had said. Since his return, he had seen few smiling faces, not from his father, not on the streets or in the café. Even Luke Bradley's good nature had seemed strained, as if he was hiding some dark truth.

The following morning, the sun wasn't even up by the time he'd cleaned the stalls and fed buckets of oats to Dolly and the two mules waiting in the corral out back. Zale appeared, scratching his beard and yawning. "Mighty early," he said. "You got way more get up and go than me." He handed Lewis a cup of coffee. "You prefer it with sugar and cream, you'll have to go down to the café."

"This is fine," Taylor said. "I'm thinking about me and Dolly taking a ride," Taylor said. "Does a man named B. J. Dixon still live on the little farm out near Timber Creek?"

"The cripple fellow, you mean? Lost a leg in that Sabine Pass battle where a handful of Confederates held off a hundred or more Union soldiers?"

Taylor nodded.

"Don't see him around much, but that's where you'll most likely find him. He a friend of yours?"

"That's what I want to find out."

At first glance, the farm appeared deserted. There was no livestock to be seen, and the field where maize once grew was fallow. Half the trees in the orchard were dead while the remainder appeared to be dying. The open gate to what was once a hogpen was swinging in the breeze.

The only signs of life were a milk goat tethered in the shade of an elm tree, a small vegetable garden, and a horse and a mule grazing down in the pasture. A weathered old wagon was parked at the entrance of a barn that looked as if it might topple in the next high wind. A rooster and several laying hens scurried from Lewis's path.

He rode to the front of the house and remained in the saddle, waiting to see if someone might step out onto the porch. Finally, he called out, "I've come looking for B. J. Dixon."

Finally, a slightly stooped lady, a bandanna covering most of her gray hair, appeared at the door. She shaded her eyes with her hands and squinted in the direction of the visitor. "My seeing isn't so good," she said, "so you'll have to state your name."

"I'm Lewis Taylor, a friend of B. J.'s from

back in the day."

A smile crossed her face. "My stars," she said, "little Lewis Taylor. You've grown a mile since I last saw you."

"Is B. J. here?"

"He's inside, putting on his britches. Sleeps late most days now. I'll fetch him."

Lewis dismounted and stood on the porch steps until the screen door swung open and a man with a tangled beard and coal black hair down to his shoulders filled the doorway. He was leaning on a crutch, his right pants leg empty from the knee down.

"Lewis. My God. If you've come looking to borrow money or run a footrace, you've got the wrong place," B. J. said. It was good to see he hadn't lost his sense of humor. "Come in this house. Sorry for the look of the place, but I haven't been able to get much done of late."

He led the way into the living room, where his mother was busily clearing a place for them to sit. "You are indeed a sight for sore eyes," Dixon said as he shook Lewis's hand, then propped his crutch on the arm of a chair. "Can't recall the last time I saw you."

"The day we signed up with the Confederates, down at the courthouse, if I remember correctly."

"I guess so. Been a good while. Last I

heard of you, you were . . ."

"In prison," Lewis said, finishing the sentence for him. "Just got out."

"Well, I'm proud to hear it and mighty glad you're back." He asked neither questions about the crime that had put Taylor behind bars nor the conditions he had dealt with during the past five years.

"I've just come to see how you're doing," Taylor said.

"Getting by. Pa passed last winter after coming down with pneumonia, so it's just me and Ma now. She's getting a little frail, so I mostly just take care of her as best I can." He laughed. "We're quite a pair, ain't we?"

The scene was a far cry from the carefree days of their youth when B. J. and Luke Bradley had been inseparable pals, then welcomed Lewis into their group. Their mothers had been young and pretty and always urged them to stay out of trouble and be home by dark. The Three Musketeers, they had called themselves.

"I'm thinking about selling the place," B. J. said. "Before Pa died, he managed to keep everything going without much help from me. Frankly, I think all the hard work contributed to his early passing. But there's just no way I can do the things I once could.

I tried for a time, but kept falling on my butt. Ever try climbing a ladder with one leg? Or plowing behind a stubborn mule?

"It's good Pa had the place paid for before he died, lest we'd be kicked off by now. I hear it's happening to a lot of folks around here. Fall behind on your lease even a payment, and the bank takes away your property without so much as a 'sorry' or 'thank you kindly.' "

"That happening to a lot of farmers?"

"The Beasleys have done left. Same with the Crowders and the Jeffersons. I don't get to town much, but last I heard, the Findleys were next. Like I said, I'm glad the note on this place is free and clear and we've got us a buyer interested."

"Who are you going to sell to?"

"A rich fellow name of Ringewald. His offer's not much, but it's the only one we're likely to get."

For the second time in as many days, Taylor had heard the name. And on neither occasion had it been spoken fondly.

Lewis stood and walked to the front door, looking out toward the barn. Just behind it was the unplowed field. He could see the weeds that were choking the garden. The pens were all empty.

"I take it that if you had your druthers,

you would prefer not selling," Lewis said. Returning to his chair, he confided the unexplainable reception he had received from his father upon his return. "I got little to do and nowhere to be. How about if I see what I can do to get things fixed up? Do some repairs and planting and fence mending. Not like I haven't done it before."

B. J. laughed. "You're joking."

"Nope. Think on it. See how your ma feels about it."

"Lewis, I got no money to pay anybody for . . ."

Mrs. Dixon had entered the room, carrying a pitcher of sweet tea. She had overheard their conversation. "I can make lots of pear pies to pay for your help," she said as she looked at Lewis. "It's my recollection you favored my pies back in your younger days. Could barely wait for them to cool."

Lewis nodded. "That I did. Seems to me a pie once a week would be fair enough payment."

Mrs. Dixon put her pitcher on a table and hugged Taylor.

B. J. started gleefully pounding the tip of his crutch against the floor. "It'll be my pleasure to tell that Ringewald fellow I've got no interest in his offer," he said.

■ ■ ■ ■

Soon, Lewis had settled into a daily routine. Before daylight, he would tend to his chores at the livery, drink coffee with Ezzie, then ride out to the farm. Daisy Dixon would have breakfast ready when he arrived, scurrying about her kitchen, insisting he wasn't to start work on an empty stomach. B. J. began rising earlier to greet him and chat briefly before Lewis pulled on work gloves and bragged on Mrs. Dixon's eggs and biscuits. He stopped short of offering praise for the glass of goat's milk she served him.

With some of his limited funds, Taylor had visited the Gila Bend feedstore and bought seed and a sack of oats for B. J.'s horse. He spent the mornings plowing and the afternoons repairing fences and weeding the garden. Before leaving, he always chopped wood and stacked it on the porch.

The work was satisfying despite the fact that spring was quickly giving way to summer temperatures. On days when the heat was unrelenting, he would take a break and ride Dolly down to the creek, strip naked, and dive into the cool, rushing water.

He was returning one afternoon to begin trimming the dead branches from the orchard when he saw three horses headed toward the house. B. J. was standing on the porch, awaiting their arrival.

Lewis slowed his pace but got close enough to hear snatches of the conversation and get a look at the visitors. One, a big man with broad shoulders and a pearl-handled pistol on his hip, wore a white Stetson and was dressed more like a businessman. He sat erect in the saddle, astride the finest-looking Palomino Lewis had ever seen. Those with him appeared to be ranch hands, their hats dusty and their boots scuffed. They, too, were armed.

The man in the Stetson climbed the porch steps and shook B. J.'s hand while the others stayed on their horses. A brief conversation quickly turned loud and unfriendly; then the visitor abruptly turned and returned to his horse. It sounded as if he was cursing. As the men rode away, their leader reined the Palomino to a stop and looked toward the barn, where Taylor was standing. He nodded slightly and appeared to grin, then rode on.

"What was that about?" Lewis said as he approached an obviously shaken B. J.

"Man came to buy the place. Brought the money with him. He was highly upset when

I informed him the farm was no longer for sale."

"What did he say?"

"That he would be back."

"I can guess his name," Lewis said.

"Yep, that was Captain Archer Ringewald himself, a man with no use for anybody who tells him no."

Chapter Four

The fire that destroyed the Dixons' barn a few nights later caused no great loss. Actually, all it did was free Lewis from the task of attempting to replace enough of its rotting timbers to make it safe and usable again.

Its charred remains were still smoldering when he arrived, and there was a lingering odor of coal oil in the air.

B. J. was standing in the yard, his eyes, red from the smoke and loss of sleep, surveying the damage. "Only thing that really angers me is that it so upset Ma. She woke in the middle of the night, screaming. Some neighbors rode over to sit with her when they saw the blaze. Just now got her settled down."

He rolled his eyes. "He said he'd be back. Just didn't figure on it being this soon."

"Want me to ride in and speak with the sheriff?" Lewis asked.

B. J. laughed. "Wouldn't surprise me to learn he was the one set the fire."

By the time they returned to the house, the neighbors had left, promising to come back and help with the cleanup once the embers cooled. B. J.'s mother was sitting at the kitchen table, an open Bible in her lap. "I was just looking for an answer," she said.

"Answer to what?" B. J. said.

"To what makes a man so evil as to do something like this to folks."

Her son was pouring coffee when he answered, "Greed, Ma. Nothing but pure blackhearted greed."

The day passed slowly for Taylor. Repeatedly, he would stop whatever he was doing to stare at the blackened remains of the barn, feeling a touch of the sadness Ezzie Zale had spoken of. Something bad was happening to the place he'd called home.

It was Friday, and Luke and Sue Ellen had invited him for supper. Lacking Mrs. Dixon's faith in the Good Book, he hoped they could provide some answers.

"It's more than just a land grab," Luke said after they had finished Sue Ellen's baked chicken, roasted potatoes, and turnip greens. He had put Little Luke to bed, the youngster tired from an hour's play with Lewis and listening to a story read by his father. "He's attempting to buy up everything in sight, seems to want to own the whole town as well as all the land around it."

"For what reason?"

"Just because he can, I guess. The way I hear it, he's already got more money than God."

"Who is he? I don't recall ever hearing the name Ringewald before."

"He came here a few years after the war ended, from somewhere back East, and started buying. I've got no idea where his money came from. Rich daddy, most likely. Anyway, before too long, he had the biggest spread and the most cattle in the county.

"I've got to admit, a lot of folks around here, me included, admired him and his success at first. In time, most people were even able to forgive the fact he fought for the Union."

"That's where the title 'captain' comes from, I suppose."

"Yes, and he's proud of it."

Luke carefully avoided mention of Ringewald's marriage to Darla. "I'm not saying he was ever a friendly sort, but what caused him to fall from the town's grace was his purchase of the bank. Suddenly, it started foreclosing on small properties that weren't anywhere near his ranch, running good folks who couldn't pay out of their homes. If you wanted a loan, you had to be prepared to pay impossible interest rates.

"Then, next thing you know, he's buying businesses in town, like the saloon and café, and the mercantile. Owners who couldn't keep up with their loan payments were foreclosed on. Others, he bought out for half what their businesses were worth. People began hating him, and he seemed to find it all amusing.

"Between you and me, I'm wondering if the man has his senses. Why would he want a little shop that sells dry goods and dresses to ladies so bad that when he couldn't convince the owner to sell, he had it burned to the ground?"

"You know for a fact he did that?"

"I couldn't prove it, but there's little doubt. Not him in person, of course. He's got some men on his payroll who cause folks to stay indoors when they come to town. 'Bad' isn't the word."

"Why doesn't the sheriff do something?" Lewis asked.

"He's scared, like everyone else. And I think maybe he's getting his palm greased.

He's got a few acres a mile or so outside of town, and the number of cattle grazing on it seems to keep growing and growing.

"Only man in town who's stood up to Ringewald is your friend Ezzie down at the livery. He's too ornery and set in his ways to be scared of anybody."

Sue Ellen returned with a pitcher of sweet tea, and the conversation ended. "In your honor," she said to Lewis, "I even baked a chocolate cake. Not a contest prizewinner, mind you, but Little Luke found it to his liking. So I'll thank you to keep it to yourself if it doesn't suit you."

The mood lightened as they sat, recalling the happy days of their youth. There was considerable laughter.

Finally, during a moment of silence, Luke asked about B. J. "I feel bad that I haven't seen him since his daddy's funeral. I need to get out to the farm and catch up."

"And maybe write a story for the *Sentinel* about somebody burning down his barn in the middle of the night," Lewis said.

With that, the mood again changed. Sorry to have made the suggestion, he soon excused himself, thanking Sue Ellen for the meal and asking that they tell Little Luke he said goodbye.

As he walked back to his storage room, he

thought about what he'd heard. There was little doubt that the tyranny of this man Ringewald had everyone scared. Including Luke Bradley.

He had been sleeping restlessly when he suddenly sat up in his cot. Even with the window open, he was bathed in sweat. What if the surprise reaction from his father upon his return had had something to do with pressure he was receiving about the family farm? Was it paid for, or was the bank still the co-owner?

Even if unwelcome, he would have to make another visit to his father.

As he'd anticipated, Axel Taylor wasn't happy to see him. He was carrying an armload of wood into the kitchen when a knock came at the door.

"Pa, it's me. We need to talk," Lewis called out.

Standing in the doorway, Axel said, "Thought we already did." The coldness remained in his gravelly voice. "I'm kinda busy right now."

"You hear about B. J. Dixon's barn getting burned down?" Lewis thought he saw a look of concern cross his father's face. "A fellow named Ringewald visited him, offering to buy his place. And when B. J. turned him down, a fire started a couple of nights later. You know this man Ringewald?"

Axel didn't respond. Instead, he moved from the doorway. "Long as you're here, you might as well come on in and have some coffee. I just made it."

As they sat at the kitchen table, Lewis told of what he had recently learned about things that were taking place in Gila Bend. "Not the same town I remember," he said. "Have you been asked to sell the place?"

"That's none of your business."

"I think it is. I was raised here. You're my pa, and my ma's buried right out there. That might not give me ownership, but it makes this place part of me whether you like it or not. Just answer my question, and if you've not been threatened by Captain Ringewald, you'll get no further bother from me."

His father went to the stove for a biscuit before answering. "Reason I ran you off when you came home," he said, "was for your own good. To keep you safe."

"From what?"

"There's folks who don't want you back in Gila Bend. Folks who have suggested harm might come to both of us if you settle back here. You got enemies, boy. Enemies you don't even know about."

Lewis felt anger beginning to boil inside.

He didn't need to ask who the enemies were. Or the reason he was unwelcome.

"Best advice I can offer," his father said, "is for you to stay clear of this place. And of that gal you were once so fond of." He pulled away when his son stood and tried to place a hand on his shoulder. "Just go," Axel said. "And don't come back."

Lewis was at the front door when he turned back to the sad-looking man at the kitchen table. "I've got some advice to pass along to you as well," he said.

"What's that?"

"No matter what happens, don't let anybody take your farm."

The Saturdays in Gila Bend that Taylor remembered were always vibrant, alive with people. Merchants did brisk business as farmers came into town, bringing their wives to shop and their kids to play with friends. Park benches would be filled with people visiting. Young boys and girls promenaded along the sidewalks, flirting and laughing, eating candied apples and ears of roasted corn.

Several of B. J.'s neighbors were coming to clean away the ashes of his destroyed barn, so Lewis decided to remain in town after fulfilling his livery duties. Ezzie Zale was busy brushing the mane of one of several horses that had been left for his tending. "I've got two needing shoeing and one that's got an eye infection I'll be medicating," he said. "Saturdays are always busy."

"Need some help?"

Ezzie shook his head. "Best you stay clear today."

Again, Lewis was being warned to stay out of sight. He checked on Dolly, then walked back to his room. On his arrival he found a basket sitting beside the door. In it was a loaf of still warm bread and a large slice of ham. Sue Ellen had visited.

He decided to spend the day stripped down to his shorts, stretched out on his cot, reading a book Luke Bradley had loaned him. It wasn't until early evening that he dressed and stepped outside. The breeze did little to offset the heat, so he dismissed the idea of taking Dolly out for a ride. Instead, he walked toward the main street, where a steady hum of noise was coming from the saloon. Another place he'd been advised to avoid.

He'd walked past the open door several times before curiosity got the best of him. Inside, he had been told, would be cowhands from Captain Ringewald's ranch. He wanted a look at them.

Unlike the weekdays, the place was filled with customers jostling for room at the bar, sitting at poker tables, or standing in small groups. The loud laughter and cursing told him that a number of the patrons were already drunk and determined to get drunker. There was no one he recognized. Apparently, even Ezzie had decided to forgo his nightly toddy.

He was deciding whether to make his way to the bar and order a beer when he heard a voice behind him.

"Way I hear it, you get yourself in trouble whenever you step into a saloon." The observation was made by a man who stood over six feet and was well muscled from years of ranch hand labor. He had a carefully waxed mustache and one gold tooth, both which he seemed to be proud of.

"Don't believe we've met," Lewis said.

"You're Lewis Taylor, aren't you?"

Lewis nodded. "And you are?"

"Name's Lyndon Greenleaf. Friends call me Lennie. I'd prefer you call me Lyndon." In the back of the room, a shoving match was about to break out into a full-blown fistfight.

"Let me guess. You're one of the hands on the captain's payroll, right?"

Greenleaf moved close enough that Lewis could smell the whiskey on his breath. "I don't see that as any of your business," he said. "At least not for now."

As he spoke, two other cowboys had moved to stand beside him. Both had simple grins on their faces and were well on their way to being drunk. "This that outlaw convict folks have been talking about?" one asked.

"He don't look so tough to me," the other said.

Taylor, seeing that nothing good would come from his remaining, dismissed the idea of a beer and turned to leave. He had no interest in getting into a fight. Not for now.

The following morning, Luke and Sue Ellen stopped by to invite Lewis to join them for Sunday services. "I fear lightning might strike me the minute I walked through the door," he said, "but I thank you just the same."

Little Luke waved goodbye to him as the Bradleys headed in the direction of the church bells. "Luke, I've got a quick question," Taylor said. "Who's this fellow Lyndon Greenleaf?

Bradley hesitated for a moment before

answering. "He's Captain Ringewald's right-hand man. You don't want to mess with him."

"I think I already did," Lewis said.

At the Rocking R Ranch, Greenleaf was doing his best to hide a pounding hangover as he walked into Ringewald's office. "Hope you and the boys didn't do too much damage to my bar," the captain said as he put a kitchen match to the end of his cigar.

Greenleaf assured him there would be no need for wholesale repairs.

"I understand you met somebody interesting last night."

"Lewis Taylor, you mean?"

"That's who. What was your impression?"

"He hightailed it out before I could really get one," Greenleaf said.

"Didn't appear to be much of a fighter, huh?"

"Can't rightly say."

"We'll see. In due time."

Chapter Five

To the residents of Gila Bend, Captain Archer Ringewald was a mystery. He had been since he bought the thousand-acre Jake Belton ranch a decade earlier and renamed it the Rocking R. On rare trips into town, he didn't speak unless it was to address some pressing business matter, he seemed to have no friends (nor, for that matter, want any), and you could count on one hand the number of times anyone had seen him smile. Laughter was a foreign language.

He was more myth than flesh and blood. A living ghost. Many of the townspeople had never actually seen him. Those who had described him in various ways. He was tall, with hard, angular features. A stout, square-jawed man one might call burly. He was handsome to some, a dandy, yet amazingly ordinary-looking to others. They guessed his age at anywhere from thirty to mid-fifties and his worth to be in the millions.

The only thing that was unanimously agreed upon was that he was a man one didn't want as an enemy.

When Dwayne Reynolds was still editor of the *Sentinel,* he had attempted to do an article on the county's newest landowner soon after Ringewald bought his ranch. His subject, he wrote, had been "cordial but publicity shy." He had served as a captain in the Union Army and come to Texas from "back East." There was not a single quote in Reynolds's brief story.

The only other mention of him in the local paper had been when Luke Bradley wrote that the captain and Darla Winslow had married "in a private ceremony at the Ringewald ranch." Thereafter, Darla's friends seldom saw her.

Though he had never written it, Bradley was certain even the captain's wife knew little about him.

He was born in New York, the son of an immigrant grocer who had begun building his fortune with a small corner store that sold bread and milk, tobacco, and a variety of hard candies. With some luck and a keen sense for business, his father soon had neighborhood groceries scattered throughout the less affluent neighborhoods in the city. Eventually, he saved enough money to purchase a small, struggling bank that catered to newcomers to America. A hard-bargain businessman, he soon had the bank making a profit, mostly because of the unsympathetic manner in which he treated his customers. If they couldn't keep up with loan payments, he filed for and gained ownership of their properties.

It was only logical that real estate would be his next financial venture. Those who bought small homes they couldn't afford eventually lost them back to the seller. The circular process of selling, taking back, and selling again was highly profitable. Some Ringewald Realty Company–owned properties had been sold a half dozen or more times.

Fellow businessmen nicknamed him "Cut-throat" Ringewald.

He pinched pennies until they bled. Said one who had done business with him: "If it's worth fifteen cents and you're willing to let it go for a dime, he'll spend all day trying to talk you down to a nickel."

In time, he became owner of a half dozen banks and lending companies, a chain of grocery stores, and the thriving real estate business, and he had moved his family from the inner city to an estate in an upscale part of New York. Few of the society elite were pleased to have him as their neighbor.

With little time for the pleasures of home life, he soon divorced his wife, offering her sole ownership of one of his less successful banks in exchange for custody of their only son. Though the elder Ringewald occasionally found time for brief flirtations, he never remarried.

He sent his son off to a highly regarded private school that specialized in providing young men a business-oriented education. By age fifty-five, Carl Ringewald was dead of a heart attack, victim of the grueling demands of his sixteen-hour workdays.

His son graduated from prep school a year later and joined the Union Army. Though he rose to the rank of captain, he participated in no memorable battles nor in any way distinguished himself as a soldier.

By the time the South surrendered, young Archer Ringewald knew what he wanted to do with his life. An avid reader since boyhood, he had devoured the romantic tales of the Old West. Texas, with its pioneering spirit and wide-open spaces, particularly fascinated him.

For a time, he grudgingly oversaw the businesses his father had built, but was unable to generate any real enthusiasm for the task. He turned over operations to a trusted partner, sold the family home, and left for Texas in search of a cattle ranch, taking with him his father's greed and business philosophy.

His quest ended outside the small town of Gila Bend.

He was leaning against the corral fence, watching as several of his newly acquired Longhorns were being branded. Standing next to him was Milton Barnes, the Gila Bend sheriff.

"You think he's back to stay?" the captain asked.

"Ain't many making him welcome, including his own daddy. He's living in a little storage shed out back of the newspaper office and, as you already know, doing work out at the Dixon place."

"He can't be making any money doing that. The cripple fellow doesn't have two nickels to rub together, so it's highly unlikely Taylor's being paid."

The sheriff nodded in agreement. "I'm guessing it's just a friendship agreement. Those boys have been running together since they were knee-high."

Ringewald cursed. "What's it going to take

to send him on his way?"

"Well, he ain't breaking no laws I'm aware of, so I've got no call to force his leaving," Barnes said. "I've seen to it that word's been spread that he's a convicted criminal, just out of the penitentiary."

"Have you suggested to Luke Bradley that it's not in the town's best interest to have an ex-convict living on his property?" He reminded the sheriff that his foreman, Lyndon Greenleaf, was always available to help if needed.

"I've been thinking about having that conversation with Bradley."

As he spoke, Darla rounded the barn, returning from the garden with a basket of tomatoes she and her maid had picked. "Morning, Sheriff," she said, peeking out from beneath her sunbonnet.

He tipped his hat and greeted her with a smile before turning back to the captain. "I'd best be on my way," he said.

"Same with Lewis Taylor," Ringewald whispered. It sounded much like an order.

Darla Ringewald stood at her kitchen window, looking out at her husband as she rinsed the vegetables. The sheriff had left, and now Greenleaf had taken his place. Though she could not hear what they were saying, she could see that the conversation was animated. At one point the captain poked a finger against Greenleaf's chest.

Darla let out a deep sigh as she watched, unable to decide which of the two she disliked more.

By early evening, Lewis had returned to his room. The pear pie Mrs. Dixon had given him before he left sat on the table untouched. He was too tired to eat after spending the day replacing burned slats on B. J.'s buggy and digging stumps from the orchard. Despite the heat, he had worked straight through the day, stopping only for an occasional drink of water.

He was feeling good about the progress he was making and suggested to B. J. that if he could afford it, he should consider purchasing a couple of pigs for the pen he'd rebuilt.

He had dozed off and was having busy dreams when he heard a knock at the door. He was surprised when he opened it to see it had gotten dark. Even more surprised that it was Ezzie Zale standing there. He had a canvas bag under one arm.

"Step inside," Lewis said. "You're my first official visitor, except for the owner of this fine place. I've even got fresh pie I can serve. What brings you out this time of the evening?"

"I was having my nightly whiskey down at the saloon," Ezzie said, "and overheard some conversation I wanted to pass along. One of the benefits of getting old is you become invisible. People don't bother noticing your presence when they think they're talking in private."

"What was it you heard?"

Zale raised a hand, as if to say he wouldn't have his story rushed. "As I was leaving, I stopped to light my pipe and noticed Sheriff Barnes talking with someone out by the watering trough. Turned out, it was that fellow Greenleaf, who works for Captain Ringewald. Don't normally see him in town except on Saturdays when he comes to get drunk.

"Anyway, it was you they were speaking about, Greenleaf doing most of the talking. I wasn't able to get close enough to hear everything he was saying, but the gist of it was that his boss is getting highly impatient with you being in town. For reasons I didn't hear, he wants you gone and apparently has no reservations about how it's accomplished.

"Does that make any sense to you?"

"I'm not sure how much sense it makes,

but what you're saying doesn't surprise me," Lewis said as he used his pocketknife to cut into Mrs. Dixon's pie. "I've got no plates, so I hope you've washed your hands recently."

They sat together on Lewis's cot, savoring the sweet pear juice that dripped onto their chins. "This is fine pie," Ezzie said. "You tell the Dixon woman if she's ever got a horse needs shoeing or an axle straightened, we can work us out a fair trade."

As he stood to leave, he handed the canvas bag to Lewis. Inside it was a Colt pistol, freshly cleaned and smelling of newly applied oil. The chamber was loaded, and there were a dozen loose bullets in the bottom of the bag.

"Hasn't been fired in a coon's age," Ezzie said, "so you might want to take a practice shot or two sometime soon." He could see the puzzled look on Taylor's face. "I just wanted you to have it. You never know when it might come in handy," he said as he made his way to the door.

For some time after the livery owner left, Lewis sat looking at the gun, slowly turning it in his hands, sighting down its barrel, feeling its coolness and weight. He hadn't fired a handgun since he was a Confederate soldier. As he'd told the judge years ago, in civilian life he'd never had a pistol of his own. No longer was that the case.

Sitting in the darkening room, he wondered if a time would come when he might have to use it.

Taylor wasn't the only one to have a visitor. Across town, the Bradley family had finished supper, and Sue Ellen was reading Little Luke a bedtime story when the sheriff knocked at their front door. He looked uneasy as he waited for Luke to answer. He had removed his hat and was slowly tracing its brim with a finger. The smile on his round face was forced.

"Come in, Sheriff," Bradley said.

"If it's all the same, I was hoping we could have a brief conversation out here."

The two men walked to the porch swing. "You look troubled," Luke said.

The sheriff cleared his throat. "As a matter of fact, I am," he said. "As you know, it's my sworn duty to see that the folks of Gila Bend are safe and free from worry any harm might come their way."

"And you do a fine job. As I've mentioned many times in my editorials."

"I appreciate it. But I've got to be honest with you regarding my concern for the boarder you've taken in. That Taylor boy."

The smile disappeared from Bradley's face. "As far as I know, he's caused no problem. You're aware Lewis Taylor is a good friend of mine, has been since we were kids."

"I know, but there's folks who don't think as kindly toward him as you do. They don't feel right about having somebody who served time in prison walking among them and being around their children."

"Lewis spent a couple of hours the other evening playing with my two-year-old, and I wasn't the least uncomfortable. Who are these people you're talking about?"

"I'd prefer not to mention names. All I'm saying is that it's my thinking it might be best for everyone, you and your family included, if he moved on, made himself a new start somewhere other than Gila Bend.

"Frankly, I'm worried that you might even get some folks in town angry with you for befriending him. I'd hate to see that happen."

Being subtle was not among the sheriff's strongest traits. Bradley stood and thanked him for stopping by. "It's getting late," he said.

Sheriff Barnes put on his hat and nodded. "You folks have a good evening," he said as he made his way down the porch steps.

Inside, Sue Ellen, already in her nightgown, was waiting. "What was that all about?" she said.

"The sheriff delivered a message. He wants Lewis gone."

"He does?"

"Well, somebody does."

"I don't need but one guess to figure who that somebody is," she said.

Her husband didn't reply.

The following day, Seth Hanson, manager of the mercantile, and Guy Anderson from the feedstore stopped by his office to inform him they were canceling their ads in the *Sentinel.*

The battle had begun.

Chapter Six

Darla Ringewald was in the ranch house reading room, a copy of the *Sentinel* spread in her lap. She had just finished Luke Bradley's editorial and was wondering if her husband had seen it. He had not been mentioned by name, but it was clear whom the editor, a friend of hers since they were children, was writing about.

It was titled "Where Has All the Laughter Gone?" and it was straightforward in message and angry in tone.

Bradley wrote:

The time has come for the *Sentinel* to stand up and be a newspaper, not just provide its readers a weekly record of the community's social events, baking-contest results, and Sunday-afternoon visits from friends and relatives.

It is time we ask hard questions about a troubling development in our town that has caused smiles and laughter to all but disappear — along with a number of our friends and neighbors.

We can remember a time when our bank was a fair and trusted community partner. It was an honest, caring institution that had faith in its customers and concern for the future of Gila Bend. We had a near-perfect working partnership.

If, in hard times, a farmer or local business owner needed a little extra time to repay a loan, a patient and understanding attitude prevailed. Ultimately, everyone — bank and townspeople — benefitted.

No more. Today there is little warmth or caring. It seems to have been replaced by a thoughtless, greedy philosophy that is driving people out of business and from our community. This is not a good thing. The smiles are disappearing; our laughter has been silenced.

The *Sentinel* wants to know why.

The writer promised it was the first of a number of important questions he would be asking in the weeks to come.

"Well, your newspaper friend's done stepped in it," Ezzie said as Lewis finished his morning livery chores. Zale read portions of the *Sentinel* editorial aloud. "I admire what he's saying. He's hit the nail smack on the head. But causing steam to come from Captain Ringewald's ears ain't exactly smart business. That's just my opinion."

Lewis agreed. He was pleased, however, at the courage Bradley had displayed in bringing the issue into the open. "I expect he's just saying what most folks are thinking," he said.

Instead of saddling Dolly and heading out to the Dixon farm, Taylor walked over to the *Sentinel* office to await Bradley's arrival. He wanted to shake his hand.

He also wanted to stop at his room and get the pistol Ezzie had given him, thinking it might be a good idea to start keeping it close.

"By the end of the day," Luke said, "there's a good chance I won't have a single advertiser left. Believe me, there's going to be pressure brought to bear. And worse things, most likely. I didn't sleep much last night, wondering if I've started a death watch for my paper and my livelihood."

"You did what's right."

"That's what Sue Ellen said. She urged me to do it. Not sure I would have if she hadn't been so insistent."

"She's a strong lady," Lewis said. "Always has been, even as a young girl.

"You recall that time when Principal Dexter threatened to remove you from the school debate team, disagreeing with the position you were taking on some issue? Remember how Sue Ellen marched herself into his office and gave him a double dose of what for, defending you at the risk of getting in trouble herself? Or how she went to the sheriff and took up for me and B. J. when we were falsely accused of swiping watermelons out of old man Silverton's garden?"

Memories of those long-ago days brought a smile to Luke's tired face. He didn't mention it, but another constant defender of him and his fellow Musketeers was Lewis's girlfriend, Darla Winslow. Instead, he said, "Those were good days, good times."

"And Gila Bend deserves to have them return," Lewis said. "Could be you and the *Sentinel* have headed the town back in that direction."

"Hope I'm not just yelling into the wind."

When Taylor stood to leave, Luke saw the handle of the sidearm that was tucked beneath his friend's belt. "I don't recall ever seeing you walking around armed before," he said.

"Hey, you said I was to be your night watchman, right? Can't very well do my job without protection."

Carrying out his duty would come sooner than he'd expected.

The night breeze that came through his open window was still too warm for comfortable sleep. Despite a hard day's work, Lewis was restless and anxious to see dark again turn to predawn gray. He was already awake when he heard a noise outside.

Quietly slipping out the door, he saw movement near the newspaper office, moonlit outlines of what appeared to be two intruders. Gun in hand, he moved closer until the images became clearer. One of the men appeared to be carrying a bucket.

Taylor stepped into the open, gun pointed, and called out, "Identify yourselves."

When he fired a warning shot into the air, the two intruders began running, leaving their bucket behind. Whitewash was spilled all over the porch steps. On the front of the building, they had painted the word "Liar."

Lewis was still trying to clean up the mess when Luke arrived. He took one of the rags and joined in.

"Looks like it's begun in earnest," he said.

Lewis had already decided he would forgo

work at B. J.'s and remain in town for the day.

In the Rocking R bunkhouse, Greenleaf was wiping whitewash from his boots when the captain entered. Ringewald was not pleased when he heard that the mission had been interrupted.

"If need be, we'll send the message louder," he said. "What I'm of a mind to do is just burn the place to the ground."

"Whenever you're ready, boss. I've got plenty of coal oil."

Taylor knew no better way to test the attitude of the townspeople than to pay a breakfast visit to the café. He'd not been there since his frigid reception on his first day in town and was surprised to find it almost empty, the lone waitress leaning against the counter when he walked in.

"Just pick yourself a table," she said. A couple of retired farmers, finishing their meals, looked up, then away.

Lewis had just ordered when Ezzie Zale came in, nodded to the other customers, then took a seat across from him. "You're late tending your chores," he said. There was more jest than chastisement in his voice.

"I'll be there soon as I've had my biscuit

and eggs. Want to join me?"

"Son, one thing you'll eventually learn is that old folks don't eat breakfast. Or much at any other time, for that matter. You start getting up in years and the appetite just seems to go away, and you slowly turn into skin and bones. You're looking at the proof."

The waitress brought him a cup of coffee and a thick slice of sourdough toast. "Need to keep your strength up, old man," she said with a flirtatious smile.

Zale gave her a wink before she turned away. "Me and her daddy used to do a lot of trotline fishing back in the day, before gout got the best of him. He passed a couple of years ago." He fell silent, chewing on his toast, then said, "Friends are getting more scarce by the day. They're burying old man Thurber this afternoon."

"Don't think I recall him."

"Not many folks do."

They were on their way to the livery when Ezzie noticed that Lewis was carrying the pistol he'd given him. "Glad to see it."

"I've already tried it out." Lewis told him about the late night visitors to the *Sentinel.*

"Soon after he bought his ranch, Ringewald came into town and made me an offer for the livery. Told me I could keep running it or come to work for him and be well paid for taking care of things that broke down or needed other kinds of fixing. When I turned down his offer, he attempted to be cordial, but I could see a cold hardness in his eyes.

"I consider myself a pretty good judge of folks, and I immediately recognized him as a man who intends no good. If I ever met someone I'd say was evil, he'd be the one. You'll do good to bear that in mind."

"I've never even met the man," Lewis said.

"You will. And if I'm right in my guessing, it won't be long."

Chapter Seven

Darla Ringewald missed attending Sunday services at the Blessed Redeemer, singing the familiar and comforting hymns, staying for the potluck picnics afterward, and visiting with friends. After she and the captain married, Pastor Daniels had come to the ranch several times, telling her how much she was missed and urging that she return to the flock. In time, however, he'd given up and no longer made the trek out to the Rocking R.

Captain Ringewald had gone out of his way to make him feel unwelcomed, strongly suggesting the promises of his sermons were the stuff of foolish myth and children's fairy tales. Like many, the preacher had decided Ringewald was a man best avoided. He resigned himself to the fact that not all souls could be saved.

Some Sunday mornings, Darla would stand on the front porch of the ranch house, hoping she might be able to hear the distant toll of the church bells. But they were too far away, like so much of her past life.

She was the daughter of Gila Bend's first licensed bookkeeper. While tending to the financial matters of almost every business in town, Stanley Winslow had raised her alone since the sudden death of her mother. Darla had been only seven at the time.

She had grown into a pretty and popular girl, excelled in school, worked part-time at the library, and been sure she was one day going to marry Lewis Taylor after the first time they danced at the harvest festival. Friends like Sue Ellen Troup urged her to postpone her decision until she had met other boys, but Darla had her mind made up. It had been love at first sight for her and for Lewis.

They began to seriously discuss marriage after his safe return from the war. And since her father was clearly lukewarm to the idea of her marrying a poor farmer's son, Lewis went in search of a career that offered stability and a decent salary.

All the while, the elder Winslow held to the hope something would occur to end the talk of marriage.

That happened on Taylor's twentieth birthday when he'd traveled to San Antonio to talk with a friend of his father's who had offered him a job working in his lumberyard. To celebrate both his birthday and his first paying job, he stopped in a downtown saloon for a beer before heading home.

Darla was at first angry that the birthday cake she had baked was unappreciated, then in hysterical tears after Sheriff Barnes relayed the message that her boyfriend was in jail, charged with attempted murder.

She refused to believe he was guilty, even when the judge sentenced him to five years in prison. She looked up the address of the state prison and wrote her first letter, telling Taylor she knew he was innocent and that he could rest assured that she would wait for him. Such was the tone of several other letters she later sent.

It troubled her that she got no reply.

In truth, Lewis had responded, with long, heartfelt letters professing his devotion and insisting he had committed no crime. None reached Darla, however, as her father routinely intercepted and destroyed them. Heartbroken, Darla had eventually given up hope and stopped mailing letters to the prison.

And in time a man named Captain Archer Ringewald had introduced himself one day when he saw her coming out of the mercantile.

Though he was clearly attracted to her, Darla didn't care for him. For one thing, he was older. For another, he had a self-important air that she found off-putting. Her father, however, saw in Ringewald's interest a great opportunity. He could provide a lifestyle few dared dream of, a secure future. Winslow realized his daughter didn't have strong feelings for the rancher but hoped that might eventually change.

He was relentless for a reason he had shared with no one. He had made several trips to San Antonio, telling his daughter he had business there. In truth, Winslow was visiting a doctor who had run a series of tests that revealed cancer was spreading quickly through his lungs and lower intestines. The prognosis was that he would soon die of the same disease that had killed Darla's mother.

Once Winslow had resigned to his fate, his concern turned to his daughter's care once he was gone. Ringewald was his answer.

Finally, Darla said yes to the captain's proposal of marriage. Feeling shunned by Lewis Taylor, something she was still unable to understand after three years of silence, she decided it was time to quit chasing the romantic dreams of her youth and embrace a secure future.

It was a decision she regretted almost immediately. Though she lived in a big house, with a personal maid and high-fashion clothing and French perfume regularly shipped to her directly from the finest stores in New York, she had not experienced such absolute misery since the days immediately following her mother's death. She was achingly lonesome, a prisoner who had made the worst mistake of her life.

Increasingly restricting her social activities, her husband forbad her traveling to Gila Bend to visit friends. To his surprise and disappointment, her own father saw her only when he was occasionally invited to the ranch, and then for only short visits. The captain was never pleased to see him.

What Winslow came to realize was that despite all the trinkets of good fortune, his daughter was being held hostage. And much of the blame fell squarely on his shoulders.

It was that growing sense of guilt and worry for his daughter's well-being that led to him visiting the editor of the *Sentinel.*

"I thought you wrote a fine and honest editorial," he told Bradley. "In my profession, I've had the opportunity to get a close look at the financial injustice that's being played out here in Gila Bend. And while you didn't mention Captain Ringewald by name, we both know he's the one responsible. Something has to be done."

Luke was surprised to hear Winslow speak of his daughter's husband in such damning terms. "What do you have in mind?" he said.

"People have to be persuaded to stand up to him. Not just a few, but enough to get the attention of him and those hired troublemakers working for him. For that to occur, folks are going to need someone to be a leader. As I'm sure you know, the sheriff will be of no help. From what I read in the *Sentinel,* it appears to me you've already taken the first step in leading the way."

Luke leaned back in his chair, pondering Winslow's suggestion. "Being honest with you, I have to say I agree with your evaluation of the situation. But I'm certainly not the man to lead any kind of revolt or showdown. But I know someone who might, if he's willing."

"Who?"

"Come back tonight after suppertime, and I'll introduce you."

Later that evening, Winslow was at first speechless when he saw Lewis Taylor walk into Bradley's office. At the same time, Lewis was equally surprised to see the man whose approval he'd once so desperately sought but never received.

Winslow composed himself. "I'm glad to see you back home," he said.

Lewis had no response.

Bradley detailed their conversation earlier in the day. "I suggested to him you might be interested in being involved."

"What would be expected of me?" Taylor said.

Winslow joined in. "I'm not sure how one combats the power of a man like Captain Ringewald," he said, "unless they shoot him dead. But I do know we need someone to unite the townspeople against him, to show that there is a strong community belief in the way of life we once enjoyed, that right will triumph over wrong."

Lewis smiled. "That's a pretty flowery speech," he said. "Maybe you should be writing some editorials yourself." He genuinely disliked the man sitting across from him. He was weak and manipulative. Stanley Winslow was no more pleased to see Taylor back in Gila Bend than he had been to have him courting his daughter.

"I admire what you want to accomplish," Lewis said, "but the notion that folks are going to follow my lead is pretty far-fetched. You can count on one hand those who are even glad I'm here. In their eyes, I'm a near killer with a prison record, not a leader.

"And if we were to take on the captain, my guess is it will quickly turn violent. You don't want innocent people getting hurt."

"So what can we do? He'll not go away willingly or change the way he's doing business."

"That's something I've already been thinking about," Taylor said as he got to his feet.

"Are you saying you're considering dealing with the matter by yourself?"

Lewis pulled on his hat and shrugged. "I got nothing to lose," he answered. "And at least in part, I can thank you for that."

The following Saturday night, Taylor walked into the loud and rowdy Captain's Bar, hoping the anxiety he was feeling wasn't obvious. As he stood in the doorway, the noise briefly quieted as eyes turned in his direction. Lewis slowly scanned the room, looking for Lyndon Greenleaf.

He located him leaning against the bar, a whiskey glass in his hand.

Taylor made his way through the crowd, never taking his eyes off the man he'd come to see.

Greenleaf nodded as he approached.

"Lewis Something, ain't it? The ex-con?"

"Been doing any more whitewashing in the middle of the night?"

Greenleaf slammed his glass down on the bar and took a step toward Taylor. He pushed his jacket back so his gun holster was visible.

"I've got no interest in dealing with you," Lewis said. "All I want is for you to deliver a message to your boss."

"And just what might that be? I ain't no messenger."

"Tell the captain I want us to have a talk, wherever's convenient and whenever it fits his schedule." He turned to walk away but a broad-shouldered ranch hand stepped up and blocked his path. Taylor pulled his pistol and slammed its barrel against the side of the man's head. He slumped to the floor, forcing Lewis to step over him as he continued toward the door.

An uneasy hush fell over the room.

Ezzie Zale had watched from outside. When Lewis walked into the darkened street, he hurried to his side. "That was about the dumbest thing I've ever seen done," he said.

"I couldn't agree more," Taylor replied.

Just before dawn, he woke to the acrid smell

of smoke and the crackling of flames biting into the sidewall of his room. Grabbing his pants, his boots, and his pistol, he rushed into the night as the fire behind him quickly spread to the roof.

It was over in less than thirty minutes, the shed was reduced to a heap of smoldering embers.

Among those who had rushed to the scene was Sheriff Barnes, who was standing next to Luke Bradley.

"Good thing the flames didn't jump to your office," he said. "It would be a shame not to get my paper this week and see what high horse you'll be riding this time."

Luke was still silently glaring at the sheriff when Taylor approached. "I'm sorry about this," Lewis said. "It's all my fault."

"Just goes to show," the sheriff said, "folks ought not ever to smoke in bed." He glanced over at Taylor. "Seems to me you got mighty lucky, waking before you could be seriously harmed."

"I don't smoke, Sheriff," Taylor said. In his hand was the bottom half of a broken bottle, blackened by the flames and smoke. He held it out to Bradley. "The smell familiar to you?"

Luke put his nose close to the bottle and inhaled. "Smells like coal oil to me."

The sheriff was already walking away as he spoke.

Little Luke sat in his lap as Taylor talked with his daddy, telling him of his earlier confrontation with Lyndon Greenleaf. "That's what set this in motion," he said.

Once sure the fire was extinguished, they had gone to the Bradley house, where Sue Ellen found him a clean shirt.

Zale had already stopped by to say Lewis was welcome to move into the livery. "If they were to decide on burning it down," Ezzie said, "they'd be doing me a favor. I'm getting mighty tired of running the place and would rather be fishing anyway."

Sue Ellen offered to cook breakfast but Lewis declined. "I've got to get on over to Ezzie's and tend to my chores," he said. "Then I'll start cleaning up behind your office."

Luke gave him a solemn look. "And then what?"

"We'll see." He hugged Little Luke and kissed his forehead, then looked across the table at the father. "Your job is to see that this little man and his mama stay safe. No more editorials, okay?"

Sue Ellen wrapped her arms around her husband and, in a mocking voice, said,

"We'll also see."

Bradley nodded his agreement.

The following week's *Sentinel* mentioned Captain Ringewald by name, asking why, with his incredible wealth, he felt the need to continue buying so much Gila Bend property. A response was requested.

Chapter Eight

Whisper's tail began wagging the instant he saw Lewis step onto the porch. "At least someone's glad to see me," he said as he took a seat next to his father. The dog jumped onto his lap and began licking at his face.

"What's that old saying about a bad penny?" Axel Taylor said. Lewis was pleased to see that he was smiling when he posed the question.

"Reason I'm here is to warn you that there might soon be some trouble with this Ringewald fellow." He told his father about the burning of Luke Bradley's shed and his saloon run-in with one of the captain's men. He'd brought a copy of the latest *Sentinel* editorial for his father to read.

"Your friend Luke doesn't beat around the bush."

"How long have you known about all this?" Lewis said.

"It started shortly after he moved here and started ranching. I had no personal dealing with him back then, but to be honest, I first thought he was okay. He raised his Longhorns, came into town for feed and medicine for his livestock, got his horses shoed, and bought grocery items for his workers. I figured since he was making a contribution to the local economy and keeping to himself, he was the near-perfect neighbor.

"Then he bought the bank and things started going bad. Bullying folks into selling or, worse, having the bank repossess property. Pretty coldhearted stuff."

"And just how badly has he pressured you?"

"His first visit was a lot of smooth talk, all friendly and polite. Next time, not so much. The last time he came with two of his men and said in no uncertain terms that he would have this place, one way or another. I've been sleeping with one eye open and my shotgun by the bed ever since."

Lewis thought for a moment, pushing back his anger as he scratched behind Whisper's ears. "What do you think he means to do?"

"He'll do whatever's necessary to take over this farm. Either run me off or kill me."

The words chilled Lewis. "Neither's going

to happen," he said. "I'll personally see to it."

"I don't want you getting in the middle of all this."

"Pa, I already am."

"That why you're now carrying a side-arm?" the elder Taylor asked.

Lewis ignored the question. "I'm moving home, whether you like it or not. If it pleases you, I'll sleep in the barn. But I don't want you out here by yourself, especially at night. From what I've seen so far, that's when Ringewald's people like to do their damage."

"Because they're cowards," Axel said.

It pleased him that his father offered only mild resistance to his plan. "You going to bring that broke-down horse with you?" he said.

"I most certainly am," his son said, breaking into the first smile since he'd arrived. "And I expect her to be welcomed properly."

Whisper barked as Axel laughed and went inside. When he returned he was holding the holster and gun belt Lewis had returned with from the war. "Long as you're going to be carrying that Colt, it's better you don't just stick it in the waist of your britches," he said.

"Also, your room inside is just as it was

before you left."

Lewis was certain Ringewald's henchmen weren't through harassing his father and would continue pushing him to agree to give up his two hundred acres.

The following day he told Ezzie and Luke he would be moving out to the family farm for a while but would stay in touch. He felt he had made considerable headway in his effort to get B. J.'s place back in working order, and explained his reason for needing to spend most of his time with his father.

B. J. thanked him profusely for all he'd done, and Mrs. Dixon presented him with another pear pie. "There's plenty more whenever you want them," she said. "I want you to know I'm most appreciative of what you've done for my boy."

Lewis promised to return soon.

At the Rocking R, Captain Ringewald was in his office, yelling at the top of his voice. It was only midmorning, and he was already drunk. "What right does that newspaperman have to be sticking his nose into my business?" He tossed a copy of the *Sentinel* away and threw an empty glass against the wall. "And now this Taylor fellow is saying he wants us to have a meeting? Who do these people think they are?"

Greenleaf stood near a window, watching his boss rail. "All I'm doing is passing along what he said."

Ringewald spat another round of curses and reached for a cigar. "We've been too nice," he said, "and allowed some folks to get uppity. We made a mistake trying to do things peacefully. It's time we show I'll not be messed with."

Darla was passing in the hallway, aware of the uproar in her husband's office. She stopped when she heard the word "Taylor." She knocked softly and entered. "Archer," she said, "maybe you should have something to eat and lie down for a rest."

He ignored her and instructed Greenleaf to see that his horse was saddled.

"Where are you going?" Darla asked.

"I'm going to town to have a conversation with your old beau. We've got some settling up to do."

Sitting in her room, she was wringing her hands, trying to comprehend what her husband was talking about. She couldn't remember the last time she had heard Lewis's name spoken. Was it possible he was no longer in prison and back home in Gila Bend? And if so, what business did her husband have with him?

Thoughts raced through her mind, pleasant memories of bygone days mixed with new anxiety. She feared something bad was about to happen, yet she had no idea what it might be.

"Boss, this ain't a good idea," Greenleaf said as the captain steadied his Palomino.

"You coming, or do I have to do this by myself?"

Greenleaf's horse was already saddled.

They first went to the *Sentinel* office, where Bradley was sitting at his typewriter, staring at a blank piece of paper. His concentration was interrupted by Ringewald's loud, unannounced entry.

"Writing another story that sullies my name?" the captain said. He was weaving slightly and placed a hand on the corner of the desk to steady himself.

"Mr. Ringewald . . . Captain . . . it doesn't appear you're in any condition to have a civil conversation right now."

Ringewald swept a hand across the desk, sending papers, pencils, and a couple of books flying to the floor. "I didn't come here to be civil," he said. His words were slurred. "I'll be seeing to you and your little pissant newspaper soon enough, but for now I'm looking for a friend of yours. This Taylor fellow." He began to laugh. "I'm told his living quarters burned down recently, so he must be hiding out somewhere else."

"Sir, I have no idea where he is, but I hardly think he's hiding. That's not his nature." Bradley was surprised at the defiant tone he managed.

Not as surprised, however, as he was when Greenleaf rushed across the room and hit him squarely in the face, knocking him to the floor. He followed it with a hard kick to Bradley's backside, then grabbed his right hand and pulled his fingers back until he heard the sound of breaking bones. The captain then pulled Greenleaf away. "That's just for starters," Ringewald said as he tossed a copy of the paper into the face of the fallen editor, who was writhing in pain.

"I need a drink before we proceed," the captain said as they walked toward their horses.

"The saloon's not open yet," Greenleaf said.

Ringewald waved a dismissive hand in the air. "Wrong. It's my saloon, and it's open when I say it's open."

Sue Ellen and Little Luke were on their way to shop at the mercantile when they decided to stop in at the paper. She was at first surprised not to find Luke at his desk, then momentarily froze when she heard a low moan come from behind it. When Little Luke saw blood on his daddy's face, he began to cry. Sue Ellen screamed and knelt on the floor beside her husband.

"I'm okay," Bradley whispered before passing out.

Sue Ellen swept her son into her arms and raced toward Doc Johnson's office. En route, she passed the saloon, where two horses were tethered at the hitching rail.

By midafternoon, the bottle of whiskey sitting in front of Ringewald was almost empty. He was too drunk to remember the reason he'd come to town or even the encounter in the *Sentinel* office. Greenleaf finally managed to persuade him to return to the Rocking R while he could still ride.

Doc Johnson, meanwhile, had determined that Luke's nose wasn't seriously damaged and only one rib seemed to be fractured. He set two broken fingers. "Typing will be difficult for a spell," he said. Bradley, heavily medicated with a painkiller, only offered a silly smile that amused his young son.

Sue Ellen, past her frantic first reaction, was livid. Though she knew it was not likely to do any good, she planned a visit to the sheriff's office as soon as she got her husband settled at home.

"He said it was Captain Ringewald and one of his hired hands," she told Sheriff Barnes.

"I reckon I can guess what started it. Those editorials Luke's been writing haven't exactly flattered the captain."

"Are you sitting there suggesting my husband was asking for a beating? In his own place of business? In broad daylight?" She was furious as she spoke, and the sheriff was briefly worried that he might be next to get a punch in the nose.

"I'll look into it," he said. "Could be it was just a misunderstanding . . ."

"That resulted in broken bones? Right. Sheriff, you need to open your eyes and get to doing your job before somebody in your town is killed." With that, she turned and stormed out.

Sheriff Barnes sat at his desk, looking out the window long after Sue Ellen had left. He knew she was right, but had no idea what his next move might be.

Lewis didn't hear about the encounter in Bradley's office until the following day. He was chopping wood when Sue Ellen steered her buggy into the yard. Whisper barked, then wagged his tail, and Little Luke's eyes lit up when he saw his newest friend.

She was detailing what had happened even before he helped her from her seat. "Luke says he was drunk as a skunk and had come looking for you," she said. "I just wanted to come out and give you fair warning."

"How's Luke?"

"A little busted up, but he's going to be okay. They broke his fingers." She paused as her rage returned. "He'll not be able to type for a while. But I sure can."

Axel Taylor had joined them and taken note of the outrage in her voice. "Come on inside," he said. "I made blackberry muffins this morning, and I bet the boy might like one with a glass of milk."

Sue Ellen was caught off guard. "You baked muffins?"

"Somebody's got to do the cooking," he said.

They sat at the kitchen table, watching with amusement as Little Luke was finishing his second muffin. There was a ring of milk around his mouth, and crumbs had spilled onto his shirt.

His mother wasn't interested in straying from the purpose of her visit. "Once violence starts," she said, "it isn't likely to end.

Setting fires is one thing. Doing bodily harm is another. I'm worried for folks' well-being, yours in particular."

Lewis reached across the table and took her hand. "You take care of Luke and your boy," he said. "I'll tend to Captain Ringewald."

Sue Ellen borrowed a damp cloth to clean Little Luke's face before leaving. "Lewis," she said, "it's not just people in town I'm worried about."

"Who else?"

"Lately, I've been thinking a lot about Darla," she said.

Lewis gave her a hug. "I do that quite a bit myself," he said.

CHAPTER NINE

Taylor had left the farm well before sunrise in an effort to avoid an argument with his father over what he planned to do. He was riding through town when Ezzie stepped from the livery door and waved him to a stop. "Mind if I ask where you're headed?"

"I'm going out to the Rocking R. I've got some things to talk with Captain Ringewald about."

"Son, you just keep having bad ideas," Ezzie said, dusting his hat against his thigh. "You even know how to get there?"

"I'll find it."

"Not without me showing you the way."

"No, thanks. This is my business to take care of."

"I've got no interest in arguing about it," Zale said.

As Ezzie led his horse from the barn, Lewis noticed that a leather scabbard hung from his weathered saddle. In it was a Winchester.

Riding southward toward the Guadalupe River, neither spoke for several miles. Only when the sun began to come up did the landscape of gently rolling hills and endless stands of cedars come into view. In the clear morning sky, a red-tailed hawk was gliding lazily, already in search of an unsuspecting rabbit for its breakfast.

"I heard about what happened to your friend at the newspaper office," Ezzie said. "He going to be okay?"

Taylor only nodded, focusing on the winding trail that was little more than side-by-side ruts worn by passing wagons.

"For a man planning on doing a lot of talking once we get where we're going, you're mighty quiet."

"Just thinking," Lewis said.

"You know no good's going to come from this, don't you? The captain's not a man to be reasoned with. And from my limited experience, he doesn't care for uninvited guests showing up at his place. I'm speaking from personal experience.

"I made that mistake shortly after he came here, thinking I'd stop in and be neighborly, making him aware that I was available for any blacksmithing needs he might have. I was run off like a kid caught turning over the outhouse."

A mother coyote and her two pups ran across the trail, then stopped briefly to watch the riders pass.

They weren't the only ones watching. From a lean-to atop a nearby hill, two of Ringewald's guards watched Taylor and Zale through binoculars. One mounted his horse and headed toward the ranch in a gallop.

Captain Ringewald was sitting on the porch, his boots resting on the railing. Unable to sleep, he'd been there all night and was now watching the sun as it began to peek over the trees that rimmed a nearby pasture. He got to his feet when the guard approached.

"I haven't even had my coffee yet," Ringewald said. "What's the problem?"

The young Mexican nervously explained that two riders were headed toward the ranch. One, he said, was the old man who ran the livery in Gila Bend.

"And the other?"

The guard wasn't sure. He was younger, he said, and he thought he might have seen once in the saloon, talking with Lyndon Greenleaf.

"It's that Taylor fellow," the captain said. "The one who says he wants to talk."

He went into the house and quickly returned, wearing a gun belt and his pearl-handled pistol. "Go make sure Greenleaf's up and about. Remind him of our plan. He'll know what you're talking about." He then returned to his chair to wait, adjusting his Stetson to where the brim sat just above his eyes.

Even before Taylor and Zale reached the entrance to the Rocking R, the best sharpshooter working for the captain had positioned himself in an upper window of the nearby barn. It was standard procedure whenever strangers or visitors whose purpose was unknown approached.

From the gaudy archway that stood as the gateway to the ranch house was another half-mile ride. By the time they reached the house, Greenleaf was standing next to the captain.

"You boys are trespassing," Ringewald said, "and I'll thank you to be on your way." He hadn't bothered to get to his feet. Greenleaf had a crooked smile on his face, and the palm of his hand rested on the butt of his sidearm.

"A friend of mine took a beating in his office the other day," Taylor said, "and he told me who did it. I've come for an explanation."

"Got no idea what you're talking about."

"No idea who's been setting fires either?"

"I'll not have some ex-convict farmer come to my home and speak to me this way," the captain said. His eyes, already bloodshot from lack of sleep, turned even redder. "Get out. Or you're liable to get yourself shot for illegally being on my property."

"Not until I say what I've come to say," Lewis said.

"And what's that?"

"That you are a greedy coward who has others sneak around in the dark of night, causing misery to people who have done you absolutely no harm. And one way or another, I aim to see that it stops. Even if it means me seeing you dead."

For a moment, Ringewald was speechless. Greenleaf had drawn his gun and was pointing it at Taylor. As Ezzie, who had said nothing since their arrival, reached for his rifle, the captain stood and removed his hat. He was giving the signal.

A second later, a shot from the barn broke the morning stillness. Dolly's head bolted to attention. Somewhere inside the barn, chickens began clucking and scattered. Ezzie jerked upright in his saddle, groaned, then fell from his horse. His rifle bounced away.

As Greenleaf was pulling back the hammer of his pistol, Taylor turned and shot him. Poorly aimed, it struck Lyndon in the thigh, spinning him over the porch rail and into a flower bed.

As a second shot came from the barn, missing its target, the captain hurried for cover inside the house, his appetite for confrontation gone.

Lewis raced toward Ezzie's rifle. He fell to one knee, sighting the figure in the barn window. More comfortable with long guns during his army days, he took careful aim and fired. And watched the sniper somersault from his perch. He was dead before he hit the ground.

Ezzie was writhing on the ground, the sleeve of his shirt soaked in blood, as Lewis knelt over him and removed his hat to shade his eyes.

"Can you ride?" Lewis said.

"Guess I'm going to have to," he said as Taylor helped him to his feet and pressed his bandanna against the wound.

"We'll get you to the doctor."

Zale was dizzy, feeling light-headed and having trouble focusing. It took him a second to realize it was Greenleaf lying in the flower bed, bleeding and cursing. Then he looked toward the barn, where a motionless body lay in front of the doorway.

"Did you shoot the captain, too?"

Taylor was steadying him on his horse. "He didn't give me a chance. He ran into the house and hid."

Even in his weakened state, Ezzie managed a chuckle. "Well," he said, "we've most certainly stuck our foot in it now."

They were halfway to Gila Bend before he spoke again. His voice was weak. "Boy," he said, "you did good. I've got to say, I am mighty proud to know you."

From her bedroom window, Darla had heard everything: the angry exchange of words, the gunshots, the horses riding away. She was still shaking as she walked downstairs to find her husband standing in his office, a bottle of whiskey in his hand. She said nothing before hurrying to the front door. She wanted to make sure Lewis Taylor, whose voice she had not heard in years, was not injured. Relieved to see he was gone, she stepped aside as Lyndon Greenleaf limped onto the porch.

He snarled at her. "Lady," he said, "you can consider your friend a dead man."

They made it as far as the livery before Ezzie briefly passed out. Lewis made him comfortable on his bed, gave him a few sips of water, then hurried off to find Doc Johnson.

Just returned to his office after delivering Gila Bend's latest resident, the doctor joined Taylor in a sprint to the livery.

By late in the day, the bullet had been removed from Ezzie's shoulder and he was medicated and bandaged, feeling little pain. The doctor had thought to bring along the bottle of whiskey the thankful new parents had given him earlier in the day and shared it generously with his patient.

Lewis rode out to the farm while there was still daylight to let his father know he would be staying in town overnight to make sure Ezzie was all right. He told him but few details of the events at the Rocking R.

"I'll be back in the morning," he said. "Meanwhile, be sure that shotgun next to your bed is loaded."

Chapter Ten

Things were quiet for the next several days. Ezzie Zale's recovery was nothing short of miraculous as he was quickly back on his feet, parading around with his arm in a sling while eagerly awaiting any customer with whom he could share details of the "wild shoot-out" at the Ringewald ranch. He particularly enjoyed telling how the captain had run for cover at the first hint of danger.

At Lewis's suggestion, Zale had replaced the doctor's bottle of whiskey.

Luke Bradley was back at his *Sentinel* office, dictating articles that his wife typed while Little Luke played on a blanket she'd placed on the floor. When Luke visited Sheriff Barnes's office to ask if there would be an investigation of the incident at the ranch, he was told it was unlikely since no one had come forward to press any charges.

B. J. and his mother rode their buggy into Gila Bend for a visit with Ezzie and the

Bradleys. Mrs. Dixon brought freshly baked pies.

At the Rocking R, Captain Ringewald moped around in a constantly foul mood, seldom leaving his office, and always kept a glass of whiskey nearby. One of his ranch hands who had helped care for wounded soldiers during the war had removed the bullet from Greenleaf's leg. It was a painful procedure, but no ligaments or tendons appeared to have been damaged and no infection had developed. Lyndon resigned himself to spending long hours in the bunkhouse and walking with a cane for the next several weeks.

Doc Johnson, when contacted, had refused to visit the ranch.

On Ringewald's orders, the dead shooter was buried without ceremony or grave marker in a grove of trees by the creek that ran through the Rocking R.

The only person who seemed uncomfortable with the welcome quiet was Lewis.

"What do we do now?" Axel Taylor asked as he put bowls of stew and a plate of corn bread on the table.

"We wait," his son said. "They'll come, sooner or later."

"From what Ezzie tells me, there's quite a

few folks in town stirred up about what happened. They're glad somebody took it upon himself to confront Ringewald." There was a trace of pride in Axel's voice as he spoke.

Lewis let the observation pass without comment, instead saying that he thought he would ride out to B. J.'s farm. "He told me he's bought himself a couple of young pigs, and they're supposed to be delivered this afternoon. I'm going to see if he needs any help getting them settled."

Axel began clearing the table. "Wouldn't mind if you returned with one of Mrs. Dixon's pies," he said.

"Knowing her, I bet you can count on it."

He just wanted to be alone, to try to grasp the unsettling events that had transpired since his return. He thought of the grip Captain Ringewald had on Gila Bend, the harm that had come to his friends, the fires and threats, and the fear that was destroying the lifestyle he so fondly remembered. And with no intention, he now found himself in the center of the storm.

As Dolly slowly made her way along the trail, he thought that little of what had occurred made sense. Yet he believed he knew the root of the evil. Certainly part of it. In addition to being a greedy and ruthless man, Ringewald was jealous of the bygone relationship between his wife and him. By returning to Gila Bend, Lewis had instantly become an enemy, a threat to be harshly dealt with. If he was right, it was just another example of the captain's unchecked passion to control, to lord it over everything around him — the land, the town, and his bride.

Stopping at a creek to allow his horse to drink and rest, Taylor sat in the cool shade of a live oak. He thought about what Sue Ellen had said: how she doubted Darla could possibly be happy living with a man like Ringewald. And he wondered if the recent series of events might have made her life even more difficult, perhaps even put her in harm's way. If so, he was the cause of it.

And so he pondered another mission, one he'd not spoken of to anyone. Before things got worse — and he knew they would — he needed to get Darla away from the Rocking R. The only question was how.

B. J. was glad to see Taylor and proudly escorted him to the pigpen to show off his new livestock. The sow, he said, would soon be having babies. "The deal we made," he said, "was that old man Stephenson, who I got them from, would get half the litter once they were old enough to be taken from their mama. He made me a generous deal, and now, before long, I'm going to be the only one-legged pig farmer in the county."

They stood at the fence Taylor had rebuilt, watching as the pigs grunted and rooted in the hay and compost B. J. had spread.

"It was good to visit with Luke the other day," B. J. said. "He and Sue Ellen promised to come out for a day real soon. Little Luke wants to see the pigs and have some of Ma's pie. You should come with them.

"I don't think I realized how much I missed him — and you. When I was in town, Luke reminded me of some of the things we used to do as kids, the fun we had. And he showed me the new editorial he'd written for next week's paper. Captain Ringewald won't be pleased."

Sue Ellen had already shown it to Taylor. It was headlined "Finally, Something to Smile About," and gave some details of the confrontation at the Ringewald ranch, most of which had been colorfully provided by "local livery owner Ezra P. Zale, who was injured during the skirmish." It also quoted Sheriff Barnes, who "told the *Sentinel* no charges would be filed." It ended with another question from Bradley: "What's next?"

■ ■ ■ ■

When the newspaper was brought to him, Captain Ringewald didn't even get to Bradley's question before angrily tossing the paper aside. However, he had been asking himself the same thing.

Retaliation, carried out soon, was essential. But what form it would take, he'd not yet decided. He called out to the maid and told her he wanted to see his wife.

Darla was out at the corral, admiring a newborn foal, when summoned. She was pleased to find that her husband was sober when she entered his office. Aside from the paper that was scattered on the floor, the room was orderly. The head of a sixteen-point mule deer hung on one wall, surrounded by framed photographs of prize Longhorns. Behind his desk was a painting of Captain Ringewald proudly sitting astride his Palomino.

"Tell me about this Taylor fellow," he said.

She feigned puzzlement. "Why?"

"I just want to know who it is I'm dealing with. You and him were once sweet on each other, right?"

"We were just kids, Archer. It was a long time ago. We grew up together."

"I know he went to prison. Is he the outlaw type? Mean? Hot-tempered?"

"Not the Lewis Taylor I remember. He was a nice and polite young man who worked hard with his daddy on their farm."

The captain leaned back in his chair, slowly lighting a cigar. The look on his face turned dark, and his eyes narrowed. "How are you going to feel when I kill him?" he asked.

Without response, Darla hurried from the room. She waited until she was in the hallway before she began to cry.

Chapter Eleven

A crowd was gathered in front of the sheriff's office, waiting for him to step onto the sidewalk and talk with them. They had been arriving since early morning: farmers, ranchers, and shopkeepers, men and women. They were orderly but getting impatient, having come to ask Sherriff Barnes what he intended to do about the growing chaos that had visited Gila Bend.

Standing among them was Luke Bradley, who had prompted the event with his latest *Sentinel* editorial. Though his fingers were still bandaged, he held a notebook, into which he was writing down quotes from those on hand. The best he'd gotten so far had come from an elderly farmer's wife who told him she prayed nightly that her grandchildren wouldn't have to grow up in a town where hateful, godless men carried out cruel deeds while the law looked the other way.

The waiting went unrewarded. The sheriff

had slipped through the jail and into the alley and was riding toward his small ranch outside of town. He preferred the quiet company of his cattle to the angry questions from those who had elected him.

As he rode, he was wishing he'd never applied for his job. Or that he'd ever met Captain Ringewald.

That evening, Ezzie had just returned from the saloon, his go-to-sleep shot of whiskey still warm in his belly. Lewis was sitting on the bench in front of the livery.

"You got no better place to be this time of night?"

"I've come to ask for your help . . . again."

"I'm not sure what use I can be since you already got me shot up and one armed."

"What I have in mind won't require much more than sneaking past Ringewald's guards." He knew that the plan he had devised was extreme, perhaps even foolhardy. But after long hours of consideration, he was determined to see it through.

Zale took a seat next to Taylor, obviously interested. "Sneaking, I can do," he said. "What else?"

"I'll need the loan of a horse with a bit more speed and stamina than mine, a can of coal oil, and a couple of torches."

Ezzie smiled. "You're going to fight fire with fire, ain't you?"

For the next few minutes, Lewis detailed a plan he had for getting Ringewald's wife away from the Rocking R. It would also involve his father and hers; both had already said they would help.

"You thinking about kidnapping the woman?"

"I'm hoping she doesn't view it that way," Lewis said, "but, yes, if that's what's necessary."

"Lord help me, where do you come up with these ideas?"

The plan was relatively simple and posed little danger for Ezzie or the others. To reach Darla, a diversion would be necessary to get everyone away from the house and the bunkhouse. In the middle of the night, Ezzie and Axel Taylor would approach the ranch's south pasture and set fires.

"I think I can map us out a route that will get us there without anyone knowing we're coming," Ezzie said. There was a growing excitement in his voice.

"Then we'll do it tomorrow night," Lewis said.

It was near midnight when the four men met at the barn. Ezzie had a young black stallion waiting in the doorway, impatiently pawing at the dirt. "I've got no extra saddle," he said, "so you'll need to use your own."

Stanley Winslow was the only one who appeared nervous.

As he removed his saddle from Dolly, Lewis went through the plan again. "Ezzie and Pa will ride down to the back side of Ringewald's pasture, where a herd of his cows will be. You'll spread coal along the fence line and set the fires. I'd prefer that none of the livestock is injured.

"Once there's a blaze, you're to get out of there as fast as you can.

"If things go as I hope, somebody's sure to notice and everybody will head that way. As soon as everyone's out of sight, Stanley and me will go to the house and get Darla. It all needs to be done quickly."

They followed the rutted trail most of the way before splitting up. Ezzie and Axel rode south, past a stand of cedars and onto the side of a rise that kept them out of sight of the ranch. Lewis and Darla's father continued down the trail for another half mile.

"There's likely to be guards on a hillside not far from here," Lewis whispered. "I'm betting they'll be sleeping, but we'll not take any chances." They left the trail and made a wide sweep past where the guards' lean-to was located.

Torches would have made the going easier, lighting the way for their horses, but they felt it safer to move along slowly and with care, hidden by darkness. Above, there was only a sliver of a moon.

Winslow hadn't said a word since they'd left Gila Bend. Lewis's only purpose in inviting him along was the hope that seeing her daddy would ease any fear Darla might have that she would be harmed when they entered the house.

They tethered their horses a short distance from the darkened house, then moved closer on foot before crouching behind the smokehouse to wait.

It was the captain, again sleeping in his chair on the porch, who first saw the orange glow in the distant sky. For a moment, he thought he might be dreaming but was soon wide-awake and on his feet. He cupped his hands to his mouth and yelled in the direction of the bunkhouse.

"Fire! We've got fire in the south pasture."

There was a sudden flurry of activity as cowhands raced into the yard, some sleepily stumbling as they pulled on their britches while running toward the barn to saddle their horses. Ringewald was leading the way. "See to the cattle," he said. "Get them to safety."

Lewis watched the melee play out. "It's working," he said.

A mile away, Ezzie and Axel had tossed away their torches and the empty coal oil can and were riding away into the night.

As the last rider left the barn, Lewis nodded to Winslow. "Let's go," he said.

They slowed as they neared the porch, holding their breath and listening for any unusual noise. The light from a single lantern was now glowing in an upstairs window. Lewis drew his pistol before carefully opening the front door and stepping inside. Winslow followed, his mouth dry, his hands shaking.

The maid, wakened by the ruckus outside, was standing near the doorway to the kitchen and screamed when she saw the two men enter.

At the top of the stairs, wearing a robe and with a puzzled look on her face, stood Darla. Her husband's yelling and the sound of horses galloping away had wakened her. She was rubbing her eyes, looking more puzzled than frightened.

"What . . . ?"

■ ■ ■ ■

Stanley's fear disappeared at the sight of his daughter, and he raced up the stairway. Lewis was momentarily motionless as he looked into the face of the young woman he'd not seen in over five years. Even with her hair in tangles and a look of bewilderment on her face, she was beautiful.

Winslow hugged his daughter. "Get dressed, honey. Hurry. We've got to go."

"Where?"

"Away from here."

For the first time, Lewis spoke. "We'll explain later," he said. "You're not safe here."

The maid was peeking from the kitchen door, her hands covering her mouth, when Darla came from her bedroom, wearing riding pants, a checkered shirt, and boots. She had opted for a hat instead of attempting to brush her hair. Stanley grabbed her by the hand, hurrying her down the stairs. She still hadn't uttered a complete sentence.

As Lewis pushed the front door open, there was the sudden sound of a shot, followed by a hollow thud as a bullet buried itself in the nearby porch rail. There was the silhouette of a man coming toward the house, limping badly. He stopped to take aim and again missed his target. Off balance, he fell.

Lyndon Greenleaf, still having difficulty getting around on his injured leg, had been left behind when the others headed toward the fire.

Lewis fired a shot above Greenleaf's head and waved to Winslow. "Get her out of here. Take her on your horse, and I'll be right behind you." He fired two more shots to keep Greenleaf on the ground as Darla and her father ran from the porch and disappeared.

When they were a safe distance away, Taylor called out to Greenleaf, who was trying to get back on his feet, "I've got no interest in shooting you again, so holster your gun and let me be on my way."

Greenleaf replied with a curse followed by another wayward shot. Lewis vaulted over the porch rail and ran toward the smokehouse.

Captain Ringewald returned to the house shortly after sunrise. Several of the hands followed while others remained behind to make certain the fires were completely out. Everyone was relieved that all of the Longhorns had been herded away, uninjured.

They were surprised to see the maid sitting in the front yard, Lyndon Greenleaf's head resting on her lap. She was wiping his brow with a wet towel. The stitches in his injured thigh had been torn away and one leg of his britches was soaked in blood. His face was ashen, and it looked as though he might pass out.

Ringewald moved his horse closer and pushed his hat back as he looked down at Greenleaf. "What happened to you? I thought you were told to remain in bed."

Greenleaf whispered something but the captain couldn't understand what he was trying to say.

"He's telling you that some men came and took Miss Darla away," the maid said.

The captain's face turned red and spittle exploded from his mouth. "Who was it?"

She leaned close to hear what Greenleaf was saying, then again looked up at Ringewald. "He says it was her daddy . . . and a man called Taylor. Lewis Taylor."

Ezzie and Lewis's father were already at the livery when Stanley Winslow and his daughter arrived. Lewis, having ridden his borrowed horse hard, was only a few minutes behind them.

Darla was drinking water from a wooden

dipper Zale had handed her and still looked in shock. But rather than apprehension, there was a peaceful, almost childlike look on her face. Her father stood at her side, bathed in sweat but smiling.

"We've got no time to stand around," Lewis said. He looked at Darla. "You'll ride Ezzie's horse and come with me and your pa." He turned and shook his father's hand. "I appreciate what you did," he said. "Now, get on back to the farm and act like nothing happened.

"Ezzie, it might be a good idea if you went on down to the café and had some breakfast, whether you're hungry or not. Visit with some folks. Make it look like you're carrying on a normal routine.

"The captain and his people will be coming this way shortly, and they won't be in a good mood."

Darla stepped toward Lewis and spoke for the first time since they arrived at the livery. "He told me he wants to kill you," she said.

"I figured as much," Taylor said.

B. J. was standing in his yard when they reached his farm. As she got down from her horse, Darla smiled at him and tried to hide her surprise. She hadn't been aware of his war injury. They hugged, and he asked if she was all right.

"Ma's inside, cooking," he said. "Pork chops, red-eye gravy, biscuits, and no telling what else. She was sure everybody would be hungry."

"That's mighty nice of her," Stanley said.

Lewis took the reins of the horses and led them to the makeshift shed he'd built to replace the barn. He was pouring oats when Darla joined him.

"It's good to see you, Lewis," she said. "I didn't even know you were back until the other day when I heard you on the front porch, arguing with my husband. Are you going to explain to me what's going on? The captain doesn't tell me much."

"You refer to him as 'the captain'?"

"When I refer to him at all." Weary, she took a seat on a nearby bale of hay.

Lewis sat beside her. "Since I've been home, a lot of bad things have been happening." He told her about the fires and Greenleaf beating Luke Bradley. Of how Ringewald's bank was treating customers. "People are scared to death of your husband and those who ride for him. He's running farmers away and stealing their land and taking over the town."

None of what he was saying seemed to surprise her.

"The more I saw and heard," Lewis said, "the more worried I got about you. How you were being treated. Your daddy was feeling the same way. That's why we came to get you."

"I've been praying somebody would since what Archer said to me the other day." She leaned forward and placed a gentle kiss on his cheek. "You know he won't stand for this, don't you?"

"Soon as it's safe, we're going to get you far away from here until things are settled," he said.

"And then what? What about you?"

Lewis touched his cheek where she had kissed him. "Right now," he said, "about as far ahead as I can think is Mrs. Dixon's kitchen table, where pork chops are waiting."

As they walked toward the house, both exhausted, he asked, "Does the captain know you and B. J. were friends back in the day?"

"I've never mentioned it."

"Then you should be safe here, at least for the time being. B. J. and his mama will take good care of you."

Later, as they walked into the yard, Stanley Winslow quickened his pace to catch up with Lewis. He squared his shoulders in an attempt to hide the pain he was feeling in his abdomen. "I can't tell you how grateful I am for what you've done," he said. He paused, took a deep breath, then added, "And I owe you an apology."

Taylor shook his head. He was aware Winslow had never approved of him courting his daughter. Now that was in the distant past, far too late for apologies.

"All you need to concentrate on now is seeing that Darla's safe. Things are going to be difficult for a while. You'll want to be with her, but you need to stay away. Go home. Act like all this never happened. Ringewald or some of his people will come looking for you, putting pressure on you, wanting to know where she is. No matter what, you can't tell them."

"That's my intention," he said. He looked exhausted, causing Lewis to wonder if he would be able to make it home alone.

"I'll ride with you," he said.

"You won't want to when you hear what I need to say."

Taylor gave him a puzzled look.

"You remember all those letters you wrote to Darla in those first years you were in prison? She never got them, Lewis. I saw to it. I intercepted every one of them and threw them away. I know you'll never forgive me, but I just want you to know how ashamed I am."

Lewis looked at him in disbelief. "Have you said anything to Darla about it?"

"No, but I'm going to."

"I wouldn't if I were you," Lewis said before riding away.

Chapter Twelve

A half dozen riders, led by the captain, arrived at the café and hurried toward the front door. They had already been to the livery and found no one there. They smelled of smoke and coal oil and had soot covering their chaps and boots. Their appearance silenced the usual morning chatter. The waitress, in the middle of taking an order, turned and stared. The cook stopped breaking eggs into a skillet and walked into the main room, curious to see what was happening.

Ringewald's eyes scanned the tables. "I'm looking for Lewis Taylor," he said. His voice was hoarse, and he was obviously angry. "If anybody knows where I can find him, now's a good time to speak up."

The room was silent. At a back table, Ezzie Zale dunked a piece of sweet bread into his coffee and avoided eye contact.

The captain had no better luck at Luke

Bradley's office. One of his men shoved a shoulder into the locked front door, tearing it from its hinges. The *Sentinel* office was empty and dark, not yet open for business.

Three of the men were ordered to check every building in town while the captain and the others went to the Bradley home. Ringewald dismounted and called Luke into the front yard. Inside, Sue Ellen was holding Little Luke, who had begun to cry.

"Where's Taylor?"

"I don't have the slightest idea."

"You sure he's not hiding inside?"

"You're welcome to come in and look, though I'd appreciate you not scaring my wife and boy any more than you have already. What's this about?"

Ringewald ignored his question and sent two men into the house to check. In a short time they returned, shaking their heads.

"You and me, we'll talk more later," the captain said as Bradley turned to go back inside.

As he lifted a boot into his stirrup, the sheriff approached. Someone from the café had come to his office and alerted him that Ringewald and his men were in town.

"What's going on?" he said.

The captain gave him a quick recap of the events that had played out at the ranch.

"They took my wife," he said. "Kidnapped her in the middle of the night. It was Lewis Taylor and Stanley Winslow, and I aim to find them. I see it as your sworn duty to help."

"Kidnapped her?"

"And they're going to pay dearly for it," Ringewald said. "You can trust me on that."

He gathered his men and outlined a new plan. Three men were to accompany Sheriff Barnes to Winslow's place on the edge of town. He and the others would head out to the Taylor farm.

Darla's father was disheveled and nervous when the sheriff appeared at his front door. The deep breaths he took did little to calm him. "Is there a problem?" he said.

"I'm told you were out at the Ringewald place last night."

Winslow shook his head. "I haven't been out there since the Fourth of July barbecue they had. You and your wife were there as well, as best I recall. Truth is, I don't get invited there all that often.

"You going to tell me what's going on?"

Ringewald's men were entering his house as he posed the question. They had no more luck than they'd had at the Bradley home.

"Your daughter's been taken," the sheriff

said, "and we aim to find her. If you know her whereabouts, I'd suggest you would be wise to tell us."

"Taken? By who?"

"You, according to what I'm being told. You and Lewis Taylor."

Winslow was uncertain whether to demonstrate outrage or surprise. "Sheriff," he finally said, "I have no idea what you're talking about. But if my daughter's in danger, I want her found immediately. What can I do to help?"

"Just stay here, in case she shows up."

Winslow took another deep breath as the men rode away. He'd pulled it off pretty well, he thought. Then, however, his hand again began to shake.

At his farm, Axel Taylor was sitting on his front porch, waiting. He knew he would be having visitors shortly and didn't bother getting to his feet when Captain Ringewald and his men arrived.

"Morning," he said.

"Where's your boy, Mr. Taylor?"

"I've got no idea. We don't see much of each other these days."

Ringewald's impatience exploded. Leaving his horse, he raced onto the porch and grabbed Axel by his shirt collar and lifted him into a standing position. Then he smashed a fist into the side of his face. He pulled his pistol and pressed the barrel against Taylor's temple. "I'd just as soon blow your brains out as drink whiskey," he said. "Tell me where he is, or you can count on never seeing him again."

"Look around for yourself," Axel said, wiping away the blood that dripped from his ear. "You'll see he ain't here. And once you're satisfied with that, I'll thank you to leave and not come back."

The captain's response was another hard blow to Axel's face, which sent him to his knees. "I'll come back whenever I want," he said. "And when this place is mine, you'll need to find yourself another porch to sit on."

He was running out of places to look. The adrenaline that had been pumping since he'd first seen that his pasture was ablaze was fading. As he and his men stopped at a stream to water their horses, Ringewald knelt at the bank and splashed water onto his face. He cursed to himself. "Where are they?" he said.

He recalled seeing Lewis Taylor once out at that crippled fellow's run-down farm, but doubted it was a place where Taylor or his wife might be. Still, he ordered two of his men to ride out there and check.

"I'm heading back to the ranch," he said, "just in case my wandering wife might have returned." His tone was hardly that of a concerned husband.

Mrs. Dixon was in her garden when she saw dust rising down the road. She ran to the house to tell her son that someone was coming. As they had already planned, Darla hurried out the back door and hid in the root cellar.

She didn't have to stay there long.

Ringewald's men, also tired and losing their enthusiasm for the hunt, only spoke briefly with B. J. No, he said, he knew nothing about the whereabouts of the Ringewald woman or Lewis Taylor.

Satisfied, they quickly left to report to the captain. No way a one-legged dirt farmer could be hiding Ringewald's wife or the man who had abducted her.

Lewis watched from a shallow ravine as the last of the captain's men rode past, on their way back to the ranch. Tired from sixteen hours without sleep, their heads bobbed in rhythm with their horses' gait. Once they were out of sight, Taylor headed for the livery.

Badly in need of sleep himself, he removed

the saddle from Ezzie's horse and leaned against the wall of Dolly's stall. Soon, he was sleeping.

He had no idea how long he'd been asleep when he woke, ending a dream in which Captain Ringewald, in full Union uniform, was standing over him, pointing a gun at his head. Lewis still had a look of relief that his mind had just been playing games when Ezzie appeared.

Lewis took the hand extended to lift him to his feet. "I just wanted to stop by and say hello to my horse," he said.

Ezzie was in no mood for levity. "What do you anticipate happening next?" he said.

"Ringewald will be back soon. In the meantime, he'll sit out at his ranch, just getting madder and madder, thinking of ways he can kill me. Then he'll come looking again. I know he'll eventually be successful in finding me, but not before I make a short trip."

"To where?"

"Best you don't know," Lewis said. "But I'd like to continue to borrow your horse for a few more days."

It was the only part of his plan he had not shared with anyone. But before he set it in motion, he wanted to alert his father that he would soon be traveling.

■ ■ ■ ■

Lewis was at first enraged, then felt a sense of guilt sweep over him when he saw the bruises on Axel Taylor's face. "I've caused this to happen," he said, "and I'll make it up to you."

"I just wish I'd had my shotgun on the porch with me when they rode up. I'd have shot him before he could climb down from his horse. I told him nothing, but he's going to keep looking for you, Son. He's madder and meaner than ever."

"I know." Taylor explained that he would be leaving soon. "I've got something I need to do. Then I'll be back and figure a way to settle this. Meanwhile, I want you to ride into town and stay at the livery with Ezzie Zale until I return." There was a firmness in his son's voice that he had never before heard. Lewis was leaving no room for argument. "You'll be safer there. It's less likely they'll hurt anyone with people in town watching."

"Seeing as it's the captain you're talking about, I wouldn't count on it. But okay, I'll see that the livestock get fed and the house is closed up. Then I'll be on my way."

"Take your shotgun with you," Lewis said.

■ ■ ■ ■

After the ranch hands had a few hours' sleep, the maid delivered a basket of fried egg sandwiches and a large pot of coffee to the bunkhouse. She told the men that Captain Ringewald wished to see everyone in his office as soon as they finished breakfast.

"I wouldn't dawdle," she said as she placed the food on a table. She then went to Lyndon Greenleaf's bunk to check on his leg. He was sitting up, pulling on his boots. Beads of sweat had formed across his forehead.

"You shouldn't be getting out of bed," she said. Even as she spoke, she knew her warning would go unheeded.

The captain was standing beneath his portrait, arms folded and a stern look on his face, as the men filed in.

"Lewis Taylor can't hide forever," he said. "I want him found soon." He outlined the plan he had devised in the wee hours. A small group would remain at the ranch, seeing after the cattle and standing guard in case another raid was attempted. He called out the names of five men he wanted to go into Gila Bend and patrol, watching for any unusual activity that might offer some idea of where Taylor was hiding. The sheriff would oversee that part of the operation. Two men, he instructed, would keep watch over Axel Taylor's farm, in case his son attempted to return home.

"Saddle up and get going," he said. Then he added, "There will be extra pay for the man who brings Taylor to me."

It was as if the captain was back in the war, giving orders to the troops. No one found it unusual that he made no mention of his missing wife. He was focused only on the enemy, Lewis Taylor.

Leaning against the doorframe, keeping weight off his injured leg, Greenleaf waited behind as the others left.

Ringewald looked at his right-hand man for a moment, then said, "Get yourself some rest. Whenever you feel able to ride, I want you to go into town and see to it no more newspapers are published. Ever. Feel free to handle the matter as you see fit."

Greenleaf nodded and limped away. Though still in pain, he was smiling.

When Lewis arrived at the Dixon farm, he was at first worried when he didn't see Darla.

"I wasn't sure it was you coming," B. J.

said from the front porch, "so I sent her to the root cellar. Ma's gone to get her."

As Darla entered the kitchen, she was brushing back her hair. She was wearing a pair of britches Mrs. Dixon had given her and one of B. J.'s shirts. She smiled at Taylor.

"I can fix some breakfast," Daisy offered. "Flapjacks and bacon, okay?"

"There's no time." Lewis quickly explained why it would be safer for her and her son to take the buggy into town and spend the next few days at the livery. "I've suggested everybody plan on staying there, at least until I get back and can come up with a plan."

"Strength in numbers," B. J. said, then asked where Taylor was going.

"I'm taking Darla someplace safe," he said.

While he helped B. J. hitch up the buggy, Mrs. Dixon was busy putting leftover biscuits and corn bread muffins into one pocket of Lewis's saddlebags. In the other, she placed a change of clothes for Darla.

"What kind of plan are you thinking about when you get back?" B. J. said. "I see no way you can avoid eventually facing Ringewald and his people."

Lewis agreed. "The only thing I have to

work out is a way to see that nobody else gets hurt."

It wasn't until they had left the farm that Darla asked where they were going. As she sat behind Lewis, her arms around his waist, a rush of excitement replaced the apprehension she had been feeling since leaving the ranch.

"You'll know soon," Lewis said. "With the horse carrying two of us, we'll not be able to travel as fast and will need more rest stops. Still, I figure with luck we can reach our destination late tonight."

"I appreciate what you're doing," she said, "but you know I can't hide forever."

"I'm aware of that. It'll just be for a little while, until things are settled and it's safe for you to return."

Darla rested her head against his back as they rode northward in silence.

The horse was weary, walking with its nose almost touching the ground by the time they arrived at the Goolsby farm. From what Lewis could tell with help from only the moonlight, little had changed since he'd last visited.

"Hello the house," he called out. "It's Lewis Taylor."

Nina Goolsby was the first on the porch,

holding a lantern that provided enough light for her to recognize the visitor. "Oh, my stars," she said, as she hurried into the yard.

Preacher was close behind, pulling the straps of his overalls across his shoulders. "Good to see you, boy."

Darla peeked out from behind Taylor and smiled. "I've brought a friend," he said as he helped her from the horse.

"Well, come on in the house," Nina said. "I bet you folks are about as hungry as you are tired."

It was almost midnight by the time Lewis had tended to the horse in Preacher's barn. As he entered the cabin, everyone was talking like old friends. The table was set, and the smell of frying bacon filled the room.

Preacher had already explained that they had not yet found a buyer for their farm. The offers they had received were lower than they felt was fair. "Could be I'm too proud of this old place," he said, "but I have no intention of just giving it away." The repair work Taylor had done during his brief stay had given the elderly Goolsby new incentive to keep things up and running smoothly. "Only thing I haven't been able to take care of is a little outbuilding down by the corral. A high wind took off the roof recently, and at my age, I'm not about to do the climbing necessary to fix it. Other than that, everything's pretty much as you left it.

"So the way things now stand, when our time comes, we'll both wind up going to our Maker straight from this farm."

As she came around the table to place a plate of flapjacks, slathered in butter and honey, in front of Lewis, Nina put a hand on his shoulder. "We'd given up hope of ever seeing you again," she said, "but we've kept you in our prayers."

Darla had waited for Lewis to join them and explain why she was traveling with him.

It was almost sunrise before he finished describing the turmoil he'd encountered on his return to Gila Bend. He left nothing out as he detailed the corruption, violence, and fear that had changed his quiet and peaceful hometown for the worse.

"And all this has been caused by one man?" Preacher said.

For the first time since Lewis had been talking, Darla spoke. "Yes," she said, "and that man is my husband, I'm sorry to say."

Nina put a hand to her mouth and shook her head. "Bless your heart," she said.

Lewis then told how he and her father had taken her from the ranch, fearful that harm would come her way. "Until this matter is settled — and I'm hoping it will be soon —

she's not safe. That's why we're here. If you could see your way to let her stay . . ."

Preacher didn't even allow him to finish his sentence. "Son, she's welcome here," he said. "And I can promise you we'll see that she's cared for properly. I'll even take to sleeping on the front porch with my shotgun in my lap if necessary."

Lewis smiled across the table at Darla. "I told you these were good folks," he said.

Part Two

Chapter Thirteen

This time it wasn't just Luke Bradley's fingers that were damaged. The Saturday-night visitors to the *Sentinel* office used a sledgehammer to wreck his printing press and typewriter. File cabinets were overturned, and papers strewn throughout the room. Windows were broken out, and the front and back doors were off their hinges. Whitewash was splashed against every wall.

Gila Bend's newspaper was out of business.

The thing that most disturbed Bradley when he surveyed the damage was the small gold picture frame that lay on the floor, its glass stomped into shards. Once having occupied a prominent place on his desk, it had held a photo of his wife and son.

"I wonder why they didn't just torch the place," Sue Ellen said as they stood amid the destruction.

"This, I suppose, is intended to deliver a

stronger message," her husband said. "They're no longer even trying to hide themselves or their intentions." He knew it was Lyndon Greenleaf and his friends who had ridden through their yard at three o'clock in the morning, yelling his name.

What Luke didn't mention, but was already thinking about, was what they would say at the bank when it learned the *Sentinel* no longer had a way to generate income.

Monday morning, loan officer R. J. O'Malley was knocking on the Bradley door. A rat-faced man who wore bifocals and was barely over five feet tall, he had a sheepish look that signaled his embarrassment over the task he had been assigned.

"I've, uh, just learned of what occurred at your office over the weekend," he said, "and wanted to stop by and tell you how sorry we at the bank are. It was such a relief to know that no one was injured." He then paused and focused on the floor as Little Luke playfully tugged at his leg. "All that said, uh, it is of some concern that your next loan payment will be due at the first of the month. Without the ability to continue publishing your paper, do you, uh, feel you will be able to address your debt in, uh, a timely manner?"

Sue Ellen seldom cursed, but when she did, it was with a heat that would scorch her kitchen curtains. Before her husband could say anything, she was ordering O'Malley out of their house. "Vultures are not welcome here," she shouted.

The diminutive loan officer turned and left quickly, looking much like a puppy that had been scolded for hiking his leg on the living room rug.

Luke couldn't help but laugh. "I've got to say, you really know how to treat company." His son was laughing along with him.

It was the following afternoon when Stanley Winslow huddled at a back table in the café, talking in low tones with a man the waitress had never seen before. He was middle-aged and overweight, and wore a black bowler hat. Their conversation lasted for some time before both stood, shook hands, and left.

Ringewald's men, watching from the nearby counter, saw nothing devious about the meeting and made no plans to report it to the captain. Instead, they followed Winslow home and watched him disappear into the side door. Later, he walked down to the mercantile, where he briefly spoke with a goat farmer they recognized, then purchased a sack of ten-penny nails. He rested on the bench in front of the store for some time, looking up and down the nearly deserted street, then slowly made his way back home.

The ranch hands agreed that if Darla Ringewald was to be found, it wouldn't be at her father's house or have anything to do with him and his daily habits.

Late on Wednesday afternoon, the farmer Winslow had spoken to in the mercantile — Gilley Dewberry — steered his wagon into town, pulling his mules to a stop in front of the *Sentinel* office. At his side was the man wearing the bowler.

His name was Archibald Miller, and he had been editor of the weekly newspaper in nearby Denton Creek before suffering a heart attack that forced him to retire. While in business, Stanley Winslow had made monthly visits to do his bookkeeping.

A tarp covered what filled the bed of the wagon — a hand-crank printing press and numerous items from his old office, including an ancient-looking typewriter and a well-worn adding machine. Winslow had used some of his savings to buy Miller's equipment and pay Dewberry to haul it to Gila Bend.

The Bradleys and Winslow were the first to greet them. Soon, several townspeople gathered to help with unloading and moving the equipment inside. Sue Ellen, almost giddy, was promising everyone a "thank you" barbecue in the park just as soon as her husband's paper was back in business. Stanley Winslow blushed when she hugged and kissed him on the cheek.

From a distance, Ringewald's men sat on their horses, watching the flurry of activity that was fast taking on the look of a celebration. "The captain ain't going to like this," one said.

"Not one bit," said the other.

Neither would he be happy to learn that Winslow had quietly organized several young men in town to begin a rotation of nightly guarding the *Sentinel* office.

The town had begun to fight back.

Even before Lewis returned from his brief trip, he had made up his mind that he would not attempt to hide from Ringewald or his men. He rode straight to the livery to exchange Ezzie's stallion for his own horse and see that everyone who had been staying there in his absence was okay.

"We've been watched like a hawk looking for a rabbit," B. J. said, "but nothing's happened except for a late-night dustup at the newspaper." He told Taylor of the destructive raid on the *Sentinel,* then of the happy ending that Darla's father had arranged. Captain Ringewald had not been seen. "I'm getting the impression the men he told to stay in town and keep watch over us are tiring of their job. They're spending more and more time down at the saloon."

In Taylor's absence, B. J., his mother, and Axel Taylor had helped Ezzie clean his stalls and work space like they'd never been cleaned before, reorganized his tools, and washed away the grime from the walls of the barn.

"I'm proud to say the place is looking like new. Mrs. Dixon is now cleaning things that have done been cleaned," Ezzie said. Then in a lower voice, he added, "But the truth is, it's beginning to feel a bit crowded. There's not much in the way of privacy." He admitted he'd been staying considerably longer at the saloon when he went for his evening shot of whiskey.

Axel greeted his son and agreed with Ezzie's observation. "I've gone out a couple of times with some folks who have stopped by, offering help, and taken care of the animals at our place and B. J.'s. But mostly we've just been visiting one another and listening to Ezzie's grumbling. Everybody's feeling closed in and homesick."

Even Lewis's dog, Whisper, who had followed Axel into town and been sleeping in Dolly's stall, seemed eager to return to the farm.

Pleased that everyone was okay, Lewis announced that it was time they returned home. "I've been thinking about it," he said, "and it doesn't seem right that we appear scared. If everyone stays alert and keeps a firearm nearby, I suggest the thing we should do is get back to as normal a routine as possible."

It was left to Ezzie to ask the question on everyone's mind. "Darla okay?"

"She's somewhere safe, probably working in the garden at this very minute," Lewis replied. He gave a quick thought to her wearing a sunbonnet, smiling and happy. He saddled Dolly, then slowly rode through town to see Luke and his new printing press.

Several people waved as he passed.

Bradley was in the back room, holding up a broadsheet he had just printed. Across it in bold letters, were the words BACK IN BUSINESS. He was obviously satisfied with his work.

"We've been wondering about you for the last few days," he said. "It's good to see you back. I guess you've already heard what happened here." He waited for Lewis to mention Darla, but he didn't.

"People are still scared," Bradley said, "but nobody's holding his breath like before. Stanley's boldness and generosity seem to have changed things some. You can even sense it in the attitude of the captain's hoodlums. Mostly, they're just ignoring us, and we're ignoring them."

He said that Sue Ellen was busy planning a weekend barbecue to honor Winslow. "Your daddy has donated a calf, Mrs. Dixon says she'll bake pies, and half the able-bodied women in town are bringing dishes. A week ago, I wouldn't have bet you could get enough folks to play a game of checkers. Now it appears the whole town's going to turn out.

"I was told earlier this morning that your friend Ezzie, colorful old coot that he is, even invited the Ringewald cowhands who have been hanging around town. He apparently extended the invitation when he was visiting the saloon last night.

"I'm feeling a change, Lewis. A good one."

So, too, was Taylor. But he knew better than to let his guard down. "The captain's nowhere through taking his revenge," he said. "Not by a long shot." As he turned to leave, he said, "When you see Winslow, assure him his daughter's somewhere safe."

■ ■ ■ ■

Saturday in the park was a different kind of celebration. The women brought bowls and plates of food and gallons of lemonade. The men brought their shotguns and sidearms. The air was filled with the sweet smell of Axel Taylor's beef cooking, and blankets were spread in every bit of shade that could be found. As the day quickly passed, appetites were satisfied, and the laughter grew. Luke Bradley made a brief speech, thanking the honored guest for his generosity.

Winslow gave a shy wave, then returned his attention to the large slice of Daisy Dixon's pear pie he was trying to finish despite having little appetite. No one seemed to notice how pale he was or that he left the festivities early.

To most, things had a look and feel of the Gila Bend of old.

As darkness approached and the cleanup was completed, a number of the men headed toward the Captain's Bar. Unlike Saturday nights past, there were none of Ringewald's men inside, noisily drinking, playing poker, picking fights, or seeing who could get drunk the quickest.

■ ■ ■ ■

At the Rocking R, the maid looked at the captain's untouched plate and quietly took it away. He had been sitting alone at the huge dining table for two hours, his staring at the wall interrupted only by sips he took from his whiskey glass.

He was taking stock of his situation and not feeling good about it. His grip on the town, once easily held through fear and intimidation, was slipping. The return of a farmer's son, a man just released from prison, had changed things. It had all begun as a bullying act of jealousy, but had grown into something entirely different. His attempted show of strength and control had been a failure he didn't wish to admit.

In truth, he didn't even miss his wife. They hardly spoke anyway. She had been just another prize he could display, like his ever-growing wealth and status as one of the largest landowners in South Texas. When she had been taken away — kidnapped, he continued to insist — all of his emotion had immediately focused on the man who took her, not on her well-being. He would admit only to himself that it was most likely that she was glad to be gone.

Seeking blame, he cursed those working for him. Lyndon Greenleaf aside, he had no employees with a taste for the violence and meanness necessary to solve his problem. They were cowhands, good at their jobs, but not outlaws. The only outlaw he had was limping around like an old man, virtually useless.

It was late when he called out to the maid and asked that she have Greenleaf come to the house. Perhaps there was something he could do that didn't require two good legs.

Though still limping badly and relying on his cane for balance, Greenleaf was on the mend. He had felt good enough to oversee the late-night attack on the *Sentinel* and had quit spending most of his days in bed.

He waited until the captain nodded toward a chair before sitting. On the table were a folded piece of paper and a bag of gold coins.

Ringewald didn't offer Greenleaf any of his whiskey, only pushed the paper across the table toward him.

"I want you to go down to Eagle Pass and find the man whose name I've written. Tell him I have a job for him and a few of his best men. This money you'll be giving him is only payment for him to come to the ranch and hear me out. Tell him the job won't take long and that the pay will be very good.

"I'm told the best place to start looking for him is the Brimstone Hotel. If he's not there, go across the border to El Casa Gallo in Piedras Negras.

"Don't let me down."

Written on the paper were but two words: El Diablo, Spanish for "the devil."

It was a name the captain had first heard during the war, while battling Confederate troops near the Brownsville shipping ports. To all who fought the war in South Texas, whether wearing Union blue or Confederate gray, the name struck fear and demanded grudging respect. To both armies, he was a constant and deadly threat, the ghostlike leader of a small band of cutthroats who came from the Mexican side of the border to rob and, when necessary, do violence.

It had been during an evening of drinking, shortly after they met, that Sheriff Barnes and the captain had been swapping exaggerated war stories when tales of the infamous bandit entered the conversation. Through others in law enforcement, Barnes had heard that El Diablo and his men had continued their criminal activities long after the war ended. Though unaware of anyone who had ever attempted to apprehend him, the location of the border headquarters of El Diablo's operation was commonly known.

Born to an American father who earned his living cheating at cards and a Mexican mother who tended bar in a shabby Laredo cantina, Dain Hayes had joined the Mexican Army as a teenager and almost immediately assembled a small group of young, rebellious soldiers who had little interest in protecting their country or lending to the Confederate cause. While the war played out around them, Hayes and his banditos made regular late-night raids on encampments to steal weapons and horses from one side and then sell them to the other. When the war ended, they turned to rustling cattle and robbing stagecoaches. On one occasion, they abducted the child of a small-town mayor and held him for ransom. If in the commission of their crimes gunfire broke out, it was simply the cost of doing business.

In time, the name Dain Hayes was all but forgotten. Though it was unsure who first called him El Diablo, it stuck. And it struck fear into the heart of anyone in his path.

He was, Ringewald decided, the perfect solution to his problems.

Chapter Fourteen

By the time summer was nearing an end, the calm that had returned to Gila Bend continued to concern Lewis Taylor. Though Ringewald's men could still be seen, slowly riding through town and along the trail that led out to Axel's farm, the townspeople no longer saw them as the menace they had once been.

Luke Bradley had curtailed his editorial campaign against the captain's power grab and returned to reporting the more mundane happenings in the community. His advertisers had come back.

Lewis fell into a daily routine of helping his father with chores and occasionally checking on B. J. and his new pigs. In the evenings he would ride Dolly into town to visit with Ezzie.

"It worries me some that I'm seeing fewer folks bringing guns to town," Ezzie said as they sat watching the moon rise over the church spire. "I'm not sure that's a good thing. It's nice to have a little peace and quiet, but we both know it isn't going to last. I guarantee you, as we speak, the captain is sitting out there on his throne, drinking whiskey and thinking up something he can do to stir things up again. He won't be satisfied until he gets what he wants."

They both knew he was referring to Lewis. "He's thinking that once he's gotten you out of his way, he can get back to doing what he wants to everyone else."

"I don't doubt what you're saying, not for a minute," Lewis said, "but all I can think of is to keep telling folks to remain alert. All we can do is stay ready."

"I'd even vote for setting another brush fire if it would hurry things along," Ezzie said.

Both were laughing when Luke Bradley approached. His hands were buried in his pockets and there was a disturbed look on his face.

"Stanley Winslow's passed," he said. "He apparently died in his sleep last night. A neighbor had been concerned that he couldn't rouse him this evening when he took him some supper. He got worried and called Sheriff Barnes, who went in and found him dead.

"Then the doctor came and discovered a half-full bottle of pain medicine used to ease the suffering of people with terminal cancer."

Taylor's thoughts went immediately to Darla. As if reading his mind, Luke handed him an envelope that Winslow had left on his kitchen table. "It's a letter he left for her," he said.

Lewis folded it and put it in his shirt pocket. "I'll see she gets it," he said as he turned back to Ezzie. "I'll be needing to borrow your horse again."

If he left right away and rode straight through, he could reach the Goolsby farm by midday. The fact that Ringewald's scouts had eased their patrolling made it more likely that he could be well on his way before any of them knew he was gone.

His mind raced as he fashioned a plan. "If I leave Dolly here, it might alert somebody that I'm gone," he said, "so I'll lead her home and, so he won't worry, tell Pa I'll be gone for a few days. He'll be able to make up a believable story if anyone asks my whereabouts."

Luke followed him as he entered the barn. "I don't know much about this sort of thing, but I'll go down to the Blessed Redeemer in the morning and begin making funeral arrangements," he said. "Lord knows, I owe him that much. He was a good man.

"I'll ask the preacher if he can schedule a service for the end of the week. That way, I can have a notice in Friday's paper."

"Write something nice," Lewis said. "If you have flowers sent to the church, I'd appreciate my name being included."

As he rode through the darkness, he was surprised at the measure of sadness he felt. And the guilt that was mixed with it. Stanley Winslow hadn't wished his daughter to marry Archer Ringewald simply for status and to get her away from him. In his secret desperation, he had seen it as the only way he had to be sure Darla would have a comfortable future in his absence.

The apology he'd made about hiding his letters suddenly seemed more genuine, more heartfelt. Too late, Lewis wished his response had been kinder.

Just as he had so often imagined, Darla was in the garden with Nina when he arrived.

Throughout every mile of his journey, he had desperately struggled to think what he might say that would somehow ease the shock and pain he would bring. For the second time in her still-young life, she had lost a parent. Lewis sent a loud curse skyward at the unfairness.

As Darla, smiling and with arms extended, raced toward him, he chose the straightforward approach. "I've come with bad news," he said, taking her hand. "Your daddy has passed away."

She was at first speechless, then began to cry. Nina was quickly at her side.

Both were holding Darla tightly as they led her into the house.

Joined by Preacher, they sat at the kitchen table as Lewis provided what details he knew. Darla continued to weep.

"I knew even before I left home that there were times when he would feel bad and have to rest in the middle of the day," she said. "But when I would ask, he would just say he thought he might be catching something, and for me not to worry. It never once occurred to me that he was . . ."

Lewis reached across the table and took her hand. "Your daddy and I recently came to an understanding," he said. "We had a good, long talk, much of it about how much he loved you and wanted to keep you safe. He's missed you."

He told her of the generous gesture that had put the *Sentinel* back in business and described the celebration at which her father had been the guest of honor. He paraphrased Bradley's speech in which he had spoken of "a man who was deeply admired and respected."

Then he reached into his pocket and held the letter out to her.

She wiped her tears and excused herself from the table, saying that she felt she should read her father's words in private.

As Nina put out a plate of cookies, the room fell silent except for Preacher's whispered prayer. On the porch, Darla sat on the steps and began to read the pained lines that had been Stanley Winslow's final act.

My Dearest Daughter:

The most difficult problems one has to deal with as he nears the end are the things he leaves unsaid and undone.

First, let me say I regret that I didn't tell you more often how very much I love you. You and your mother are the greatest things to ever happen to me. I wish you had gotten to know her better. The two of you have provided me wonderful memories to take with me (wherever I'm going).

Another thing that I probably should have done was to make you aware of my illness sooner. I gave it a great deal of thought, wondering if knowing I was nearing the end would have been better than the sudden shock you are now feeling. All I can say is that it was my hope to delay your pain for as long as possible. The last thing I wanted was for you to worry and feel sorry for me. Please don't be angry — and if you are, I hope you can soon see your way past it and reach an understanding about my decision.

As parents, no matter how loving, we make mistakes. Some of them big ones. How I regret my urging you to marry someone who turned out not to be good for you. I don't think it will hurt your feelings when I say I came to realize, far too late, that your husband is not a good man.

Which brings me to something I need to say about Lewis Taylor. I was terribly wrong about him. I've gotten to know him better and believe him to be a fine and decent person. You know, don't you, that it was his idea to take the risks necessary to get you safely away from the situation you were in? I'll be eternally grateful to him for his courage. Perhaps you'll want to thank him, too, if you haven't already.

I've tried my best to apologize to him for the worst sin I've ever committed. Now I must do so to you, hoping that you will not spend the rest of your life hating me. Ask him about what happened to the letters he wrote to you while he was away. I simply lack the courage to tell you myself.

I know there is more I should say, but I'm feeling tired and should lie down. (Must be catching something . . .) If there really is a heaven, your mother and I will be waiting for you — but don't feel the need to hurry.

I love you, dear daughter, with all my heart, and though I'm not a religious man, I pray, pray, pray that you have a wonderful, happy life in the days and years to come.

Your Father

She gently folded the letter and walked into the yard, alone with her thoughts. Her entire body shook as she cried like she never had before.

In time, she felt an arm across her shoulder and turned to see that there were also tears in Lewis's eyes. He found her grief unbearable and begged for a way to offer comfort.

As she touched his face, wiping away a tear, she said, "You did write to me?"

He only nodded and held her more tightly.

"When is my daddy's funeral?"

"Luke's seeing to it with the preacher at the Blessed Redeemer. The service will be day after tomorrow."

"I'm going back with you," she said. The strong resolve in her voice left no room for argument.

The pews of the church were filled, and the smell of fresh flowers and scented candles wafted through the old building. The Blessed Redeemer ladies' choir sang "Amazing Grace," all verses.

As Reverend Daniels took his place at the lectern, a low murmur suddenly filled the room.

Darla Winslow, wearing a Sunday dress borrowed from Sue Ellen Bradley, walked slowly down the aisle. For a moment she stood, head bowed, at her father's casket, then turned and took a seat in the front row.

Lewis, who had escorted her to the church, was in the back of the room, near the door. Outside, a dozen young men he and Ezzie had assembled were standing guard. Each with a firearm, they watched to see if any of Captain Ringewald's men might attempt to interrupt the service.

None did.

The pastor offered a prayer, asking that the departed be welcomed into God's kingdom; then he read a series of Bible verses. His brief sermon was the same he'd given numerous times before when a member of the community had died.

Luke Bradley closed the service with an abbreviated version of the speech he'd given in the park.

By the time the mourners filed out of the church, the men who had stood guard had discreetly put their weapons away and were thanking the preacher for his sermon, though they had not heard it.

Many in the congregation participated in the procession to the nearby cemetery, where Stanley Winslow would be buried next to his wife. It was Darla's wish that Lewis, his father, Ezzie Zale, and Luke Bradley serve as pallbearers. After a closing prayer, dozens of well-wishers quietly formed a line to express their condolences to the grieving daughter.

In less than an hour, it was over.

Miles away, Captain Ringewald had little interest in the report he was given about his father-in-law's funeral. Instead, he sat in his office, anxiously awaiting the return of Lyndon Greenleaf and the man he had been sent to find.

Later in the day, Darla and Lewis stood in the living room of the Winslow house. The air was stale and smelled of the sickness that had taken her father's life. She went from room to room, surveying the clutter of a place that had seen no woman's touch in years. Memories cascaded as she entered the room that had been hers when she lived there, before things had so dramatically changed. It was the only part of the house that was undisturbed, still looking as though it was awaiting her return from school or a Saturday-night dance.

In the room her father used as an office, papers and files were stacked on every flat surface. For all the praise he received for his work, Stanley Winslow had not been an orderly man. The kitchen was littered with unwashed dishes, and the single closet in his bedroom had become more a place of impromptu storage than one in which to hang clothes and put away shoes.

In the main room, she let her fingers trace the titles of books that filled a shelf near the fireplace. Most were either on finance or histories. One, however, was the novel *Moby-*

Dick by Herman Melville, which she had given him for Christmas long ago. At a table where he had left his reading glasses, she lingered over two small framed photographs: one of her mother, the other of her. There were no other pictures in the house.

It had been, she decided, a sad and lonely place for one to spend his final days.

Lewis watched in silence as she made her nostalgic tour.

"I'm so glad I came back," she finally said. "It was a lovely service, didn't you think? So many people. Daddy had a lot of friends."

Weary, she motioned for him to sit with her at the kitchen table. "I just feel numb, empty, like I have nothing left inside me. I'm so tired, I didn't shed a single tear at the church or cemetery. I wanted to cry, but just couldn't. Does that make any sense?"

"At a time like this, little does," Lewis said.

"I feel badly that even during the service, I was having thoughts about myself, wondering what I'm going to do now. I know things are unsettled here and Lord knows what my husband might do next, but, Lewis, I can't keep hiding.

"The Goolsbys have been wonderful. They've treated me like I'm part of their family. I love them both, but I just can't go back."

"Maybe you won't have to," Lewis said.

He had a plan that might address the problem. He stopped short of admitting to her that he, too, didn't like the idea of her being so far away.

Before the funeral service, he had met with Reverend Daniels and was surprised to learn how much the pastor knew about the events that had been taking place in Gila Bend. He was keenly aware of the fears and frustrations of the townspeople and understood the cause. The changes he'd seen in members of his flock troubled him.

"I don't think people realize that a man of the cloth can be just as angry and discouraged as they are," he said. "Those of us in the ministry take a solemn oath to turn away from violence and thoughts of revenge, and I do my best to follow that creed. But God help me, it isn't always easy. I've seen what has been done to this town and its people, and I am distressed that there is little I can do but pray things get better and offer comfort when and where I can."

Lewis was pleased by the pastor's awareness and willingness to help. "It's that offer of comfort I would like to speak with you about," he said.

He then explained Darla's situation. "Among those deeply concerned for her safety was the man you will bury later today. We spoke shortly before he died, and he told me how worried he was that her husband, Captain Ringewald, might do her harm."

Reverend Daniels's knowledge surprised him again. "And I understand that's why you took it upon yourself to rescue her from harm's way."

"But only for the time being," Lewis said. "Ringewald's not likely to rest until he finds her or until this dispute is somehow ended."

"It was very brave of her to come out of hiding to attend her father's funeral. God bless her for that." Reverend Daniels paused and looked out of the rectory door and saw that people were already arriving for the service. "Is there some way you think I might be of help?"

Taylor was struggling for words. "To be honest, I'm not much of a spiritual person. . . ."

The pastor lifted a hand to interrupt him. "Oh, I think you are. You just haven't yet found your way through the front door of the church. From what I've heard, you are a man of strong and admirable faith. At least in your fellow man — which is as good a start toward salvation as I know of.

"Now, tell me what's on your mind."

As a boy, long before Daniels became the pastor at the Blessed Redeemer, Lewis recalled times when down-and-out strangers would find their way to Gila Bend and be taken in by the church. It would provide them food and clothing and, for short periods of time, shelter. On more than one occasion, he, B. J., and Luke would sneak to the back of the church to steal a look into the window of the small room where the latest transient was staying.

"Do you still have that room?" he asked.

"Yes, but it's rarely used these days. I sometimes go there when I feel the need for a private place to collect my thoughts." He smiled, anticipating Taylor's next question.

"Darla is going to insist on staying here in Gila Bend," Lewis said, "regardless of the danger she might face. But her husband's men would find her in no time if she . . ."

Reverend Daniels placed a hand on Taylor's shoulder. "Tell her she would be most welcome here. I'll start tidying the place immediately after the funeral. And I thank you, Mr. Taylor."

"For what?"

"For affording me an opportunity to finally feel of some use in this battle being fought for the soul of the community."

■ ■ ■ ■

Convincing Darla to stay in the Blessed Redeemer sanctuary, at least for a while, was easier than Lewis had anticipated.

"If a person has to hide," she said, "where better than a church?"

Chapter Fifteen

Other patrons in the El Casa Gallo bar sat as far away as possible and spoke only in hushed tones. Alone at a back table, the man all called El Diablo was cursing, his hands clenched around the neck of a tequila bottle, his brown eyes ablaze. His prized game rooster, which had been earning celebrity status at border cockfights for months, had just been defeated. When the lifeless carcass of his rooster had been unceremoniously tossed away and the opposing entrant declared the winner of the to-the-death contest, El Diablo had angrily pitched a handful of gold coins, the cost of his losing bet, into the dirt ring and stormed from the courtyard.

He had not even bothered to cut the custom-made silver gaffs from the spurs of the losing fowl.

And now, sitting alone in his misery, all he wanted to do was get drunk. He wasn't pleased when the stranger approached him.

"You're a hard man to find," Lyndon Greenleaf said. He had started his search on the American side of the border, visiting the Eagle Pass hotel the captain had suggested, but had no luck. A man there had suggested one cantina; another said he might try yet another. At every stop, the name of the man he was looking for was well-known, but he'd not been seen for some time.

Several wanted to know if Greenleaf was a lawman and spoke only after getting his assurance that he wasn't. Twice, information had been given only after he paid.

Finally, he crossed the Rio Grande and continued his search along the dusty streets of Piedras Negras. Learning of the cockfight that was underway, he reached the shaded courtyard only to find that it had just ended. The only person remaining at the blood-splattered ring was an old Mexican woman who was eagerly putting dead birds into a gunnysack. They would make fine meals for her family, she told him in halting English. She also knew where his man was likely to be.

By the time he walked into the dimly lit and rancid-smelling bar, his bad leg ached and he needed a drink. As he limped toward

El Diablo, he had his saddlebag draped across one shoulder.

When Greenleaf started to speak, two men were quickly at his side. "He's drinking," one said, "and isn't interested in company."

He showed the bag of money, shaking it so they could hear the rattle of the coins. "This," he said, "should be worth a few minutes of his time."

El Diablo, who had not even raised his head when Greenleaf first spoke, took a long drink from his bottle. "Sit," he said as he waved the others away. He pulled his side-arm from his holster and placed it on the table, then opened the drawstring of the bag. The expression on his face did not change.

"I've been sent by a man named Archer Ringewald to ask that you come to his ranch to talk business," Greenleaf said. "He has a job offer he would like you to consider."

"What's the job?"

"That's not for me to say. I'm to tell you he'll explain it when you meet. That's what the money here is for, payment just to talk. He did say to tell you that what he wants you to do shouldn't take much time and that you will be paid well. I should add that he's one of the richest men in South Texas."

He offered El Diablo a map he had drawn.

"This will show you the way. It's no more than a two-day ride."

As a young woman placed another bottle of tequila on the table, El Diablo's eyes were fixed on his visitor. Though he would not admit it, for the first time in his life, Greenleaf felt intimidated.

"Leave the money."

"So I can tell him you'll come?"

"Just leave the money" was El Diablo's only reply as he folded the map and put it in the pocket of his leather vest. He then sent his visitor away.

Despite his knowledge of the captain's impatient nature, Greenleaf felt he had earned himself some time to relax. Crossing back into the States, he sought out a place to drink that was more welcoming and well lit than those across the border. Before heading back to the Rocking R, he deserved to rest and get pleasantly drunk, allowing the whiskey to erase the image of El Diablo that was still dancing in his head.

Swearing her to secrecy, Lewis had told Sue Ellen Bradley of Darla's new hiding place. On the pretense of visiting the pastor, she would take extra clothing, food, and books to the church. She was always careful to carry her Bible with her.

Both women looked forward to their secret meetings. The room where Darla was staying was small but neatly kept. Plain white curtains, sewn by the women members of the congregation, hung from the window, and the quilt that covered the bed was also their handiwork.

Occasionally, in the evening, Reverend Daniels would knock on her door and invite her to join him in the vestry to talk and have a glass of his homemade wine. A few times, after he assured her that the town was quiet and sleeping, she would venture into the darkness outside and walk among the grapevines in the churchyard, feeling the cool night breeze on her face and inhaling the sweet aroma of late-blooming flowers.

Lewis didn't risk visiting. Instead, he relied on Sue Ellen to report on how Darla was doing.

"I took her a copy of the *Sentinel* the other day so she could read the obituary that Luke wrote. She seemed very pleased. She talks quite a bit about her daddy, mostly remembering things from when she was a little girl. It seems to make her feel good.

"She reads and takes afternoon naps. Reverend Daniels is good about checking on her, seeing if there's anything she needs.

He said the other night she dusted the pews and set out the hymnals. Then they sat and talked for a while. I'm sure he's trying to convert her.

"You needn't worry, Lewis. She's doing fine," Sue Ellen said. Then she smiled. "Of course, there's always the possibility she'll go stir-crazy if this lasts too long."

"I'm hoping it won't."

"One thing I almost forgot to mention. She asks about you every time I visit."

That clearly pleased him.

"Hey," Sue Ellen said, "maybe you could start passing notes, like we did back in school."

Lewis knew she was joking, but gave a serious reply. "I wouldn't know what to say."

He didn't bother to knock, nor did he introduce himself when he entered the captain's office. Lyndon Greenleaf had said that he was sure El Diablo would come for the meeting, but had no idea when to expect him.

It was dusk when he arrived, accompanied by the same two men who had watched over him in the Piedras Negras bar.

"So you decided to come," Ringewald said as he offered his guest a drink. El Diablo, seeing that it wasn't tequila, shook his head.

"Tell me why I'm here."

Ringewald looked across his desk at the legendary outlaw and immediately determined he was an even more imposing figure than the stories had suggested. He was well over six feet tall and had obviously done enough hard labor at some time in his life to develop muscular arms and a broad chest. His coal black hair hung straight, touching his shoulders, and, just next to a large, sweeping mustache, a small, jagged scar was visible on his left cheek.

But it was his eyes that most caught the captain's attention. If, indeed, they were the window to a man's soul, El Diablo didn't have one.

He took a seat and began dusting his boots. "My men outside are hungry," he said.

The captain called out to Celia, the maid, and instructed her to bring some food. He didn't even bother to taste his own drink before he began to tell El Diablo of the difficulties he was having with a group of rebellious people in Gila Bend, of the editorial lies that had appeared in the newspaper, and of the kidnapping of his wife. His life had been threatened, and one of his best cowhands had been killed. It took some time before he mentioned Lewis Taylor by name.

"He's the cause of all this," Ringewald said. "He comes back home after getting out of prison and wants to take over. He's who I want dead, as soon as possible. And there might be a few others who also need killing."

El Diablo said nothing while the captain talked. Nor did he say anything for some time afterward. Finally, he spoke. "What's this worth to you?"

Anticipating the question, Ringewald had written a figure on a piece of paper. He slid it across the desk.

Instead of picking it up, El Diablo leaned forward to read the numbers.

"We will return soon," he said.

It was Stanley Winslow's funeral that caused Sheriff Barnes to begin taking a serious look at his own life. He wasn't pleased with what he saw. Comparing the people who had come to sing Winslow's praises and mourn his passing to the angry group that had recently gathered in front of his office, demanding that he get control of his town, depressed him.

When his time came, he wanted to be remembered fondly by the residents of the town he had watched over for almost two decades. He'd never been the kind of lawman the dime novels were written about, but he had been fair and firm. Townspeople had trusted and depended on him, until he became one of Captain Ringewald's puppets.

There were times when he couldn't even remember how it had happened. At others, it replayed like a bad dream that visited in the darkness, night after night, until he came to dread sleep. The sheriff would relive it and curse the weakness that had turned him down a wayward path.

It had begun a few years after Ringewald came to South Texas.

Two of his Rocking R cowhands had instigated a drunken brawl that resulted in a serious injury to one of the saloon patrons. Unlike most Saturday-night scuffles, there had been an unusually ugly level of violence involved. The hands had beaten a young farmer until his face was masked in blood and then tied a rope to his feet and dragged him behind a horse.

Had Sheriff Barnes not arrived when he did, it is likely the man might have died.

The two drunk cowboys were arrested and taken to the Gila Bend jail. One began cursing and took a swing at the sheriff. In return, he was hit across the back of his neck with the barrel of the lawman's shotgun. Several onlooking saloon patrons applauded.

Once the men were locked in their cell, the sheriff summoned Doc Johnson to care for the injured farmer.

It was typical of the manner in which Barnes carried out his elected duties.

The prisoners had been behind bars for almost two weeks when the captain visited the jail. Polite and businesslike, he introduced himself to the sheriff and asked if there was something he could do to have them released. If it was a matter of paying some fine, he had brought money. He badly needed them to return to work on his ranch.

"I don't know how they are sober," the sheriff said, "but drunk, they're bad people. You sure you want them around?"

"I think I can straighten them out. And I'll make you a promise that you'll never see them in town again."

Sheriff Barnes, tired of getting food from the café to feed them and weary of their constant moaning and arguing, agreed to their release in exchange for payment of a fifty-dollar fine. "They're lucky the boy didn't want to file charges against them," he said. "Take them, and tell them I don't want to ever see their ugly faces again."

The captain smiled, paid the fine, and invited the sheriff to a barbecue at the Rocking R the following weekend.

It was during that visit that things began to change.

Barnes was surprised when, upon his arrival, he found that he was the only guest. Still, the food was good, and his host was generous with his whiskey. Ringewald gave him a tour of the ranch, showing off his prized Longhorns.

As the day faded, they adjourned to the captain's office, where they were joined by Lyndon Greenleaf, who was introduced as the ranch foreman. They drank more whiskey while Ringewald discussed future plans he had for his cattle enterprise.

"Also," he said, "I'll want to get more involved in the community since Gila Bend is now my home." He was evasive about what that "involvement" would include, but made it clear he would need the sheriff's help. "I understand you've served the town for many years and are routinely reelected. That tells me you have people's respect."

Warmed by the liquor, Sheriff Barnes welcomed the praise.

"It's my hope to earn similar respect," the captain said. "I'm a very rich man, Sheriff.

I've got more money than I can spend, and I'd like to see some of it put to use to benefit the town. To accomplish that, I'll need the help of someone with your standing in the community."

Barnes was flattered that Ringewald was interested in him rather than the town's mayor. "Anything that will make life better — and safer — for folks, I'm in favor of," he said.

"That's what I knew you would say. Good, we can consider ourselves partners."

He turned to Greenleaf, who had said nothing since they had entered the office. "From time to time," the captain said, "it will be Lyndon here who you'll be dealing with when I'm involved in other matters."

The sheriff nodded as Ringewald refilled his glass and extended his hand.

A day later, the sheriff rode out to inspect the small pasture he owned just outside town and found that a Longhorn cow and her calf had been added to his modest herd.

Ultimately, his relationship with Captain Ringewald had come to this: Favors became demands. Gifts turned into bribes. Handshakes disappeared, and threats took their place. Sheriff Barnes was no longer the intimidator. He was the intimidated. He had looked away while his friends were badly treated: their barns burned, farms and businesses stolen, and lives threatened.

Looking townspeople in the face had become all but impossible. Same with looking at himself in the mirror.

The news that Greenleaf had just brought to him was the final straw. Some men, he said, would soon be coming to town to "take care of Lewis Taylor." The captain, he said, suggested that it might be a good time for Barnes to pay an overdue visit to his sister in Fort Worth.

He pulled a handful of gold coins from his pocket and placed them on the desk. "Enjoy your vacation," he said as he headed for the door.

Sheriff Barnes sat silently at his desk long after Greenleaf was gone. He knew the quiet in Gila Bend was about to end. So was his relationship with Archer Ringewald.

Taylor was mucking Dolly's stall when the sheriff arrived at the farm. "You coming to arrest me for something?" he said, expecting a smile in return.

"We've got to talk," Barnes said as he dismounted and tethered his horse near the watering trough. "I think big problems are coming."

It was a warning that Lewis had expected and dreaded. He set his rake aside, removed his gloves, and motioned for the sheriff to take a seat on a nearby bale of hay.

He listened as Barnes related his conversation with Lyndon Greenleaf. "I've allowed things to get out of hand," the sheriff said, "and I hope to God it's not too late to set them right. We need to see that the town's prepared for whatever's coming."

"When's this supposed to happen?"

"He didn't say, but my impression is that it will be soon. Arrangements with whoever it is coming have already been made."

"I have to admit, Sheriff, that I'm surprised that it's you giving me a warning. I was under the impression you and Ringewald are . . ."

"Were," Barnes replied. "I've made some bad mistakes and used poor judgment. I owe apologies to you and everyone in Gila Bend and plan to do whatever I can to make amends."

As he spoke, Axel Taylor entered the barn, a look of concern on his face. "What brings you out, Milton?" he said. They had once been friends, but Barnes's bold allegiance to the captain had changed things.

He repeated the warning he'd already given Lewis. "Something I need to do immediately," he said, "is deputize some men. If this thing gets as bad as I fear it might, I can't handle it alone."

Lewis Taylor immediately volunteered.

"Son, you would be my first choice if it wasn't for the way the law works. You being a felon — and understand, I'm not saying I think you were guilty or deserved being in prison — you can't legally wear a badge. That's a rule I have to follow, or I'll lose my own badge."

"Well, I've never been to prison," Axel said. "Since Lewis isn't allowed, I'll volunteer." Before Sheriff Barnes could argue, he began suggesting others he thought would make good deputies. Oran Dalton's boy, Raymond. Vince Williams. Cutter Clayton. "They're able-bodied, levelheaded, and fearless," Axel said. "And they've all got one grudge or another to settle with Captain Ringewald. They'll jump at the opportunity if asked."

The sheriff nodded in agreement. "I'll be in touch with them. Maybe a few others. I want the town battened down and ready for whatever's coming. And I want it done now."

He told them he had already visited the bartender of the saloon and ordered the place locked up until further notice. "That way, Ringewald's cowboys won't have reason for their Saturday-night visits to town," he said.

"That's going to make some folks mighty unhappy," Lewis said. He smiled as he imagined the Rocking R crew being told that the door of the Captain's Bar was locked and an armed deputy would be sitting out front.

Barnes shook both men's hands. "Lewis, I don't need to tell you to keep your eyes open. You're who they're coming after, but we want to make it so they have a lot of other folks to go through first. Axel, I'll see you at my office first thing tomorrow morning for a swearing in. I'll see that the newspaper's there to report on it. For now I've got another thing I've been needing to do for some time."

As the sheriff rode away, Axel Taylor shook his head. "Can't say I expected that," he said.

It was late in the afternoon when one of Ringewald's guards hurried up the front porch steps, sweating and out of breath. "Something strange is happening, Captain. There's cattle coming."

Minutes later, they stood watching as Sheriff Barnes and two wranglers he had borrowed herded a dozen Longhorns through the main entrance and into a holding pen near the barn. When the cattle were locked away, Barnes sent his aides back to town.

He turned his horse toward the house and tipped his hat to the stunned captain. “I’ll not be needing your livestock any longer,” the sheriff said. He then pitched the bag of coins Greenleaf had delivered to him onto the porch. “Or your money,” he added.

Before Ringewald could reply, Barnes was gone.

Chapter Sixteen

The sheriff wasn't the only one who had been taking stock of his life. Since being ordered to find El Diablo and summon him to the Rocking R, Lyndon Greenleaf had felt a growing resentment and no small degree of anxiety about his boss's obvious decision that he could no longer be depended upon to do his job. Now he had been reduced to the role of an errand boy.

For a time, he tried to mask his uncertainty by blaming it on his bad leg. But since it was healing nicely, it had become an unsatisfactory excuse. The truth was, he was being replaced.

Once El Diablo returned and bunkhouse rumors began to circulate about his purpose, Greenleaf's standing was certain to be diminished. The men who had feared and respected him would soon be laughing behind his back. And the prospect of such a downfall tore at him.

Since coming to work for the captain immediately after the war, he had been willing to carry out any assignment given him. He had intimidated farmers hesitant to let go of their land, using physical violence whenever necessary. At the captain's request, he had threatened lives, burned buildings, broken bones, and, on one occasion, committed cold-blooded murder.

When a poor Mexican family had been traveling south, one of the sons had made a late-night visit to a far corner of a Rocking R pasture, cut the fence wires, and stolen a calf. He and his family, he later tried to explain, were starving. Captain Ringewald showed no sympathy for their dire situation, saying only that it was important a strong message be sent that rustling his cattle would not be tolerated. Greenleaf was ordered to kill the young man and did so.

However, his evil deeds had apparently not been enough to satisfy the captain. He wanted someone even more ruthless to do his bidding. He wanted the infamous El Diablo to kill Lewis Taylor. It didn't matter that Greenleaf deserved revenge for Taylor shooting him in the leg.

That he was being robbed of that satisfaction angered him most. His only recourse, he decided, was to find a way to deal with Lewis Taylor before El Diablo could.

In Gila Bend, defensive preparations were underway despite the fact that no one seemed to know exactly what to expect.

The sheriff swore in three deputies on the porch in front of his office as a small crowd, including *Sentinel* editor, Luke Bradley, looked on. One was immediately assigned to stand guard in front of the boarded-up Captain's Bar.

While the ceremony was underway, Lewis found Reverend Daniels sitting beneath the grape arbor in front of the Blessed Redeemer, preparing his sermon. "It's a pleasure to see you, Mr. Taylor," he said. Even before he was asked, the pastor assured him Darla was in good spirits and dealing with her isolation well.

"I think it helps a great deal for her to see Mrs. Bradley now and then."

"I hope she'll soon be able to move around freely," Lewis said. Then he explained that it would be necessary to watch over her even more carefully in the days to come. "Trouble's coming, but nobody seems to know exactly when or from what direction."

"That," Reverend Daniels said, "seems always to be the nature of trouble."

■ ■ ■ ■

By the time Lyndon Greenleaf reached the entrance to the Taylor farm, his anger had boiled into rage. Sweat beaded beneath his eyes, and he was grinding his teeth. He, like the captain, had reached the conclusion that it was the presence of Lewis Taylor alone that had brought all the misery into his life. During his ride from the Rocking R, he shouted curses into the morning breeze, anticipating a confrontation that would put an end to the man who had caused him so much grief.

The surge of adrenaline momentarily slowed when he found that no one was home. He carefully searched the cabin, then the barn. He rode down to the creek and through the small pasture, finding nothing but a few grazing cattle and a flock of wild turkeys that skittered from his path. There was no sign of Lewis's horse.

He would have to wait for his return.

For days, Greenleaf had imagined a variety of scenarios. He could patiently hide and ambush his adversary. He could wait until night and kill Taylor while he slept. Or he could set fire to the cabin and shoot him as he ran to escape the blaze. None satisfied him.

He wanted to look into frightened eyes as he fired his kill shot. He decided he would wait in plain sight and make his intent known. Lyndon Greenwood was no coward.

Absent from his plan was Axel Taylor. He had given little thought to a two-against-one situation. But seeing no horses in the barn or the pasture, he realized that wherever Lewis was, his father must have accompanied him. And that they would likely return together.

So he would have to kill them both, and he soon convinced himself that could be even better. By doing so, he could regain the favor of his boss. With both Taylors gone, adding their farm to the Ringewald holdings would be a much easier task.

Impatience got the better of him.

Just as Lewis and Axel came into sight, slowly riding side by side, Greenleaf moved from the porch into the yard and fired off a series of shots. Though one brushed Lewis's shoulder and another clipped the brim of his father's hat, no damage was done.

The riders quickly headed their horses into the cover of a nearby thicket as Greenleaf continued to shoot wildly. "I've come to kill you, Taylor," he yelled, "and I'm not leaving until it's done. Sorry about your daddy, but he'll have to die, too." There was a maniacal tone of one who was fast losing control.

The response was a single gunshot that only kicked up dust in the yard, causing Greenleaf's horse to tear the reins from the porch railing and run. Furious, Greenleaf stomped his feet and called after the animal, then fired a shot in its direction.

Whisper, who had hidden under the porch, yelped and ran for the safety of the barn.

"I think we've got a crazy man on our hands," Axel said as he knelt behind the trunk of an oak tree. "Is that who I think it is?"

"Yeah, Lyndon Greenleaf," Lewis said, "Ringewald's henchman." He briefly recounted their confrontation at the Rocking R, during which he'd shot Lyndon in the leg. "He's obviously wanting to settle a grudge."

"And he's come here alone in broad daylight? It doesn't make much sense." As Axel spoke, Greenleaf fired more shots while running toward the cabin. "At this rate," Axel said, "all we need to do is wait until the fool runs out of ammunition."

Inside the cabin, Greenleaf paced as he

reloaded his pistol. His leg was starting to ache, and his mouth was dry. Things were not going as he had planned.

Hidden in the weeds no more than a hundred yards away, Axel tried to make light of the situation. "I've been a deputy, what, no more than two, three hours, and here I am already in a genuine shoot-out. I'm not real sure I'm going to like this job."

Lewis watched the cabin closely, trying to figure what Greenleaf's next move might be. Taking the offensive, he decided, was what he and his father should do. "You fire a shot now and then to keep his attention, and I'm going to see if I can make my way around to the back of the barn.

"Whatever you do, don't make yourself an easy target."

Lewis got to his feet and ran to their horses, giving each a hard swat on the hindquarters that sent them galloping away, safely out of the range of Greenleaf's shots.

It had reached the heat of the day by the time Lewis made his way to the barn. Entering through a back window, he climbed the stairs that led to the loft, hoping the sudden flight of startled pigeons rousted from their perch in the rafters didn't draw Greenleaf's attention.

From his vantage point, he could see into the cabin below. There was shadowed movement as Greenleaf moved from one window to another in an attempt to locate his targets. Twice, shots from Axel pounded into the front door.

Lewis cupped his hands to the sides of his mouth and called out, "Greenleaf, unless you're figuring on taking up residence in there, you might just as well come on out. You might be here to kill me, but that's not going to happen. Put your gun down and step out onto the porch so we can put a peaceful end to this."

A loud boom came from a window, followed by a puff of white smoke. Greenleaf had found Axel's shotgun inside, and probably the stash of ammunition he kept on a kitchen shelf. Things were obviously not going to end as quickly as Lewis hoped.

"I'm not leaving until I've done what I came to do," Greenleaf yelled before firing another shotgun blast in the direction of the barn. It was followed by a poorly aimed pistol shot.

Lewis moved behind a mound of hay he had shoveled into the loft just days earlier and tried to imagine how the encounter would end. Greenleaf, he knew, was furious and fast losing touch with reality. At the moment, his sole purpose in life was to see Taylor dead. It was, he knew, a wish shared by the captain, but for some reason, this didn't seem like something Ringewald had ordered.

Greenleaf was operating on his own, and Lewis couldn't understand why. He didn't see him as a man who would make a move without his boss's order and approval.

He decided to taunt him and see if doing so might produce an answer.

"I wonder what the captain would think if he was to see his toughest hand hiding here in a cabin, borrowing an old man's shotgun to protect himself," he shouted. "Why are you doing this?" Pellets from another shotgun blast peppered the side of the barn. "I'm not sure Ringewald would be too pleased, Lyndon."

Inside, Greenleaf's shoulders slumped, and he rubbed at his aching leg. Lewis was right.

While Lewis had Greenleaf's attention, Axel Taylor made his way closer to the cabin. He had reached the back wall of the smokehouse, which was just a few steps from the corner of the porch. Anyone walking out of the cabin would be an easy close-range target. He signaled his position to Lewis.

"I'm coming out into the yard," Lewis shouted, "and I'll give you the opportunity to do the same. Sidearms holstered until we're both in the open, okay? Then, man-to-man, we can settle this. That sound fair?"

Greenleaf considered the offer and liked his odds. He found himself suddenly laughing at the idea of a contest matching a professional gunman against a pissant dirt farmer. Taylor was making things easy for him.

"Show yourself first," he called out.

Once he saw Taylor standing in front of the barn, gun holstered and arms at his side, Greenleaf emerged from the cabin. He made an effort to disguise his limp as he slowly walked down the porch steps.

The two men were just yards apart when Greenleaf, focused on the man he planned to finally kill, heard his name called. Turning toward the smokehouse where he saw Axel kneeling, he began firing wildly in his direction. Soon, the two men were in a frantic gun battle as Lewis looked on, frozen in place. Finally, one of Axel's shots found its mark, and Greenleaf's head exploded into bloody pieces of bone and skin. As if in slow motion, he sank to his knees, then fell prone at Taylor's feet.

Axel was still pointing his pistol as he stepped from behind the building and approached. Lewis, his firearm still holstered, was speechless.

The elder Taylor stood over Greenleaf and, for a moment, stared down at his body. "I'm now a duly sworn deputy sheriff," he said, "and I'd be placing you under arrest if you weren't already so dead."

His son looked at him with a mixture of disbelief and admiration. A befuddled smile was beginning to form.

"What?" Axel said as he saw his son's expression. "I wasn't about to let some lowlife trespasser come onto my place and shoot my own flesh and blood."

Lewis left to go round up the horses. Whisper emerged from his hiding place and followed.

It was late afternoon when they rode through town, Greenleaf's horse trailing behind, his body covered with a blanket and draped across the saddle. They stopped at the sheriff's office to report what had taken place.

At the time, Sheriff Barnes was scolding a couple of ten-year-old boys who had been caught stealing fruit from the widow Singleton's orchard. She stood at Barnes's side, barely satisfied with the degree of fear he was instilling in the young thieves. "If my Robert was still alive," she said, "he would be tanning their hides something fierce."

The sheriff rolled his eyes and turned his attention to the Taylors and what was obviously a body beneath the blanket. He sent Mrs. Singleton and the boys away, and when he heard Lewis's explanation of what had taken place at the farm, he, too, gave Axel a surprised look.

"Just doing my job," the elder Taylor said, tipping his hat.

Barnes didn't even bother leaving the sidewalk to look beneath the blanket. "I've got to admit, you've done folks around here, myself included, a sizable favor. Now what?"

"Seeing Greenleaf to his final resting place isn't my concern," Lewis said, "so we're taking him back to where he came from."

"Out to the Ringewald place?"

"Yep."

"Want me to ride with you?"

Ezzie Zale, seeing the commotion from his livery, had rushed to the sheriff's office and asked what had happened. When told it was Greenleaf's body beneath the blanket, he immediately invited himself along.

"The more, the merrier," Lewis said as Ezzie went to saddle his horse. When he returned, he was carrying his rifle.

A small group of curious onlookers had gathered by the time they rode out of town. Word that Lyndon Greenleaf was dead would no doubt spread quickly through Gila Bend.

Nearing the small hill where Ringewald's guards were stationed, they stopped and waited. "They're probably sleeping," the sheriff said, "so unless we make them aware of our presence, we might have a long, hot wait." He pulled his pistol and fired a shot into the air.

Soon the guards approached, guns drawn and looking nervous.

"We want no trouble," Lewis said. "We've just brought one of your people home."

One of the guards dismounted and warily approached the trailing horse. He slowly lifted the blanket, then turned away and was sick to his stomach.

"Looks like he recognized him," Ezzie said.

Lewis let the reins of Greenleaf's horse fall to the ground, then waved the others back toward town.

Chapter Seventeen

Axel Taylor was surprised at how little regret he felt for taking Greenleaf's life. He had not served in the war and therefore had never even shot at another man, much less killed someone. This, he told himself, was an instinctive act that was unavoidable. Had he not pulled the trigger when he had, it might have been his son dead. That thought alone provided all the righteous justification he needed.

The father and son had unsaddled and fed their horses and were sitting on a bench near the doorway to the barn. Whisper, now calm, made his way between them and rested his head in Lewis's lap. It was dusk, and the familiar night sounds had begun down by the creek. Frogs croaked, wings flapped as waterfowl settled, and a gentle rustle of leaves added to the chorus.

Earlier, Lewis had suggested that his father go inside and put on some coffee, a pretext that allowed him time to clean away the bloody debris that had been left in the yard.

They sat for some time, saying nothing. Finally, it was Lewis who broke the silence. "What you did . . ."

His father interrupted. "I'm not proud of it, nor am I ashamed of it. It's just what had to be done."

"You saved my life," Lewis said.

With nerves still raw, he reached for his pistol when he heard someone riding toward the barn. Whisper jumped to the ground and bared his teeth. Both calmed when the rider called out, "Don't shoot. It's just me, Ezzie, looking to wet my whistle."

Axel laughed and was already on his way to the cabin for his bottle of whiskey before Zale dismounted.

"Since the sheriff has seen it necessary to lock up the saloon," Ezzie said, "I've got no place to get my nightly toddy." In truth, he had ridden out to the farm to see that his friends were okay after their nerve-racking day. And he wanted Lewis's opinion on how Captain Ringewald would react to Greenleaf's death.

"I know it's not proper to speak ill of the dead, even if it's somebody worthless and needing to be killed," he said, "but, boy, I'd have given my horse and saddle to see the captain's face when they brought what was left of Greenleaf to the ranch. I bet if we'd listened close enough on our way back, we could have heard him cussing."

When Ezzie glanced at Axel, it suddenly occurred to him that he was making too light of the ranch hand's death and had not considered the emotional toll it had taken on his friend. "I'm proud that you stood up for your boy," he said. "I admire what you did.

"You can sleep well tonight, knowing you did what was right."

Lewis tried without success to change the course of the conversation as the men drank their whiskey from Axel's fruit jars.

"Every time something like this happens," Ezzie said, "I find myself hoping that's the end of it."

"Well, it's not," Lewis said. "We both know that. What puzzles me is that I'm all but certain Greenleaf wasn't here on the captain's orders. It seemed more like a personal thing, just him coming for me on a wild impulse. I'm not sure he even gave a lot of thought to what he planned to do or why.

"There's got to be something else, something bigger, brewing. I just wish I knew what it could be."

By the time they finished the bottle, it was pitch-dark and late. "You've got no moon to help you find your way back," Axel said to Zale. "Plus, you're probably either near blind or seeing double by now. Best you stay here tonight."

Ezzie's eyelids drooped and his chin was already pressing against his chest as Taylor extended the invitation.

El Diablo had not liked Captain Ringewald from the moment they met. He saw him as a devious man who used his wealth as power, one who attempted to show strength by having others do things he lacked the courage to do himself. On his own, he was weak and unsure, without the genuine confidence he worked so hard to display. And he was a fool to think that through intimidation alone he could indefinitely rule an entire town.

Still, one did not have to admire a man to take his money. El Diablo would do what the captain wanted, but only after showing him who was in charge. His first move in that direction was to take his time returning to the ranch. Let the man worry and wonder.

And, indeed, he did.

Twice in recent days Ringewald's position had been challenged: first by the sheriff returning the cattle that were supposed to assure his allegiance and then by the brazen delivery of Lyndon Greenleaf's body.

The ranch hands, aware of his foul mood, avoided him whenever possible. Celia, the maid, dreaded hearing her name called. All were relieved when the captain shut himself away in his office, lost in deep thought, sipping whiskey and smoking one cigar after another.

No one was foolish enough to think that the death of Greenleaf was the cause of Ringewald's dark mood. In fact, his only reaction when the guards had brought the body to him was to tell them to take him away and bury him.

A full week had passed before El Diablo and his two men — Esteban and Ernesto, twin brothers — arrived. The captain was pleased to see them and did his best to hide his disappointment that there were only three men.

"I'll see to it you have space in the bunkhouse," the captain said. "Get settled. Then Celia will fix you something to eat."

Before Ringewald could give anything resembling an order, El Diablo spoke. "After we've rested for a day," he said, "we will acquaint ourselves with your town. And you'll need to provide directions to the farm where this man Taylor can be found."

Knowing the captain was eager to hear how long it might take to find and kill Taylor, El Diablo gave a nod. "We will not be here long," he said.

That night, as he prepared for bed, the captain felt a wave of calm sweep over him for the first time in longer than he could remember. Once asleep, he dreamed.

He was young again, proudly walking into a gaily decorated room where a military ball was underway. People were dressed in their finest, laughing and enjoying themselves. When he entered, proudly wearing his Union uniform, everything stopped — the music, the laughter, the dancing — and all heads turned in his direction.

Across the room, dressed in a flowing red gown, was the most beautiful woman there. With an inviting smile, she was looking directly at him, as if hoping he would walk her way.

It was Darla.

In the dream, he made his way through the admiring crowd, finally getting close enough to ask if she might like to dance. Just as she prepared to answer, a Confederate soldier stepped between them. He was dirty and smelled, his uniform in tatters, yet the young woman seemed to find him handsome and gallant. All attention turned to him. "If you so much as touch her," he said, "I'll see you dead."

It was Lewis Taylor.

Suddenly awake, the captain bolted into a sitting position and tossed aside the sweat-dampened covers, trying to erase the bizarre image from his mind. His fists were clenched, and he had a copper taste in his mouth. The calm was gone.

In the darkness, he angrily called out Taylor's name. It sounded more like a curse.

In the bunkhouse, the cowhands watched as the new arrivals entered and carefully surveyed the room. Conversations went silent, card games ended in middeal, and those already stretched out on their bunks were suddenly on their feet.

These, they knew, were not men who had come to help with herding and branding cattle.

"There's empty beds over there," one of the men said, pointing toward a corner of the room. He didn't bother to make known the fact that two of them had once been occupied by workers who had recently lost their lives, Greenleaf and Waymon Tuttle, the unsuccessful sniper.

El Diablo gave no response and instead slowly walked the length of the room, looking each man in the eye as he passed. The twins followed in lockstep.

They finally stopped at the opposite end of the room, away from the noise of the poker table and where two windows allowed a hint of night air. "We'll use these three," El Diablo said.

Without argument, the occupants gathered their belongings and gave up their beds.

And with that, there was a new leader among the ranks.

Since the death of Lyndon Greenleaf, the men sent to town to keep watch and report to Ringewald had disappeared. A welcome rumor spread that since the captain's chief enforcer was dead, a truce had been declared, and life could return to normal. Sheriff Barnes was even considering reopening the saloon.

Most anxious to accept the new state of affairs was Darla Ringewald.

"I made the mistake of telling her about the shooting at your place," Reverend Daniels said. He and Lewis were sitting beneath the church's grape arbor, watching as early-morning rain clouds approached.

"I'm afraid she took my news to mean that she is now free to come out of hiding and resume a more normal life."

"Not yet. You've got to convince her it's still not safe. It's hard to explain, but as I've told you before, I've got this feeling something bad is coming."

The pastor assured his visitor that he had faith in his instincts. "As I'm sure you know, Darla is a wonderful woman with many admirable traits. Not among them, however, is the fact she lacks patience and is quite stubborn. I'm under the impression that when she sets her mind to something, there's little that will change it. And regardless of what you or I might think best, I can't force her to stay."

Taylor stood and watched as the oncoming clouds boiled in the distance. "Rain's coming," he said. Then he added, "Tell her I'd like to speak with her tonight."

"She will be delighted to see you," Reverend Daniels said.

Chapter Eighteen

A pounding rain beat against rooftops, and rumbling claps of thunder rattled windows, making Dolly nervous. The trip from the farm into town had been a test of will. Instead of going directly to the Blessed Redeemer, Lewis took his horse to the livery, where he removed the soaked saddle and dried her coat.

"Anybody out in this weather is a fool ten times over," Ezzie said. "You're lucky you and your horse didn't both drown."

Taylor shook water from his hat and slicker. "I can't argue that," he said. "But at least it's highly unlikely there was anyone crazy enough to follow me." As he prepared to venture back into the storm, he told Ezzie he would be back shortly. "If it's all the same to you, I'll bed down here for the night."

"Your snoring won't keep me and the horses awake, will it?"

Lewis was laughing as he ducked his head and ran into the rain. The street was a rising river.

Reverend Daniels was waiting in the doorway, towels in hand, when Taylor arrived. "This rain is a godsend for the farmers and ranchers," he said, "but it would have been nice if He had held off for one more day. I wasn't sure you would make it.

"Darla's in her room, anxious to see you."

She was standing by the window, watching the storm, when he entered. Hearing the door open, she turned and smiled. "You look like a drowned rat," she said, then hurried across the room to hug him.

He hadn't seen her since her father's funeral and offered an explanation for why he had not visited her since she had taken up residence in the sanctuary.

"I heard what happened out at your place," she said. "I'm sure Reverend Daniels wouldn't approve, but the truth is, I'm so glad Lyndon Greenleaf is dead. He was an evil man who made the hairs on the back of my neck stand up every time I saw him.

"But now that he's gone . . ."

Lewis anticipated her next thought and gently put his hand to her lips. "Darla, it still isn't safe," he said.

He could see the defiance in her eyes. The pastor was right. She had made up her mind.

"I can't go on living like this," she said. "I'm tired of hiding like it's me who has done something wrong. You don't know how it feels." She stopped and put her hands to her mouth, realizing what she had said. Of course, he knew. He had spent five years knowing how it felt. "Lewis, I'm so sorry," she said.

He shrugged it off. "What would you do? You can't be thinking of going back to the ranch."

She laughed at the absurdity of the idea. "Honestly, I haven't thought everything out yet," she said. "Sue Ellen and I have been talking, and she and Luke will let me stay with them for a while. It would be good just to be around friends, smell some fresh air, and go where I please.

"What I'll do in the long term, I don't really know. That's one of the things that's hardest. Not having any idea what my future holds."

Lewis was losing the argument. "What concerns me," he said, "is once it's known where you are, your husband —"

"He'll not be my husband much longer. One of the things I have thought out is that

I never want to see Archer Ringewald again. My daddy left me some money, not much, but enough to pay a lawyer to help me get a divorce."

Taylor thought of the reaction the captain would have to such an idea, but said nothing.

"When do you plan to move in with the Bradleys?"

"Just as soon as it stops raining," she said.

The look on Taylor's face when he returned to the livery told Ezzie everything he needed to know. "You're old enough," he said, "to know better than to argue with a woman."

The rain had ended by the time Zale rousted Taylor from his sleep. The morning sun peeked through, and there was a clean smell to the air. "I thought for a while last night we were going to wash away," Ezzie said as he held out a cup of coffee.

Lewis dusted hay from his britches and reached for his mud-crusted boots. Before his friend could ask, he said Darla was planning to come out of hiding and move in with the Bradleys.

"Little Luke will be pleased," Ezzie said.

"That's something he and I don't have in common." Lewis was already planning to visit the sheriff. They needed to talk with Luke about a way to assure that his new boarder would be protected.

"By the way, I saw something interesting early this morning," Ezzie said. "I went out to see if the street was draining and saw three men riding into town, two Mexicans and one who looked to be a half-breed. They didn't seem in any hurry, just sort of looking things over."

"Any idea who they were?"

"Well, I didn't take them to be selling Bibles. In fact, they were pretty rough-looking. Hats pulled down on their faces, guns on their hips. I didn't bother saying hello since it would probably have been a waste of breath."

"Which way did they come from?"

Ezzie's expression was serious. "The way you're thinking," he said.

Little Luke was scampering around the room, doing all the things two-year-olds do to impress someone they are meeting for the first time. And he clearly wanted the attention of the young woman who was moving in with him and his parents.

"I think he's in love," Sue Ellen said.

Out on the front porch, Sheriff Barnes listened to the plan Taylor and Bradley had earlier discussed. It was far from ideal, but the only one they thought might meet the approval of both Darla and the sheriff. Since Barnes had, in fact, made the decision to allow the saloon to resume business, one of his recently sworn-in deputies could be used to make it work.

"What Luke and I have discussed," Lewis said, "is using two men to alternate keeping watch over the house, one doing it days, the other at night. I'm sure Darla's going to insist that she be allowed to move about town to shop and visit her friends, but we have to convince her to do so only with one of the men accompanying her wherever she goes."

"Who are the men you have in mind?" the sheriff said.

"Me and my father," Lewis said. "He'll do the day shift, and I'll replace him at night."

"I've got no better idea," Barnes said.

The unusual thing about the Saturday-night reopening of the saloon was that there were no Rocking R cowboys among the crowd. While local customers, enjoying their first drink in over a week, assumed that word simply had not reached the ranch, the truth was Captain Ringewald had ordered his men to stay away. He had already lost two hands and didn't want to risk losing another. At least not yet.

In an effort to appease his disappointed crew, he personally delivered several bottles of whiskey to the bunkhouse.

Meanwhile, the farmers and ranchers were in a mood to celebrate. The rain had ended a summer drought, and a quiet peace seemed to have finally been restored to Gila Bend.

Even B. J. Dixon drove his buggy into town. Lewis had told him that Darla was living with the Bradleys and reminded him he hadn't seen her in a while. "She's wanting to be around friends," Taylor said.

Indeed, she was thrilled to see him, waiting in the doorway when he arrived. B. J. tossed his crutch aside and wrapped an arm around her. In the other he held a pie his mother had insisted he bring. Sue Ellen and Luke invited him to join them for supper as Little Luke held out a small book he hoped the visitor might read to him.

Lewis, who had arrived to replace his father as lookout, joined in the happy reunion. Shortly, nostalgia filled the room as childhood memories flooded back. The Three Musketeers, older, wiser, and now a bit frayed at the edges, were together again. And for the moment, all seemed right with the world.

While Sue Ellen and Darla were in the kitchen, cutting into Daisy Dixon's pie, B. J. bragged to Lewis and Luke about his new litter of piglets.

The pleasant evening lasted until Little Luke's bedtime.

"On the way here," B. J. said, "I stopped to say hello to Ezzie Zale. We agreed to meet at the saloon for a drink. Then I'm going to bed down at his place. In the morning I need him to doctor a bite on my mule's hind leg."

At the Captain's Bar, they were enjoying the rowdy gathering. B. J. spoke with numerous friends he'd not seen in some time, and Ezzie was in fine form, entertaining a table of farmers with one tall tale after another. A steady sound of laughter and good cheer filled the room. Dixon was having a second beer, bought for him by a neighbor, while Zale nursed his nightly toddy.

It was getting late when a sudden hush fell over the room. The three strangers Ezzie had seen earlier in the day stood near the entrance, their cold eyes roaming from one table to another. They acknowledged no one as they made their way through the crowd.

When the bartender greeted them, the tall, dark-haired man was the only one who spoke.

"Tequila," he said.

For a reason no one seemed to understand, his presence drained all joy from the room.

Chapter Nineteen

A light sleeper, Ezzie was aware of the intruder even before he felt a rough hand pressing against his shoulder and heard someone say, "Get up, old man. We need to talk." When his only reply was a loud grunt, El Diablo grabbed him by the front of his long johns and pulled him into a standing position.

"I'm not interested in buying no Bible, especially at this time of night," Zale said before being slammed against the wall. El Diablo, not understanding the biblical reference, looked momentarily puzzled.

"I watched you down at the saloon earlier," he said, his words slightly slurred after the half bottle of tequila he had consumed. "It seems you know everybody in this town. So I figure you're the person who can tell me where to find a man called Lewis Taylor."

Ezzie shook his head. "The name's not

familiar to me. You sure you've come to the right town?"

El Diablo backhanded him across the face. "I'm not here to play games or listen to your smart-mouthing," he said. "Where can I find him?"

Zale felt dizzy, the sudden awakening and the blow to the head making it difficult to focus. "Beat on an old man all you want," he said, "but I don't know this Taylor fellow. Even if I did, I doubt seriously I would be inclined to tell you.

"Who are you, by the way?"

His attacker delivered a hard punch to the midsection that took away Ezzie's breath.

As he clutched his stomach, Dixon appeared from the stall where he had been sleeping. "Hey, what the . . . ?"

One of the twins rushed toward him and kicked his crutch away. El Diablo released Ezzie, letting him slide to the floor, and turned his attention to B. J. "Lewis Taylor, where can I find him?"

Dixon, balancing himself against the stall door, shook his head. "Not here," he said, "unless he came in while I was sleeping. Last I heard, he was in prison for almost killing somebody."

El Diablo placed his palm against Dixon's chest and shoved him to the floor. Then he placed a boot on his chest and bent forward until his face was close enough for B. J. to smell his foul breath. "It's not in my nature to harm women or cripples," he said, his voice barely a whisper. "So consider yourself lucky. And when you see this Taylor fellow, and I'm sure you will, make him aware I'm looking for him."

He then walked back to Zale, who was still struggling to regain his breath. "I'm called El Diablo," he said before turning to leave.

The twins, not having said a word, were right behind him.

As dawn was approaching, B. J. found his crutch and checked on Ezzie. "You hurt bad?"

"I'm okay, except for these stars I'm seeing. Just let me sit here for a few minutes to convince myself this isn't just a nightmare caused by bad whiskey. Meanwhile, you might go see if the sheriff's in his office yet. Tell him somebody calling himself El Diablo is in town, and his manners are just awful."

Like most Texas lawmen, Milton Barnes was aware of the legend and had heard the litany of stories about the infamous outlaw. "If half of them are true," he said, "he's a man who will shoot you dead just for looking at him wrong. And from what I've heard, he'll laugh while doing it.

"Go back and check on Ezzie. I'll send Doc Johnson."

Then he would go in search of Lewis Taylor.

Lewis was in the Bradleys' front yard, promising Little Luke that he would return soon, when the sheriff rode up. Taylor was surprised that he was on horseback and hadn't walked the short distance. "I see you're getting your morning exercise," he said.

Barnes was in no joking mood. "We've got to talk inside."

He relayed the information B. J. had given him and assured Taylor that the doctor was on the way to the livery to look after Ezzie.

"I've never heard of anybody called El Diablo," Lewis said. "The way you're describing the man makes him sound like some character out of one of those dime novels I read when I was in prison."

"He's real, Lewis, and he's not going to stop looking until he finds you."

"Well, at least we now know who the enemy is. His being here helps make sense of what's been happening lately." He laid out his theory for the sheriff. He had been right: Greenleaf hadn't come to the farm at the captain's instruction. He was simply crazed and angry about being replaced as the Rocking R's top gun. Ringewald, for whatever reason, had lost faith in him and hired someone to take his place.

"This is someone who makes Lyndon Greenleaf look like a Sunday school teacher," the sheriff said. "And he's brought two others with him."

Luke Bradley stood in the doorway, listening. "What can I do?" he said.

"You and your paper can get the word out to folks that things aren't as calm and peaceful as they seem," the sheriff said. "Alert them to be on guard, watching out for one another, because something's about to happen and it's not likely to be pretty."

"And," Lewis added, "see that your family and Darla are kept safe."

"What are you going to do?" Luke said.

"I'm going to try to find this El Diablo before he finds me."

In the days to come, tension and fear returned to Gila Bend. There was far less casual activity on the streets, women stopped bringing their children with them when they ventured out to do shopping, and in the evenings the saloon was visited by only the most die-hard patrons.

The new edition of the *Sentinel* made it clear to readers that all was not well. In a carefully worded editorial, Luke Bradley wrote that there was reason to believe that a real menace might be afoot and that the heart and soul of the town could be at stake. It was time for God-fearing, law-biding people to make it known that outsiders and carpetbaggers would not be allowed to destroy their community. He ended it by urging his readers to be vigilant but, under no circumstances, to attempt to take matters into their own hands. "Leave that to Sheriff Barnes and his capable deputies," he wrote.

At the Blessed Redeemer, the Sunday congregation was smaller than usual as Reverend Daniels used Bradley's editorial as the basis for his sermon, adding his own praise of the virtues and values of small-town life. He then invited Sheriff Barnes to the pulpit.

Rarely a churchgoer, he was clearly uncomfortable as he spoke, yet made it clear the only role residents had in the matter was to protect themselves and their loved ones. "We've never been a town of vigilante justice," Barnes said, "and we're not going to start now. It's the job of me and my men to provide protection and make Gila Bend safe. And that's what we're going to do."

As people filed out, talking and squinting into the bright sunlight, two men on horseback watched from the shadows on the opposite side of the street. They were Mexican and looked so much alike, they could be twins.

Ridley Merriwether, Esq., was a diminutive man, balding before his time, who walked as if he was always running late. Even with his wire-rimmed spectacles his face was always drawn into a permanent squint. His voice was high-pitched and annoying to most. But his business thrived because he was a good and trustworthy lawyer.

It was easy to see he was nervous as he climbed onto the Ringewald porch. By the time Celia greeted him and escorted him to the captain's office, his hands were moist and beads of perspiration were visible across his forehead.

Ringewald was not pleased to see him. "I'll not invite you to sit," he said, "since I'm busy and have little interest in talking to any lawyer not working for me."

"I understand," Merriwether said. "Yes, sir, I certainly understand. I can see you're a very busy man. Very busy, indeed." He was reaching into his satchel as he spoke; then he laid several sheets of paper on the desk.

Ringewald read slowly, silently mouthing the words. His cheeks began to redden. "A divorce? She wants a divorce?"

"Sir, yes, sir, that's the case. I think by reading the document carefully, you'll see that your wife has adopted a very generous stance in this matter —"

The captain interrupted him with a stream of curses.

"She is not asking to share in any of your holdings or —"

Ringewald crumpled the papers and threw them toward the young lawyer. "Get out. And don't come back. You can tell your client she's a fool to think I would agree to this."

"But, sir —"

"I said get out. If you can't find the door, I'll have someone come throw you out the window."

Long after the attorney had left, Ringewald sat, stewing. Finally, he took several deep breaths to calm himself, then scolded the maid for allowing Merriwether into the house.

"And find me El Diablo," he said.

■ ■ ■ ■

El Diablo was quietly amused as he watched the captain storm from one end of the room to another, then back again. He kept lifting a clenched fist above his head and shaking it as he paced. "A divorce," he said. "She'll have to see me dead first. My mother hated my father like he was a dreaded disease, but she never once asked for a divorce. Not once. No, sir, this is not going to happen to me."

"Maybe you should be talking to your own lawyer instead of me," El Diablo said.

For the first time since the outlaw's arrival, Ringewald stood his ground. "You be my lawyer," he said. "Make sure she knows what a big mistake she's making. And see that Mr. Merriwether never sets foot on this place again."

El Diablo had the sudden feeling that the captain's urgent wish to have Lewis Taylor dead and his wife's request for a divorce were somehow connected.

As he turned to leave, he knew one thing for certain. In recent days, Ringewald had begun to lose control as one bad thing after another occurred. Just the day before, he had learned of the rallying cries of the sheriff, the preacher, and the *Sentinel.* If something wasn't done soon, he could be facing a full-scale rebellion from the town he had so carefully planned to one day own. It frustrated him that Lewis Taylor was nowhere to be found. And now this from Darla, the woman he'd given everything.

Before the day was over, the captain would be so drunk that none of it would matter. But for the moment, the pain he was feeling was almost physical.

Chapter Twenty

The one-room office of Ridley Merriwether was above the mercantile, small and well-kept. Were it not for a filing cabinet, a typewriter, and a shelf of neatly arranged law books, it could have been the living room of an old maid. Everything on the desk was precisely arranged: papers in small stacks, pens and pencils side by side like tiny soldiers. Aside from a map of Texas that hung above the cabinet, the walls were bare.

The man who occupied the space was an early riser who lived his life by clockwork routine. He was always one of the first to arrive at the café each morning, ordering the same buttered biscuit and scrambled eggs, before walking the short distance to the stairs that led to his place of business. Once at his desk, he would spend several minutes cleaning his glasses, rearranging the items on his desk, and checking a note-pad on which he had a list of things that would occupy his day.

With no family and few friends, he worked long, tedious hours, drafting wills, preparing mostly trivial lawsuits for one Gila Bend resident angry with another, and, on occasion, guiding divorce proceedings along their bitter path.

On this day, when he entered his office, he realized immediately that his routine would not be the same. Sitting in the leather chair that his father had given him when he graduated from law school was a man he had never seen before. His boots were propped atop the desk, disrupting the careful arrangement that had been laid out the previous evening.

He was reading a copy of the document the captain had wadded up and thrown in the lawyer's face.

"As much money as Captain Ringewald has," the man said, "you would think his wife would be asking for more. Maybe some of his cattle or a sizable piece of land or . . ."

"Who are you, and how did you get in here?" Merriwether was already beginning to sweat.

The intruder slowly twirled the small dagger he had used to pick the lock of the office door. "I came in just like anyone would," he said. He didn't bother giving his name.

Merriwether's legs felt suddenly weak, and he put his briefcase aside and made his way to the chair generally used by clients.

"I guess you could tell yesterday that you caused the captain a great deal of grief, you and his woman. He hasn't stopped drinking since you left."

"I'm just doing what I was hired to do."

"I was sent here to tell you that no divorce is going to happen."

"But, sir . . ."

El Diablo swung his feet to the floor and stood, sweeping the papers and writing materials from the desk. He walked to the filing cabinet and began opening drawers, tossing files across the room. With a foot, he pushed against the typewriter, sending it smashing against the wall.

"Tell me about this woman. Is she pretty?"

"Yes, she's an at-at-attractive lady." Merriwether had not stuttered since childhood.

"I'd like to see for myself. Where can I find her?"

"You . . . you . . . you have to . . . to understand. The privacy of my clients is . . ." The remainder of what he had to say was drowned out by the sound of books tumbling to the floor.

"I'll ask one more time. Where can I find her?"

Not a courageous man, Merriwether's only wish was to get this man out of his office as quickly as possible. An odd and ill-timed thought flashed through his mind — that he would have a great deal of cleaning up to do once this disturbing encounter was over.

He told El Diablo that Darla was currently living at the home of the newspaper editor and his wife. "I hope you'll do . . . do . . . her n-n-no harm. She's a very nice lady."

"One more question," El Diablo said. "Do you know a man called Lewis Taylor?"

"I . . . I . . . I've heard the name, but, no, I've had no business dealings with him."

They were the last words Ridley Merriwether, Esq., ever spoke.

With a single blow to the face, El Diablo knocked the lawyer unconscious. Then he placed his gloved hands around Merriwether's throat and lifted him from the chair. His feet, several inches off the floor, kicked wildly for a while before his body went limp. Finally, the low gurgle in Merriwether's chest ceased and his face began to turn blue and his tongue began to swell. El Diablo released his grip and let the body fall to the floor among the scattered papers.

Before leaving, he stood before the framed map of Texas, a finger idly tracing the Mexico border. He was getting anxious to return home.

It was late in the day before Merriwether's fate was discovered. Zeke Ashfield, a farmer considering suing a neighbor he'd caught hunting on his property, almost broke an ankle as he hurried down the stairs en route to the sheriff's office.

He was in a daze as he entered, breathing heavily and having difficulty speaking. Finally, he managed to get the words past his lips.

"Lawyer Merriwether's dead," he said. As an afterthought, he added, "And it wasn't me who killed him."

Sitting with Sue Ellen at her kitchen table, Darla began to sob. "This is my fault," she said.

Luke was standing on the back porch with Lewis, discussing what the sheriff had told him about Merriwether's death and the state his office was in when he was found. "Why would anybody want to kill him?" Luke said. "He was a gentle little man who people hardly knew. He went to school with us, and I bet you don't even remember him."

Taylor shook his head. "My question is, why is Darla blaming herself?"

"She was just telling Sue Ellen that she went to him last week and spoke about getting divorce proceedings started. She didn't tell anyone. Apparently, he was supposed to deliver the papers to Captain Ringewald yesterday."

"And today he's dead," Lewis said. Darla's tears now made sense.

She joined the men on the porch. "I should have waited," she said, "but I was just so anxious to put that part of my life behind me. I knew the captain would be angry. I even warned Mr. Merriwether, but I had no idea he would do something like this."

She, like Lewis, had no doubt who was responsible for the attorney's death.

"Your husband doesn't sound like a man in his right mind," Lewis said. "But if you're looking for someone to blame, it's me. Taking you away from the ranch is what seems to have set all this in motion. It's me who has created this mess.

"And I've got to figure a way to put it to an end before others are killed."

He knew it was highly unlikely that Ringewald himself had come to Merriwether's office and strangled him. It was the sort of thing he would have had Lyndon Greenleaf do when he was still alive. Now the only logical suspect was El Diablo, a man Taylor had yet to even see.

Ezzie Zale, who had come in search of Lewis, agreed. "When I was headed to the café earlier today," he said, "I saw him riding out of town, headed in the direction of the Rocking R."

Taylor felt bad that he'd not seen his friend since he was attacked in the livery. "How's your head?" he said. "I'm the cause for what happened to you and B. J.," he said. "I'm sorry, and I'm going to find some way to make it up to you."

"Well, killing the guy seems fair," Ezzie said.

For two days, Esteban and Ernesto had been riding along the Guadalupe River, searching for a location that fit El Diablo's description. Upon his return from Gila Bend, he had instructed them to look for an isolated, well-hidden cabin that could be reached in a day's ride. Deserted, if possible. But if it was occupied, they were to kill whoever lived there.

What they found was a run-down log

cabin, the home of a weathered old hermit. He was on a small raft baiting his trotline for catfish when they happened on him. He never made it back to the bank of the river. Instead his body floated downstream, past a bend and out of sight.

When they returned to the ranch and described what they had found, El Diablo was pleased. It fit perfectly into his plan.

He, too, had developed a likely sequence of events, and it revolved around the wife of Captain Ringewald.

For whatever protest he might display, the captain obviously had no genuine affection for this woman Darla. She was nothing more than a prized possession that had been stolen from him. On the other hand, the man who rescued her from the Rocking R must care for her. Otherwise, he would not have risked his life to save her.

El Diablo was betting he would do so again. Soon, Lewis Taylor would have to come to him.

Leaning against the fence of the corral, away from prying eyes and ears in the bunkhouse, he outlined his plan. Ernesto was to return to the riverside cabin and wait. El Diablo and Esteban would soon bring the woman there.

▪ ▪ ▪ ▪

There was no funeral for Ridley Merriwether, just a brief graveside service at which Reverend Daniels struggled to find much to say to the few assembled. He read more scripture than usual and extended the length of his prayer, asking that the gates of heaven be opened for the deceased. He didn't want to appear dismissive. Few of the lawyer's clients even bothered to attend.

Though she had spoken with the lawyer only the one time, Darla felt she should be there, and Lewis had insisted he accompany her.

"Too much time's been spent in the graveyard lately," he said to the pastor after the service.

Reverend Daniels agreed, then said, "Keep Darla safe."

Two days later she was gone.

She had promised Little Luke a new ball to replace one that he had lost, and with Axel Taylor escorting her, she made the short walk to the mercantile. As they stepped onto the sidewalk, she assured Axel she would not be long and suggested he wait for her outside. "Take a seat on the bench and light up your pipe. Enjoy the sunshine," she said. "No need for you to watch me shop."

Inside, the only other customer was a young Mexican man who, in excellent English, had asked where he might find rope and metal spikes for a tent he was erecting for his boss. After pointing the way, manager Seth Hanson smiled and returned to the front of the store.

Darla had just selected a brightly colored rubber ball when Esteban placed his hand over her mouth and showed her his knife before pressing it against her ribs. "This way," he whispered, moving her toward the back door.

The ball, which had fallen from her hand, bounced lazily down the aisle.

Outside, Esteban hurriedly wrapped his bandanna over Darla's mouth, then lifted her onto El Diablo's saddle. Riding behind her, he wrapped an arm around her waist before digging his boots into his horse's hindquarters. Esteban was already a few yards ahead, leading the way.

They were on the outskirts of town in minutes. Despite their conducting the abduction in broad daylight, no one had paid them notice. That was part of El Diablo's plan: Whenever possible, do whatever you have to at a time when your enemy least expects it.

They were a mile from town by the time Axel's patience ran out. He entered the store to find Hanson sitting near the front window, reading the *Sentinel.* Both were surprised to see they were the only people in the store.

"Where did she go?" Axel said.

"She was here just a minute ago. Only customers I had were her and this young Mexican fellow."

"Oh, my God," Axel said as he ran toward the back of the store and out a door leading to an empty alley.

Lewis had just finished giving Dolly a brushing and feeding Whisper when his father arrived, dismounting before his horse could even come to a full stop. The look on his face signaled that he had bad news.

"Son, she's gone," he said. "They've taken her." It was the first time Lewis had ever seen tears in his father's eyes. "I've already told the sheriff. He and the other deputies are trying to figure where they went. Ezzie's helping."

"Is anybody headed to Ringewald's ranch?"

"Not that I know of."

"Then I'm going. I'll need to use your horse."

Lewis pushed his way past the maid, and the captain looked perplexed when he burst into his office, pointing a rifle. "What?" he said.

"Where is she? What have you done with her?"

"Boy, I've got no idea what you're talking about. If it's my wife you're looking for, I haven't seen her since back when you came and kidnapped her."

Lewis had the sense Ringewald was being truthful for once.

"What about that outlaw you've hired? The Devil, El Diablo, whatever he's called."

The captain, not quite drunk, not quite sober, was enjoying the panic he could hear in his visitor's voice. "He's not here. I haven't seen him in a day or two. If he's doing his job properly, he's out looking to find you and shoot you dead."

Taylor chose to ignore Ringewald's threatening tone. "If he harms her . . ."

"You saying you think he's got Darla?"

"I know he does," Lewis said.

Several of the captain's men were gathered near the front porch by the time Taylor was leaving. Seeing them, he cocked his Winchester and watched as they slowly backed away, providing him a path to his horse.

In the house, Ringewald was trying to determine whether to be angry with El Diablo or to laugh out loud.

Chapter Twenty-One

The horses, particularly the one carrying two riders, were tiring. "We'll rest for a few minutes," El Diablo said as he helped Darla to the ground and removed the bandanna from her face. "I don't think we've been followed." Kneeling near a spring-fed pool, he dipped his hat into the clear water and held it out to her. She slapped it away.

"Why are you doing this?" she said.

"You have no reason to be afraid. We're not going to hurt you." He took a step back and looked at her. Though windblown, her hair glistened in the sunlight. Despite her anger, she had a face that was almost angelic. She was, just as the lawyer had said, a pretty woman.

"I'll ask again, why are you doing this?"

Rather than answer, he asked a question. "What can you tell me about this man Lewis Taylor?"

Darla glared at her abductor, her cheeks

turning red. "You want him to come find me. You're using me to set a trap."

El Diablo smiled. She was also smart.

The trip took most of the day as Esteban led them past vast cedar breaks, through shallow gorges and fields of tall grass, and over small streams that fed into the Guadalupe. Though she was relieved to no longer have her mouth covered by the sweat-smelling bandanna, she said nothing.

By the time they reached the river, the day was ending. An early-rising moon reflected on the swiftly moving water. They rode along the bank until the cabin came into view. Inside, a single lantern glowed. Outside, Ernesto sat beside a firepit, cooking a catfish he had pulled from the old hermit's trotline.

"Hola," his brother said. "What you're cooking smells good."

Ernesto, who rarely spoke, only nodded.

While the brothers sat by the fire, El Diablo took Darla into the one-room cabin. It was sparse, with only a bed, a single chair, and a small table on which the lantern sat. There was an odor of mildew and lingering pipe smoke.

"You'll not be here long," El Diablo said. "While you are, my men will watch over you and see that you are well cared for. They will sleep outside, leaving you to your privacy, and they have been told you are not to be harmed in any way.

"My only request is that you not try to run."

Darla spoke for the first time since they had stopped to rest the horses. "This is my husband's idea, isn't it?"

El Diablo smiled. "Your husband is a sad and foolish man, not smart enough to plan anything but his next drink of whiskey. Why would a woman like you marry him?"

She turned her back, offering no reason. In truth, she didn't have one. All she was certain of was that she was tired of being hidden away.

The fire had faded to sparkling embers as the three men sat silently, each wishing someone had thought to bring a bottle of tequila. A gentle breeze rustled the tree leaves, and there was an occasional splash in the river as frogs searched for food.

El Diablo explained that he would leave at daylight and return to the ranch. The brothers would stay, watching over the woman, until he returned.

In the cabin, the lantern was out. The sour smell of the bed made Darla choose to sleep on the floor.

Miles away, Whisper whined as he watched his master pace and pound a fist against the wall. Lewis had no idea where to look for Darla. The sheriff's men had ridden out of town in all directions and found nothing that would tell them the route El Diablo had taken.

"I'd like to help," Axel said, "but I've got no idea what I can do."

"Neither do I," his son said. "He wants me to come looking for her . . . and him . . . but how can I do that when I have no idea where to look? All I know is that when I do find him, I'm going to kill him. I promise you that."

"And I hope to be there to see it," Axel said.

Luke Bradley was also frustrated as he sat in front of his typewriter, trying to write a story for the *Sentinel* about Darla's abduction. It was almost midnight, and the words were coming painfully slow when Sue Ellen arrived with a sandwich and a jar of sweet tea.

"The neighbor's watching Little Luke," she said. "I just wanted to come over and see if you needed some company."

Luke stood to give her a hug and stretch his legs. Then he heaved a sigh and nodded toward his typewriter. "This isn't going to do any good," he said. "I'll write this story. Then a few people will read it, but all it will accomplish is making them grateful it isn't them or one of theirs who has been taken.

"Darla needs help. So does Lewis. And I'm sitting here doing absolutely nothing for them."

A single tear ran down Sue Ellen's cheek. "I feel the same way," she said.

Bradley wasn't completely right when he assumed his effort was futile. The day the *Sentinel* was published, a farmer came to the sheriff's office to report something he'd seen a couple of days earlier.

"I came in this morning to visit the feed-store and read about that woman being taken away," he told Sheriff Barnes. "Day before yesterday, I was down by the creek, hunting for squirrels, when I saw these two horses pass in the distance. They weren't close enough for me to tell who they were, but it looked like there were two people on one of the horses. One could have been a woman.

"They were headed south and seemed to be in a hurry."

He gave the sheriff directions to the place he'd been when he saw the riders. "Better than this, I'm headed home as soon as my wagon gets loaded. I'd be glad to take you there."

"I know where you live," Barnes said. "I've got a stop to make. Then I'll meet you at your house as soon as I can get there."

He considered locating one of his deputies to accompany him, but decided against it and rode straight to the Taylor farm.

Lewis was saddling Dolly with plans to make another visit to the Rocking R when the sheriff arrived. "Old man Lindsey, who farms south of town, says he thinks he saw something," he said.

Soon, they were walking through the farmer's cornfield toward the grove of oak trees where he had been hunting. Once there, Lindsey pointed to the south. "Over there," he said, "just before that little rise. That's where I saw them."

Taylor shook the farmer's hand and Barnes thanked him.

As they walked back to the farmhouse, Lewis kept turning to look in the direction Lindsey had pointed toward. "What's that way?" he said.

"Nothing much, until you get to the Guadalupe River. Then a long ride farther down, there's the border. You think maybe they're taking her to Mexico?" Lindsey asked.

Lewis shook his head in frustration. "I have no idea," he said. "I've not done any tracking since the war. But since we've got no better plan, I'm going to give it a try."

"Want some company?"

"Thanks, but it could be I'm going to be chasing my own tail. I think it would be best if you stay in town in case something develops there."

Sheriff Barnes took his rifle from its scabbard and handed it to Lewis. "Mind that you take care," he said.

It was coming back to him as he rode toward the rise. Look for fresh tracks made by two horses, one carrying a heavier load than the other. Watch for broken twigs, bent grass, stones out of place, boot prints near a resting place, a burned-out campfire, anything that would show that someone had recently traveled this way. He had done the same back in his army days when he was assigned to chase Yankee prisoners who had escaped.

Knowing that it would be slow going, he had decided to ride Dolly. She hadn't had a great deal of exercise lately and would enjoy the new scenery. Farmer Lindsey had loaned him a canteen and given him a bag of beef jerky. "Be careful," he had said as Lewis rode away.

Though not much at praying, he gave it a try. "Please, Lord," he whispered to the wind, "let her be safe."

Darla had not slept at all. As she lay on the dusty cabin floor, her mind raced, not so much because she was worried about her own safety but rather that she had put others in harm's way. A wave of guilt swept over her as she thought of Lewis being lured into a deadly situation.

When the first rays of sunlight came through the cabin window, she went outside and sat on the porch. The twins, already up, watched her carefully. Both, she saw, had pistols tucked into the waists of their britches.

She watched the horses as they drank from the nearby river, their hooves hidden beneath the racing water.

"I'd like to go down there and wash my face," she called out.

Ernesto got to his feet, ready to follow her. She brushed her hands against her dress as she stood and gave him a stern look. "I'll need a few moments of privacy," she said.

"I promise not to run away."

Her captor seemed to be blushing as he watched her quickly make her way to the river's edge.

Chapter Twenty-Two

The farther he traveled, the more confident Lewis was that he was on the right trail. As far as he could tell, the riders he was pursuing were the only ones who had come this way in some time. Theirs were the only hoofprints he could see.

That he had come upon no campsite or burned-out fire indicated they had not stopped for any length of time along the way. Wherever they were headed, he decided, wasn't too far. Still, he resisted the urge to speed Dolly along. He was on a methodical journey until he reached whatever destination waited ahead.

As the sun began to set, he reached the Guadalupe and found a spot where horses had pawed at its muddy bank. Nearby were boot prints and indentations where knees had sunk into the mud while someone bent forward to drink. Looking closer, he saw smaller footprints, likely made by a woman.

He was close.

The signs slowly led him along the river. It was getting dark, and he was contemplating making camp and waiting until daylight to continue. Just as he stopped, however, he glimpsed something in the distance. At first, it was only a dark shape, perhaps an outbuilding of some sort. The more he focused, the more clearly it came into view. A deserted cabin, maybe. Quickly he discarded the notion that it was deserted when he thought he could see a flicker of light coming from inside.

Tethering Dolly near the water, he took the sheriff's rifle and slowly moved toward the light. Kneeling in chest-high weeds, he was aware of his heart racing and his boots sinking into the muck. He held his breath and listened and in time was aware of men's faint voices speaking in Spanish. He couldn't determine how many there were.

Moving closer, he saw that two men were sitting by a dying campfire that no longer warmed the kettle dangling above it. They were eating something that smelled of boiled cabbage and wild onions, and their hats were pulled low on their brows.

Lewis wished that he knew what El Diablo looked like.

■ ■ ■ ■

If Darla was here, she was probably inside the cabin. Was she alone? Or was there someone in there guarding her? To find out, he carefully made his way toward the back of the small structure, hoping not to alert the men sitting out front. He moved the final fifty yards on his hands and knees.

There was a small window on one side, and he went to it. A lantern on a small table lit the room, but at first look, he saw no one. His heart sank as he saw the empty bed and was unaware of any movement. He was about to move away when he heard a faint moan. Just a few feet below him, curled up on a tattered floor rug, was Darla. He watched her for a minute to make sure she was breathing normally; then he stepped back into the darkness and pondered his next move.

There was no way to sneak her from the cabin. Waking her would most likely alert the men out front. Even if he could get her attention, the window was too small for a person to fit through. The well-guarded front door was the escape route.

Lewis made his way to the corner of the cabin, where he could see the two men. One was talking while the other's head bobbed as if he was about to fall asleep.

With the rifle in one hand and his pistol in the other, he stepped from the shadows. Neither of the men noticed him there until he said, "Anybody who reaches for a weapon is dead."

The men jumped to their feet and stared at the intruder. The man who had just moments ago been nodding off had lost his hat in the sudden movement.

For an instant, Taylor thought he was seeing double. The young men were mirror images. "I want your hands high above your heads," he said. Without taking his eyes off them, he called Darla's name. "It's me, Lewis. Come on out."

The sound of his voice alerted the nearby horses. Taylor glanced toward a sprawling cottonwood tree and was relieved to see there were only two, nervously pawing at fallen leaves and pulling against the ropes that tethered them to a low-hanging branch.

Still, he needed to be sure. "Anybody else with you, except the woman?"

"The other one left." It was Darla standing on the porch, disheveled and shivering. "I heard him say he was going back to the ranch."

"El Diablo?"

"Yes."

In his haste to locate her, Lewis had given little thought to what he would do with the two men now standing in front of him. He considered tying them up and taking their horses, leaving them to wait until El Diablo became concerned enough to come looking for them. Or he could take them back to Gila Bend and let the sheriff deal with them. The law wouldn't look kindly on the kidnapping of a woman.

The decision was made for him.

In a single motion, Esteban lowered an arm and reached for his pistol. He already had it drawn and pointed before Lewis could react. Gunshots echoed through the trees and across the river. Esteban's shot grazed Lewis's shoulder, tearing away a piece of his shirt. Lewis's shot hit Esteban squarely in the chest. He rocked dizzily for a second, then fell back into the remains of the campfire.

Ernesto screamed at the sight of his fallen brother and ran toward the porch. His gun already drawn, he would make Darla his shield.

As he reached the top step, she lifted her leg and gave him a kick that spun him around. Again facing Lewis, he aimed his pistol. This time, Taylor was not slow to react. Not bothering to aim, he fired two quick shots that found their target. Ernesto's gun fell to his side as he grasped his chest, took a single step, then fell, dead before he hit the ground.

The acrid smell of gunpowder filled the air as Taylor holstered his pistol and walked toward Darla. Her hands covered her mouth, and her eyes were closed in an attempt to hide the horror that had just played out. He put his arms around her. "It's all right," he said. "You're safe now."

Before she could reply, she fainted.

Lewis lifted her, carried her into the cabin, and laid her on the old hermit's bed. The quilt was filthy, but better than the floor where he'd first seen her. With water from one of the dead men's canteens, he gently bathed her face.

She woke with a jerk, her fists clenched and fright showing on her face. Then she looked up at Lewis, and there was the beginning of a smile.

"Are you all right?" he said.

She nodded. "Just how many times are you planning on rescuing me?" she said.

"As many as it takes, I suppose."

While she rested, Lewis went outside and dragged the bodies toward the river so she would not have to look at them as they left.

Then he saddled the Mexicans' horses. "We'll ride these," he said.

Dolly had done her job and would be allowed to follow behind as they made their way home.

They reached Gila Bend just before dawn and rode straight to the Bradley house. Sue Ellen was watching Little Luke eat his breakfast when they walked in. She screamed, "Hallelujah," as she attempted to hug both of them at once. Then she called out to the bedroom, "Luke, come see who's here."

Entering the room, he was speechless.

While Sue Ellen hurriedly prepared eggs and biscuits, Darla played with Little Luke. Lewis explained to his friend what had happened in the past few days.

"Without you," hc said, "it wouldn't have been possible." He explained how farmer Lindsey had gone to the sheriff after reading the story in the *Sentinel.* Darla reached over and took Luke's hand, then kissed him on the forehead.

Not since the birth of his child had the newspaper editor felt so proud.

After clearing away the dishes, Sue Ellen sat down by Darla. "You have no idea how glad I am to see you," she said. "Come with me. Let's get you cleaned up and into some clothes that don't smell like you've been wallowing in a pigpen."

"I'll leave her in your good hands," Lewis said as he prepared to leave. "I've got some things I need to do."

He rode Dolly to the livery, the two dead men's horses trailing behind. "I've got a couple of good-looking mares for you," he said as Ezzie approached, smiling. "Their previous owners no longer have any use for them."

"I'm glad to see you back."

"We just got here, right before sunup."

"We?"

"Yep, Darla's over at the Bradleys, healthy and happy." He then had to again tell the story of how he found her.

Minutes later, he was in the sheriff's office, repeating the story yet again. "I should inform you that there are two bodies down on the Guadalupe," he said. "I killed them in self-defense."

"That's far out of my jurisdiction," Barnes said, "so I'll not worry about it."

"Got time for a quick ride?"

"Where are you headed?"

"I need to stop by and let my daddy know I'm back. Then I'd like to ride out to see

Mr. Lindsey. I need to return his canteen . . . and shake his hand."

Chapter Twenty-Three

Sue Ellen was planning a big supper of pork roast, mashed potatoes, string beans, and freshly baked bread to celebrate Darla's safe return. She had invited Luke, Axel, Sheriff Barnes, Ezzie, B. J., and his mom. "Perhaps I shouldn't admit it," she said, "but one of the reasons I asked B. J. to bring his mother is because with her coming I won't have to worry about fixing dessert. She'll bring pies."

Darla requested that one more be invited. "Would it be okay if Reverend Daniels joins us?"

"Absolutely. He can give the blessing and pray that my roast isn't too dry."

"I'm thinking about returning to my room at the church," Darla abruptly said.

It wasn't her own safety she was concerned about. She realized that her husband and El Diablo would continue their quest for revenge, and she didn't want to be responsible for putting the Bradley family in harm's way.

She had already discussed her plans with Lewis, and he had agreed it was a wise thing to do. "I think this will all be over soon," he said. "Then everyone can get on with their lives."

"What plans do you have for the future, Lewis?" she said.

The question was surprising and made him a bit uneasy. He thought for a minute before answering, "Just to be happy," he finally said.

"Me, too," she replied.

It was a cool evening, so Luke washed down the wooden table in the backyard and borrowed extra chairs and a couple of lanterns from the Blessed Redeemer. Sue Ellen had decided she wanted to serve her celebration supper under the stars.

Everyone seemed to make a concerted effort not to talk about what everyone was thinking. At least for the evening, they wanted to put the nightmarish events of recent days out of mind. Nor, on this night, did they wish to contemplate what the future might hold.

Ezzie did his best to keep the mood light, spinning funny yarns and outrageous tales.

"You ought to write a book," B. J. said.

"I probably should read one first," Ezzie said.

Reverend Daniels and Darla spoke briefly while in the kitchen helping Daisy as she prepared servings of pie. "I'm delighted you'll be coming back," the pastor said. "The room is just as you left it.

"I'm so pleased you returned home safely. I prayed for you in your absence. And for the brave man who went to find you."

She thanked him as Daisy handed her a tray filled with plates of pear pie. "Mr. Zale always eats two slices," Mrs. Dixon bragged.

The pastor smiled at Darla. "We members of the clergy pick up on things, you know," he whispered. "Your Lewis Taylor is a good man. He protects you for a very special reason."

She waited until Daisy was out the door. "Yes, I know," she said. "And I hope you will keep praying that he's protected, too. He's had enough unfair heartache in his life. I'm not sure I could stand it if something else bad were to happen to him."

"Just trust that God is watching over him," Reverend Daniels said.

Darla smiled. "Keep this up," she said as she headed back into the yard, "and you're going to convert me."

"That," he replied, "wouldn't be so bad, would it?"

The only mention of the abduction and escape came as everyone was leaving. The sheriff and Taylor called Luke aside. "We'd appreciate it if you didn't write anything about Darla's return," Barnes said. "The longer El Diablo thinks she's being held captive, the more waiting he's going to do. Let's let him figure Lewis is getting anxious and will come looking for him soon.

"That will give us more time to figure what our next move will be."

Luke, the newspaperman, was disappointed. Luke, the friend, promised he would write nothing.

At the Rocking R, El Diablo was, in fact, getting impatient. His mood was more sour than usual, causing the cowhands to stay clear. He cleaned, then recleaned his pistol and carried a rifle everywhere he went. He rarely slept or joined the others at mealtimes. Several times a day, he rode out to the guard stand to see if anyone had been sighted, returning disappointed.

He wanted a showdown, had expected it. But where was Lewis Taylor? Had he misjudged him? Was he so cowardly that he had no concern for the woman who had been kidnapped? El Diablo cursed and kept a wary eye on the horizon.

The captain found him sitting on the fence of the corral. He, too, was losing patience. "I'm not paying you to sit around all day, staring at my cows," he said. He demanded to know what El Diablo was planning. And where were the Mexicans?

El Diablo's dislike for Ringewald had grown daily. "I know what I'm doing," he said. "My business here will be finished soon. Until it is, leave me alone."

Ringewald stood his ground. "I just hope to God I didn't make a mistake, bringing you here." He again asked about El Diablo's men.

"They're part of my plan. That's all you need to know."

Lewis Taylor was also apprehensive. The calm that he'd felt after Darla's safe return had been replaced by an ever-present awareness that the worst was yet to come. He tended chores in an effort to take his mind off the man who planned to kill him, but got little relief. Even Whisper sensed the uneasiness and didn't let him out of his sight.

"You muck that stall one more time," Axel said as he entered the barn, "and it's going to be cleaner than my kitchen. Come up to the house and sit."

The sound of his father's voice triggered a new train of thought. It was Reverend Daniels who had urged Lewis to look to the positives in his life, suggesting that by weighing the good against the bad he would find new peace. It made sense. Since his return to Gila Bend, his relationship with the man who had raised him had greatly improved. The townspeople, many of them at least, had put aside their concerns that an ex-convict was walking among them. He had renewed old friendships. And Darla was back in his life in a way that he found as confusing as it was comforting.

Yes, there was plenty of good to consider. But he wouldn't be able to fully savor it until the other matter was finally dealt with.

Whisper's tail wagged as he followed the two men to the porch. They sat side by side, eyes roaming the small piece of land that had been the only home either had ever known.

"It'll be good when fall comes," Axel said, breaking a long silence. "That's the best time of the year. Harvesting, always having a fire going in the fireplace, the crisp, new smell in the air. Your mother and I always liked it when time came for her to bring out the extra quilt for the bed, and going to sleep knowing we would wake up to frost in the pasture the next morning.

"It's my favorite time of the year, even better than Christmas."

Lewis smiled, knowing that his father's intent was to have him focus on a future that was free of constant turbulence and trouble.

"You miss her, don't you?"

"Every day," Axel said. "Up until the time she passed, my life was about as perfect as a man can hope for. We didn't have much money and times got hard now and then, but she would always smile and assure me better days were coming. Your mother brought sunshine in the daytime and a million stars at night. If it hadn't been for you needing some help growing up after she passed, I'm not sure I would have had any reason to stay around." He turned and looked at his son. "But I'm glad I did."

Lewis said nothing, but wondered if there would ever be a time in his life when he would know such perfect joy.

El Diablo was done waiting. The sun had gone down, and he was halfway into town before realizing his trip had no real purpose except to show the people of Gila Bend that he had not gone away. Nor that he would. It was time to announce to one and all his reason for being there.

Again, a silence fell over the saloon when he entered and slowly walked to the bar. Instead of asking for tequila, he drew his pistol and fired two shots into the ceiling. A few men closest to the door quickly made their way into the street. Others sat frozen to their chairs. The bartender was on his hands and knees, crawling toward the kitchen.

"For those of you who don't already know," El Diablo said, "I'm here in this rat hole of a town to see a man I have business with. He's called Lewis Taylor, and it seems he's too cowardly to come out of hiding and face me." Though menacing, his voice was shrill and high-pitched. He sounded like a man who was at desperation's edge.

Suddenly, a voice came from the back of the room. "Speaking of cowards, why don't you go on back out to the ranch and tell your Captain Ringewald to tend his cows and leave folks here in town alone? He's the one needing killing, not Lewis Taylor."

Ezzie Zale was on his feet, shaking a finger toward El Diablo. He was stone-cold sober but livid. "It seems to me you could find better things to do than be a hired gun, pestering and threatening folks who have done you no harm. We're getting tired of it, and sometime, when you're not looking, it just might be you dead. Like those Mexican boys you brought with you."

The second the angry words left his mouth, Ezzie knew he had said too much.

El Diablo hurriedly walked toward him, slapping bottles and glasses to the floor along the way. His gun was still in his hand. "What are you saying, old man?"

Now frightened, Ezzie cleared his throat before replying, "All I'm saying is they aren't likely to be helping you out anymore."

"What's happened?" El Diablo was screaming.

"Maybe you should leave us be and go find out for yourself."

A crazed look crossed El Diablo's face, and he was cursing as he turned away and hurriedly left the saloon. No one moved until he was out of sight.

In time, the tension waned, and several admiring patrons offered to buy Ezzie a drink. He thanked them but said it was time he got to bed.

He was walking alone toward the livery, replaying his verbal confrontation, when a dark figure suddenly stepped from an alley. There was a flash of a pistol shot that knocked Ezzie to his knees. Then the attacker continued to cock and fire until his gun was empty.

The gunshots were heard inside the saloon, and several patrons rushed into the street, where they found Ezzie's bloodied body.

By the time Sheriff Barnes arrived at the scene, he found no one who could identify the person who had ambushed and murdered his friend. Adding to his frustration was the fact no one had seen the gunman flee. It was as if a ghost had emerged from the alley, then just vanished.

Zale's funeral was conducted two days later. According to a wish he had expressed in a letter the sheriff found among his belongings, it was held not at the Blessed Redeemer, but instead at the livery. People crowded into the building, many standing, some sitting on hay bales or the stall gates. A couple of youngsters straddled a donkey that nibbled at an oats bucket, paying little attention to what was going on around him. Ezzie's bed had been pulled from his sleeping room to make a place for the elderly and frail to sit. The women from the church had provided a clean quilt to cover his tattered bedding.

Flowers lined one wall, masking the odor of horses, hay, and saddle soap.

Despite the anger and grief that hung over the room, Reverend Daniels made an effort to keep his message light and uplifting. Several humorous stories he told about the deceased brought chuckles from those on hand.

Toward the end, after "Amazing Grace" was sung and a prayer said, the pastor pulled a folded piece of paper from the pages of his Bible.

"I can give you no better example of the kind of loving and generous man Ezzie Zale was than by reading to you from something he wrote. He never came to my church and made no apologies for it. But in my humble judgment, he was as fine and caring a person as I've ever known.

"It isn't traditional to read a last will and testament during this kind of gathering. No more than it is for me to be performing a funeral in a livery barn," he said as he pulled his glasses from his vest pocket.

He then began to read:

> This old place has long provided a worthwhile service to the people of Gila Bend, always with work well-done and being mindful of fair prices. I would like

to see that tradition carried on. Thus, I wish to turn ownership over to my friend Lewis Taylor, who I know will work hard to see that it remains useful to the town. He knows little about blacksmithing, but in time he'll learn.

There is a small, empty parcel of land just on the other side of the corral that is in my name and fully paid for. I wish to pass it on to Daisy Dixon, along with a small amount of money I have in savings at the bank. The idea came to me a while back that the location would make a fine place for a pie shop.

The pastor removed his glasses and looked into the crowd. Many were crying, including Daisy Dixon.

"God bless you, Ezra Zale," Reverend Daniels said. And it was over.

The only people not at the funeral were Sheriff Barnes and his deputies, who were on their way to the Rocking R to arrest El Diablo. Though no one had seen him fire the shots that killed Ezzie, there was little doubt about his guilt.

The captain was in the barn when they arrived. "He's not here," he said. "I haven't seen him in a couple of days."

The sheriff gave Ringewald a disgusted look. "Any idea where he might be?"

"Nope. But if you do find him, tell him he's no longer welcome on my property. He's fired."

Barnes turned away, then stopped and moved close to the captain. There was the smell of whiskey on Ringewald's breath. "A bit early to be drinking, isn't it?" the sheriff said. "I've got more important matters to see to right now, but rest assured I'll come back soon. And you won't like what happens when I do."

At that moment, El Diablo was sitting on the bank of the Guadalupe, a half-empty tequila bottle balanced between his legs. He had dragged the bodies of Esteban and Ernesto away from where animals and insects had begun to prey on them and shoved them into the fast-flowing river.

For a moment, he wished he could feel some degree of sadness but quickly dismissed the thought. He preferred the white-hot anger boiling inside him.

Rather than thinking of his dead companions, he was imagining the slow and painful way he would kill Lewis Taylor.

Part Three

Chapter Twenty-Four

Trapped birds flittered through the rafters as Lewis stood alone in the livery. Aside from regular trips to town to tend the livestock, he had spent little time there since learning it now belonged to him. The quietness was saddening as he found himself hoping to once more hear the sound of Ezzie's laughter. As he had done repeatedly in recent days, he was remembering the good times.

"Still missing your friend, aren't you?" It was Darla, standing in the doorway. "I was getting a breath of fresh air in the churchyard and saw you ride past."

"This place just isn't the same without him. Yes, I miss him. Ornery as the old coot was, I expected him to outlive us all."

Darla could hear the lingering pain in his voice. "Lewis, you can't blame yourself," she said.

His rebuttal was simple. "That man El

Diablo didn't come here to kill Ezzie. He came to kill me. And everyone's suffering because of it."

She moved closer and placed a hand on his arm. Smiling, she changed the subject. "So you're now one of Gila Bend's proud business owners . . ."

"Who barely knows how to shoe a horse. But I'm going to learn. I'm going to figure out how to mend a broken axle, what doctoring a sick animal requires, and how to keep the forge properly hot. Ezzie's got books here that tell you how to do things, and I'm studying them. I'm going to make him proud."

"It seems to me you've already done that," she said. "Otherwise, he'd have given this place to somebody else."

Turning to get back to the Blessed Redeemer, she waved. "I hope you have lots of customers."

From the front window of the sheriff's office, Milton Barnes watched Darla leave the livery. He had been awake since long before dawn and had ridden out to his pasture to check on his small herd while the moon was still high and bright. Sleepless nights had become commonplace.

And now, as he stood there, he was letting

self-pity consume him.

He had let his town slip from his grasp and was obsessed with finding a way to remedy the situation. There had been too many killed, too much fear. And there was the haunting realization that the people of the community had lost their trust in him.

Somehow, he had to get it back. The first step toward redemption was to find El Diablo and put him in jail. Then, once he was transferred to San Antonio, where he would be tried for the murder of Ezzie Zale, only one thing would be left to do. To finally remove the cloud that had hung over Gila Bend for far too long, he had to deal with Archer Ringewald.

Once that was done, he had decided, he would turn in his badge. He was tired. The enthusiasm he had brought to the job as a young man was long gone. His bones creaked when he got out of bed, and even with his reading glasses, his eyesight was beginning to fail him. Stamina and a steady hand were things of the past. He rarely had much of an appetite, and now all whiskey did was give him a headache. Getting old had slipped up on him, arriving before he could properly prepare for it.

Still, he was determined to muster the strength and resolve to end his career on a high note. But how to do it?

He had thought of putting together a posse to go in search of El Diablo, but really had no idea where to look. Since the outlaw was apparently no longer welcome at the Rocking R, there was little need to go there. The only recourse, Barnes knew, was to wait until he showed himself. And that required a great deal of patience, another thing the sheriff was running short of.

He walked down to the livery and found Taylor rummaging through a barrel of discarded horseshoes. "Looks like he kept every one he ever replaced," he said as the sheriff approached. "What does a man do with worn-out horseshoes?"

"I guess he melts them down and makes new ones. That or uses them to weight down trotlines. Beats me."

Lewis was embarrassed that he didn't know the answer to his question. "I've got a lot to learn," he said.

The sheriff removed his hat and ran his fingers through his graying hair. "I'm more than a tad older than you," he said, "but can still make the same observation. The fact is, I've come to ask for your advice."

"I'm all ears, and there will be no charge."

"You do have a lot to learn," Barnes said. "Now that you're a businessman, I'd suggest you quickly eliminate the words 'no charge' from your vocabulary."

They walked out into the morning sun and sat on Ezzie's favorite bench.

"This El Diablo fellow has gotten into my head and keeps grinding away, night and day. And I can't figure him out, can't get an idea of who he is or what his next move might be. As long as I've been doing this, you would think I could anticipate what's in a lawbreaker's head. But not this one.

"All I know for certain is he likes killing people. If somebody's willing to pay him for it, so much the better."

Taylor's response was silence.

"What I'm asking," Barnes continued, "is what you think of him. I've heard the stories, but they don't really tell me much. All I know is that sometime soon, he's going to show himself and start raising holy what for. And I want to be ready."

Lewis chose his words carefully. "When I was locked up in Huntsville," he said, "I met men like him. They might not have been as smart as El Diablo appears to be, but they thought like him. The only life they valued was their own. Their only regret was that they got caught and were being punished for it.

"Most who kill a man, accidentally or on

purpose, in wartime or peace, carry a scar. You know that, so do I. It stays with you, haunts you, leaves a dark spot on your soul. And just when you think you've finally put it out of your mind, something happens to trigger a memory, and all of the ugliness comes back.

"In that sense, El Diablo's lucky. He's not haunted. I doubt he has troubling dreams. He feels no guilt or shame. He has no interest in being a better person because he likes having the reputation of a ruthless, mean-spirited outlaw. That's who he is. He's the devil, El Diablo, just plain bad, and that's as simple as I can put it.

"Even killing me won't satisfy him for long."

Barnes got to his feet and looked out into the street as if lost in thought. "He'll not get that satisfaction. It's my job to see that he doesn't."

"One other thing, as long as I'm running off at the mouth," Lewis said. "Despite his reputation, El Diablo is a coward. That's his big secret, and it's what we have to take advantage of."

"How?"

"By showing him we're not afraid."

El Diablo remained at the hermit's cabin

for several days, hoping the solitude would allow him to determine what the days ahead would bring. He found coffee and tobacco that was left behind and foraged in the old man's garden to satisfy his hunger. Mostly, however, he slept restlessly or sat by the river, silently watching its shallow waters boil over the rocks and rotting tree trunks.

On the morning after he had disposed of the bodies of Esteban and Ernesto, he sat for an hour, watching squirrels play their games of chase through the cottonwoods, amused by their high-pitched barks and quick movements.

He wondered why he didn't just go back to Mexico and put this fool's game behind him. It had been a mistake to take the captain's money, to pursue a person he didn't even know. In recent days, in fact, his anger had been focused more on the man who hired him than it had been on killing Lewis Taylor.

And with the arrival of night, he did, in fact, dream. Not of murders and mayhem but of long-ago days before he was known as El Diablo. He was still Dain Hayes then, living in a carefree time when he played with friends, watched his mother make tamales and sweet bread, and hunted crayfish along the banks of the Rio Grande.

He would always awake angry that those days were now far gone. And his thoughts would return to the decision he wrestled with.

If he did stay, if he decided to honor the agreement he'd made, he would also kill Captain Ringewald before heading home.

In the *Sentinel* office, Luke Bradley was finishing an article about the new schoolteacher who had just been hired when Lewis knocked on his door.

Luke was glad to see him. "I hope you've come to buy an ad for the livery," he said. "Ezzie never would. I couldn't even talk him into buying a subscription."

"Are you planning to write something about his funeral?"

"It's going to be my editorial. I talked to a lot of people at the service and got some nice quotes I'll use."

"Can I give you one?"

Luke was surprised by the request and searched his cluttered desk for a pencil. "What do you want to say?"

"Write that I think killing Ezzie was the most cowardly thing I've ever heard of. And be sure you use my name."

Luke finished writing and looked up at Taylor. "This is going to get back to him.

You sure you know what you're doing?"

"I hope so," Lewis said.

"Want to go down to the café for some lunch?"

Lewis shook his head. "I don't have time," he said. "I've got to get back and learn some more about horseshoeing."

That night, after Little Luke had been put to bed, Sue Ellen listened as her husband told her of Lewis's visit. "He's calling El Diablo out, challenging him," he said.

"You can't print that, Luke. He's going to get himself killed," she said.

"He wants me to. Pretty much insisted."

Two days later, when the new issue of the paper was distributed, Axel Taylor was livid when he read the quote from his son. Adding to his rage was the fact Bradley had paraphrased it in the headline above his editorial. "Act of a Coward," it read.

Though the *Sentinel* sold out in a matter of hours, its editor felt little reason to be pleased. He feared that he might well have written his friend's death notice.

Chapter Twenty-Five

Captain Ringewald threw the newspaper across the room toward El Diablo. "I didn't pay you to come here and shoot old people," he said. "It's been weeks, and you've still not done your job. You're fired. Get your belongings and get out. Go back to where you came from and drink tequila until you're blind as a cave bat."

The peace of his Guadalupe stay quickly erased, El Diablo ignored Ringewald and instead focused on the headline in the newspaper that lay at his feet. All he could see was the word "Coward," and it enraged him.

For a few seconds, he stood his ground, glaring at the captain; then he turned to leave. As he walked toward the bunkhouse, he was aware of cowhands stopping their work to look at him. Their fear seemed to be gone. So was the fear he had commanded.

He gathered his few things and stuffed

them into a saddlebag, still aware that curious eyes were watching. As he made his way to the door, he had no idea where he would go, yet he knew one thing for certain.

"I'll be back," he said to no one in particular.

In Gila Bend, things seemed normal. There was bustling activity at the mercantile and the feedstore, wagons rolled along the main street, and the bells of the Blessed Redeemer were ringing. B. J. Dixon stood in the wilting sun, supervising the clearing of the plot where his mother's pie shop would be built.

She had decided she would call it Rainbow's End.

Lewis left the livery and walked over to join his friend. "This will be a fine thing for your ma," he said. "She will do well. I just wish I knew half as much about running a livery as she does about baking pies."

Dixon laughed and slapped Lewis on the back. He, like most, had read the *Sentinel* editorial. "You doing okay?"

"Fine."

"I wish there was something I could do to . . ."

"I'm fine," Lewis repeated. "Before you know it, everything is going to be like old times."

"From your lips to God's ear," B. J. said.

Dixon was explaining how Ezzie had left his mother enough money that he would be able to hire someone part-time to help out at the farm when the sheriff joined them.

"I've decided to post deputies at each end of town," Barnes said. "A couple of other fellows have volunteered to take turns sitting up on the roof of the saloon, keeping watch. We've also rounded up some torches to keep lit at night, making it harder for someone to sneak around in the shadows."

"So," Taylor said, "you think he's finally coming?"

"I honestly don't know what to think. I'm just trying to be as ready as possible. And I suggest you do the same."

From a ridge, too far away to be seen by rooftop lookouts, El Diablo knelt behind a boulder with his spyglass slowly roaming the main street of the town. He stopped momentarily to focus on three men standing in a vacant lot near the livery. He recognized the one leaning on a crutch and, seeing the glint of a badge on the vest of another, assumed he must have been the sheriff.

The third one, he guessed, was Lewis Taylor, the man who had called him a coward.

He cursed and gripped the spyglass until his hands ached.

With El Diablo gone, the captain didn't know whether to feel relief or anger. He sat behind his desk for a long time before coming to a decision. He had waited too long for someone else to do his work. Lyndon Greenleaf had failed him, and now so had this half-breed from down on the border.

It was time he took control himself.

He waited until the hands had finished supper before making a visit to the bunkhouse. There, he announced that it was high time their Saturday-night visits to the Captain's Bar resumed. He wanted his men to again become familiar faces in Gila Bend, to give people cause for concern.

"Tell the bartender," he said, "that the first drink is on me."

Ringewald had thought things out carefully. He wouldn't accompany his men on their evening of celebration, but since it was highly likely some would wind up in jail for various degrees of drunken behavior, he would ride his Palomino into town later to pay their fines. By doing so, everyone would see him and know that the captain was hiding from no one.

As it had neared midnight, finding a sober customer in the saloon was impossible. Laughter and swearing had grown louder, fights were breaking out, and the few locals who had been there when the Rocking R crew arrived had long since gone home. Doc Johnson was summoned when one cowboy's hand was stomped after he had been accused of cheating at five-card stud. The injured man was still ordering more whiskey when the doctor told him that several bones appeared to be broken.

It was when things spilled out into the street and random shots were being fired into the air that Sheriff Barnes arrived.

He began taking firearms away and announced that the saloon was immediately closing. To demonstrate his authority, he placed three of the drunkest offenders under arrest and ordered the rest back to their bunkhouse. Some who had long since passed out would have to wait until they came to. Barnes lifted the men from where they slept at the bar or slumped over poker tables and dragged them out to the sidewalk.

"We were just having us some fun," one of those arrested said as he was being taken to jail. "Seeing that El Diablo fellow on his way is cause for partying."

The sheriff stopped the drunken cowboy

in the middle of the street and slapped him to get his attention. "What do you mean, he's on his way?"

The cowboy laughed as if something funny had just occurred to him. "The captain fired him, told him to clear out," he said, slurring his words. "And a mighty good riddance, I'd say." With that, his wobbly legs failed him, his eyes rolled back, and he fell into the sheriff's arms.

Barnes was still weighing the news as he locked the men up. One was already in the corner of the cell throwing up, while the other two were fighting over who would get to lie on the bunk. No doubt, the captain would be arriving soon to take them back to the ranch. The sheriff would ask him about El Diablo then.

Barnes and Taylor were standing in the doorway of the livery on Monday morning when Captain Ringewald arrived. They had already discussed the news that El Diablo was gone.

The ranch owner's appearance was much like a grand entrance. Sitting erect in the saddle, his white Stetson riding high on his head so the smile on his face was visible, Ringewald was followed by the two men who normally stood guard outside the ranch entrance. Both were carrying rifles.

He reined his horse to a stop in front of the livery and stared silently at Taylor for several seconds before turning to the sheriff. "I've come to get my boys," he said, "and to apologize for their misbehaving."

"I hear they were celebrating you firing one of your people," Barnes said.

"El Diablo wasn't the kind of person we want out at the Rocking R," Ringewald said. "As soon as I learned what he did to the old man who once owned this place, I wanted him out of my sight. I think he must have gone stone-cold crazy, and I'm sorry about what happened. I wish you could have arrested and hanged him. All I can say now is that taking him on in the first place was a big mistake."

He returned his attention to Taylor, then added, "And truth is, he wasn't getting his job done."

Lewis finally spoke. "Got someone to replace him?"

"Could be," the captain said before riding toward the jail, the sheriff close behind.

From his spot on the nearby ridge, El Diablo watched the conversation play out, wishing he could hear what was being said.

Rather than leave immediately after his ranch hands were released, the captain led his men on a slow parade along the Gila Bend street, occasionally nodding to those who noticed his passing. He made certain to ride by the newspaper office and was disappointed to find it not yet open. Still, the smile never left his face.

As they turned to head back toward the ranch, Ringewald slowed when he again passed the livery. He tipped his hat in Lewis's direction. "Yep, could be," he said before kneeing his horse into a gallop.

Barnes waited until they were well out of sight before rejoining Taylor. "If he's to be believed, maybe we've got one less worry," he said. "If El Diablo is gone, I've got to admit I would be mighty relieved. On the other hand, I didn't like that look the captain gave you. And the way he strutted into town gives me cause for concern."

"I think it should," Lewis said.

The sheriff nodded and forced a smile as he turned to leave. "For now there's another thing I'm dreading. I've got to get back and clean out a jail cell that stinks like a hog-pen."

Taylor kept the exchange light. "My pig farmer friend, B. J., won't appreciate your reference."

Had Ringewald timed his visit to Gila Bend

a bit differently, he would have encountered another familiar face. Minutes after he and his men paraded through town and left, his wife was walking from the Blessed Redeemer toward the Bradley home. Feeling increasingly bold about occasionally leaving her room, Darla was taking a birthday present to Sue Ellen.

When she arrived, Little Luke was having breakfast.

"You need to be more careful," Sue Ellen said. "Not more than ten minutes ago, your husband and some of his men were riding through town. My neighbor came and told us. Luke's gone to see what it was all about.

"If the captain had seen you, you would be on your way back to the ranch right now, kicking and screaming, instead of standing here in my kitchen."

The thought terrified Darla, and her hands shook as she handed Sue Ellen her gift, a small crocheted doily. She knew full well the risks that had been taken to keep her free from Archer Ringewald, and she suddenly felt foolish and ashamed for her careless behavior.

As she slumped into a chair next to Little Luke, the youngster, puzzled by the sad look on her face, reached a small hand out to gently touch her arm. "Is this ever going to be over?" she said.

Sue Ellen was wondering the same thing.

"Someday," she said. It was the best consolation she had to offer.

From his rocky hideaway, El Diablo had watched as the men rode from town, a small cloud of dust trailing them. Even from a distance, the urge to confront their leader pounded in his head. He would have no peace until Captain Ringewald, the man who had brought so much grief into his life, was dead.

He, too, was anxious for it to be over.

Chapter Twenty-Six

Axel Taylor had forgotten the amount of work he had done alone before his son's return. Now, with Lewis tending to the livery, keeping the farm had again fallen to him. Still, despite blisters and aching muscles, he thanked his stars daily that he hadn't allowed Archer Ringewald to cheat him out of his land.

He did, however, occasionally worry that his farm chores left little time for his responsibilities as a deputy sheriff. Fortunately, he had not been needed lately.

The weariness he felt at the end of each day was quickly forgotten when he saw Dolly approaching. He always had a meal prepared and a lantern lit and sitting on the porch railing. Dusk, with its sweet scents and gentle sounds, had become his favorite time.

"It's got so Dolly knows the way home," Lewis said. "I don't even have to direct her.

I just lock the barn door and get in the saddle, and she starts heading here."

"Smart animal," Axel said. "Of course, as long as she's been around, she should have learned a few things by now."

Lewis had gotten used to good-natured kidding about his aging horse.

They had finished their venison stew and corn bread and were cleaning the dishes away when Lewis mentioned having had a visitor earlier in the day.

"Why was the captain in town?" Axel said.

"He came to pay the sheriff some fines so he could get his cowboys out of jail. Apparently, they got a little rowdy Saturday night."

"Interesting that they've returned to their routine of raising Cain at the saloon."

It was, however, the news that El Diablo might be gone that really got Axel's attention. "Do you think it's true?"

"I'd like to, but I'm sure not going to bet this farm on it. From what I've learned about him, he doesn't seem the type to just walk away from things. For the time being, I'm going to continue to sleep with one eye open."

Axel looked across the table at his son and felt a swell of pride. How had he allowed so many years to pass before seeing the strength and courage of his own boy? How had he missed the fact that he had grown into such a good and decent man? And how, belatedly, would he be able to make up for such an oversight?

"The night's pleasant," he finally said. "Let's go out on the porch and sit for a while."

The moon was high, a bright silver beacon that lit El Diablo's way. Despite the fact it was almost midnight, he avoided the trails most often traveled, carefully guiding his horse through underbrush and over shallow streams. Occasionally, a prowling coyote or a skittish fox would abandon its hunting and run from perceived danger.

While he was camped on the ridge, El Diablo had given much thought to what he planned to do. This, he had decided, would be carried out with the utmost care and preparation. For several days his only nourishment had been wild berries and cold spring water. There was no alcohol in his system to cloud judgment or slow reflexes. He was rested, and his thoughts were clear and focused.

Tonight, with the moon full and a soft breeze blowing, he was ready.

It took over an hour for him to get close enough to see the dark outline of the guard stand where he expected to find the two men he'd seen in town with the captain. He was certain they were sleeping but would take no chances.

Leaving his horse behind, he slowly walked the remainder of the way, stopping occasionally to listen for voices or movement. Aside from the gentle wind and an owl calling out to its mate, there was only silence.

Nearing the lean-to where the guards were, in fact, sleeping, he pulled his knife from its sheath and covered the final few yards in a slow, quiet crawl.

Then, moving quickly, he was astride one, pulling his head back by the hair. Though the man was still not fully awake, his eyes widened as he looked up at his assailant. He was about to speak when the blade swept across his throat. There was a gurgling sound deep in his chest as the other man, startled awake, sat up.

El Diablo stabbed him in the chest, burying the knife to the hilt.

It had taken only a minute, maybe two. Using the blanket one of the dead men had slept on, he wiped blood from his hands, then cleaned the knife before going to retrieve his horse. This time he was walking upright and smiling.

The first stage of the plan had been accomplished.

When he reached the gateway to the Rocking R, he dismounted again and slowly made his way through the shadows toward the ranch house. There was no light coming from inside, and the porch was empty except for a half-full whiskey glass sitting on the arm of the captain's favorite chair. A hanging wind chime made a tinkling noise that momentarily startled him.

Across the way, the bunkhouse was also dark.

El Diablo had his pistol drawn when he tried the front door and found it unlocked. Inside, it was pitch-black, causing him to stand for several minutes, allowing his eyes to adjust. The thought occurred to him how foolish it was for a man so concerned for his own safety to leave his house open and unprotected. But then, he had never thought that Captain Ringewald was a smart man.

For a time, he roamed the massive house, finally finding his way to the office. For a moment he stood in the empty room, breathing in the stale smell of cigar smoke and the leather that covered the captain's chair. He ran a hand over the liquor bottles that lined one shelf and, for once in his life, was glad there was no tequila. A drink would have to wait until later.

In a drawer of Ringewald's desk, he found a cloth sack of gold coins and took them. He also put several of the captain's cigars and a small box of matches in his shirt pocket.

He walked down a hallway toward the kitchen and found the door that led to the maid's living quarters. It, too, was unlocked, and he made his way in, moving toward Celia's bed. She didn't wake until he put a hand over her mouth.

"I'm not here to hurt you," he whispered. "If you stay here in your room and don't make a sound, you'll be safe. Okay?"

Celia was vigorously nodding her head, barely breathing. *"Sí, señor,"* she said as he moved his hand away.

El Diablo left her room, quietly closing the door behind him; then he walked toward the staircase leading to the second floor.

Archer Ringewald lay on his bed, still fully clothed except for one boot he had managed to kick away. His loud snoring was the only sound, and the moonlight, shining through a nearby window, bathed the room in a ghostly gray.

For several minutes, El Diablo stood silently at the foot of the bed, watching as the sleeping man fitfully tossed.

Finally, El Diablo tapped the barrel of his pistol against the captain's bare foot.

When he woke, the first thing Ringewald saw was El Diablo's face. Though his eyes were open, the rest of his body was frozen. In time, he managed to lift an arm and wipe a hand across his face, as if attempting to brush away a nightmare.

"What the . . . ?"

"Let's talk a bit before I kill you," El Diablo said.

"I've got . . . I can give you money. . . . I will. . . . Please . . ."

The laughter interrupted him. "You have nothing I want. Unlike you, I am not a greedy man. I will be satisfied just to listen to you beg for a while and watch you suffer."

"I am begging you. Just tell me what I can do. Anything . . ."

Captain Ringewald, a man of great wealth and perceived power, was suddenly cowering and pathetic. Tears had begun to stream down his cheeks, and he was prepared to give up everything in exchange for his life, miserable though it had become.

"How does it feel to no longer be in control? To be the one made to look small and scared?" El Diablo said. "I am a bad person who will have no place in heaven. I know that. But you are even worse. You delight in the misery you cause others. . . ."

"I'm sorry. I . . ."

El Diablo was fast growing weary of the conversation. Impatience was getting the better of him. "Get up," he said.

Pressing his gun to Ringewald's ribs, he marched him to the window. Outside, it was still dark, but the shady outlines of the barn, the bunkhouse, and the corral were visible. In the distance, still masked by the night, were the endless pastures, miles of fence, and hundreds of prized cattle. "Take a good look. For this, you sold your soul. For this, you will die."

Before the captain could make one last plea, El Diablo pulled a knife from his boot, and the blade slashed across Ringewald's throat. As he slumped to the floor, he frantically clawed at the deep gash, blood oozing through his shaking fingers. He tried to say something but could make only a wheezing sound before his body went limp.

El Diablo left the house and calmly walked to where he had tethered his horse. Then he rode to the Rocking R barn, where he located a container of coal oil. He lit a torch, then one of the captain's cigars, and approached the bunkhouse.

He made his way around the perimeter, splashing the liquid against the walls. Since he had no intent or reason to kill the cowhands, he fired several warning shots into the air. Then he touched the torch to the front wall and watched as groggy and frightened men rushed out in various stages of undress, yelling and cursing as they ran.

Quickly, the bunkhouse was engulfed in flames. Embers floated high into the night sky, like runaway fireflies.

Sitting astride his horse, watching, El Diablo puffed on his cigar and smiled. Then, before riding away, he shouted out for all to hear, *"I . . . am . . . El Diablo. . . ."*

Word of what had happened at the Rocking R didn't reach town until midafternoon when the ranch maid slowly rode into town on the captain's Palomino. She was in shock, a faraway look on her face. Still in her nightgown, she rode bareback and seemed to not know where to go.

Sheriff Barnes was the first to see her, and he hurried into the street. It was several seconds before she recognized him.

"Are you all right? What's wrong? Tell me what's happened."

Her stare seemed to be focused on something miles away, the sheriff's questions sounding as if they were coming from deep in a well.

Finally, in little more than a whisper, she answered, "El Diablo."

Celia's arrival triggered a flurry of activity. Doc Johnson came and escorted her to his office while Lewis led the captain's horse to the livery and placed him in one of the stalls. Sheriff Barnes began organizing a posse to ride to the ranch.

No one was prepared for what they found upon their arrival.

The bunkhouse was little more than a pile of smoking embers. Cowhands mingled about, some quietly talking in small groups, others just aimlessly pacing in the yard. Though they knew what was likely to be found inside the house, none had entered.

It was the sheriff and Lewis who found the body.

"Lord, I never expected things to take a turn like this," Barnes said as he spread a bedsheet over the captain. "I'm not saying I'm sad to see him gone — I don't know anybody who will be — but he was one of those people you figured would be around forever. I thought the man was bulletproof."

Lewis didn't say what he was thinking:

Maybe that was why El Diablo had cut Ringewald's throat instead of shooting him.

Back outside, the sheriff called out to Bill Claxton, one of the cowhands he knew. "Who's foreman now that Greenleaf's passed?"

"We ain't got one."

"You do now," Barnes said. "You're taking over, in charge of seeing that the livestock is cared for until we can figure all this out. You'll see that the everyday work gets done and that no one leaves the ranch until I say they can."

Since the bunkhouse was destroyed, the sheriff said it would be okay for them to use the bottom floor of the ranch house. "But," he warned, "I'm leaving deputies here to see that no one enters the captain's office or goes upstairs."

Barnes was operating on instinct, evaluating the situation and giving orders on the run. This was far beyond anything he had ever dealt with. And things would only get worse.

As he spoke, a member of the posse assigned to look for El Diablo arrived with more bad news. Two more bodies had been found up at the guard stand.

Claxton's face turned ashen when the sheriff told him to send a couple of hands to dig two graves down by the creek.

"What's going to happen to the captain?" he said.

"We'll bring him down to the barn and find some stout canvas to wrap him in. As soon as what remains of the bunkhouse cools down, pile charcoal over and around the body. Then bust up some of those salt blocks out in the corral and mix it in."

It was, Barnes knew, the way bodies were preserved when a member of a wagon train passed away and friends or loved ones didn't want the deceased buried in the middle of nowhere.

"I've got my doubts anyone's going to request a funeral," he said, "but we'll wait and see."

At the moment, his priority was finding El Diablo before he could do more damage. He was well aware of who was next on the list. He glanced across the yard at Lewis Taylor, who was talking with one of the wranglers.

As soon as he got back to town, the sheriff would send telegrams to authorities in San Antonio, Brownsville, and Galveston, advising them to be on the lookout for the man who had just murdered one of the richest men in Texas.

There would soon be a widespread manhunt underway, he knew, but he had the strong feeling it would be a waste of time and manpower.

The sheriff was convinced that El Diablo wouldn't go far.

Chapter Twenty-Seven

Over the next few days, a mixture of shock and relief swept through Gila Bend. That Captain Ringewald — evil, rich, and bigger than life — was dead was difficult to believe. Rumors spread quickly. He had been found dead hanging from the rafters of his barn after long hours of merciless torture. He had taken his own life with one of his famed pearl-handled pistols. He had been bound and left inside the bunkhouse when it was set on fire and died in the blaze.

It was left to Luke Bradley and his *Sentinel* to set the record straight. The headline he chose read simply, "Captain Murdered," and his story relayed the few details Sheriff Barnes would provide him. His final paragraph read, "The killer has been identified as a notorious South Texas man who uses the name El Diablo. He currently remains at large and is likely to be heavily armed. The sheriff has advised that everyone in

Gila Bend be on high alert."

Bradley at first had written that "the captain is survived by his wife, Darla Ringewald," but omitted the sentence at Sue Ellen's insistence.

After an impassioned plea from Ringewald's maid, Reverend Daniels reluctantly agreed to travel to the ranch and officiate at a brief graveside service. Darla was torn about what she should do and was relieved when both the sheriff and Lewis advised her it might not be safe to attend.

With ranch hands serving as pallbearers, Captain Archer Ringewald was laid to rest in the shade of a sprawling oak tree no more than a hundred yards from where he had died. Attending the service were other members of the ranch workforce, a couple of officials from the captain's bank, and the bartender from his saloon.

Sheriff Barnes, feeling his presence was required, and Luke Bradley, there to do a story for the *Sentinel,* watched the service from the porch of the ranch house.

There were no flowers, no hymns were sung, and the only prayer offered by Reverend Daniels was the Lord's Prayer.

"I think the captain would have expected more," Barnes said as he watched two cowboys lazily shovel dirt into the grave.

■ ■ ■ ■

For the next week, men gathered in front of the sheriff's office to get their daily instructions. In small groups, they would ride off in different directions, searching for any indication of El Diablo's route. On the third morning, the hiding place where he had watched activities in town was discovered, but it had long since been abandoned.

Ringewald's killer had vanished.

In law enforcement offices throughout the state, old stories of El Diablo's past misdeeds were revived, some true, others pure fantasy. Wanted posters appeared, promising a reward for the killer's capture. Reporters from big-city newspapers began arriving in Gila Bend, eager for any new details about the crime. When none were available, they improvised.

One reporter, after spending only a day in town, filed a glowing biography of the victim that painted Captain Ringewald as a "much-loved resident" who was the town's chief benefactor. The story, filled with flowery prose, described a community in mourning over the death of a "legendary war hero." Celia, his "loyal and devoted housekeeper," was elaborately quoted despite the fact that she spoke virtually no English and had not been seen since Doc Johnson took her to his office.

When none of the visiting journalists could find her, Darla became "the grieving widow." One story even suggested the "loving couple" was expecting their first child at the time of the captain's death.

Though he refused all requests for interviews, Milton Barnes was portrayed as "a dedicated lawman who always gets his man." He was quoted as having said he would "see El Diablo hang from the highest tree in Texas" once he was captured.

A man named Ned Buntline arrived from New York City, smartly dressed in a suit and bow tie, and was telling everyone that he was there to gather material for a book.

All that was missing from the lurid story was a dramatic ending. Only the capture of the killer could provide that, and as the days dragged on, that was looking less likely.

Luke Bradley viewed the visiting newsmen, who had set up headquarters in the saloon and rarely ventured from it, with great disdain. If he had ever entertained romantic aspirations of working at a big-city paper, the dream was now gone.

"They'll get tired of our little town soon,"

Sue Ellen said, "and be gone, off somewhere else to make up a new story."

They were sitting on the porch, enjoying their first chance to really talk since the captain's murder. Luke had been spending long hours at his office, and when not watching their child, she had been making regular visits to the church to check on Darla.

"How's she doing?" Luke asked.

"Feeling like a prisoner. She's afraid to even step outside for fear of running into one of those reporters. And I think she's needlessly dealing with some guilt."

"About what?"

"Being relieved that her husband is dead and wanting to break out in song to celebrate her new freedom. But that's not the way a wife is supposed to react, is it? No matter how bad he was or how mistreated she was, a wife is supposed to feel sad when her husband passes. That's just what people expect."

Luke put his arm across his wife's shoulders. "There's no one in this town who would begrudge her a little singing and dancing."

"I know that. You know that. All we have to do is convince Darla."

"Maybe now that she's no longer married,

Lewis can help," he said.

The suggestion brought a smile to Sue Ellen's face.

In a dark and run-down bar on a backstreet of Fort Worth, a man sat alone, staring at the near-empty bottle of tequila in front of him. His hair was cut shorter than it had been just days earlier, and his mustache had been shaved. To anyone who asked his name, he answered truthfully.

He was Dain Hayes, and like many who came to the neighborhood known as Hell's Half Acre, he was hiding.

Located adjacent to the town's stock pens, where cattle drives from deep in Texas ended, the Half Acre was row after row of saloons and gambling houses. A pungent odor of trail-weary cowboys, spittoons, tobacco smoke, and stale beer hung over the places where men came to gamble or drink their money away. Few asked or answered questions.

This, too, had been part of El Diablo's plan.

Fleeing from the Rocking R long before he could be followed, he had ridden his horse to the point of near heart failure to get to Fort Worth. Though he had heard of the place, he had never been there before, and he was reasonably sure he would not encounter anyone who might recognize him.

His fame and reputation had been earned along the southern border, not in a North Texas cow town.

Still, he had altered his appearance and reclaimed the name he'd not been called by since his teenage years. There would be men looking for him, he knew, but without success soon, their attention would turn to other things. In time, the death of Captain Ringewald would be little more than a passing thought. And then he would return to Gila Bend to finish his business.

Taking a room in a small hotel, he resigned himself to a long, quiet wait. With the money he had stolen from Ringewald's office, he could afford to be patient.

Chapter Twenty-Eight

Once the reporters were finally gone, Darla felt free to venture from her church hideaway. She was, however, always accompanied by someone handpicked by Sheriff Barnes. On numerous occasions, it was Lewis.

Several times, she had mentioned to him that she would soon be moving from the Blessed Redeemer. It was time she rejoined the outside world.

The tumult over Captain Ringewald's murder had quieted, and his killer seemed to have vanished, exhausting much of the darker conversation at the café in the mornings and the saloon at nights. Many in Gila Bend believed the bad times were over and had returned to their day-to-day lives.

The most exciting item in Luke Bradley's *Sentinel,* in fact, was the announcement that Rainbow's End, Daisy Dixon's pie store, would soon hold its grand opening. All who stopped in were promised a free sample.

She had spent every waking hour preparing for the big day. The shop itself was small, barely larger than a smokehouse, but inviting. Its walls were whitewashed, curtains Daisy had sewn bordered the two windows, and a small flower garden had been planted near the entrance.

Under B. J.'s direction, display shelves for his mother's pies — pear, blackberry, and, his favorite, buttermilk — were built and lined the back wall. To one side, displayed for all to see, hung Ezzie's weather-beaten old hat, a loving tribute to the man who had made the store possible.

Since she would do the baking at home, her son had built racks onto the back of the buggy to carry her wares into town each morning. He had also bought several new laying hens to be sure she had plenty of eggs and, with the help of his new farmhand, saw that sacks of flour were neatly stacked in a corner of her kitchen.

"I think it's marvelous," Darla said as she and Lewis joined B. J. out front. "The name she's chosen for the place is perfect, just perfect." She had purposely waited until the shop was completed before coming to see it. As they admired the newest addition to the town's landscape, several children hurried past, checking to see if it had opened yet.

"The café has already told her it will buy three pies every morning," B. J. said. "The waitress down there said she was tired of tossing out what the cook tries to pass off for pie. She says they look and taste more like cow patties."

At Darla's suggestion, Celia, who had returned to her duties as the Rocking R maid, would drive the buggy to town once a week and purchase pies for a treat.

As they stood in the warm midday sun, sharing in the anticipation, Sue Ellen joined them, Little Luke at her side. "What thrills me most," she said, "is that I won't have to do any more pie baking. I'll just send Luke down here to pick whatever he has a taste for."

Little Luke climbed into Darla's arms as Lewis said it was time he got back to the livery.

Sue Ellen touched her friend's arm. "If you've got a minute," she said, "I'd like to talk to you about something." She had watched Darla closely since Captain Ringewald's death, careful to let her deal with the matter in her own way and in her own time. She couldn't imagine the stress and fear Darla had endured from her former husband's threats, the kidnapping by El Diablo, and the murders at the ranch. And though she knew Darla to be a woman of strength and resolve, she also saw the scared and fragile side. To move on with her life, Darla needed a friendly push.

"I've got somebody you should meet," Sue Ellen said. "He's a friend of Luke's from San Antonio who we've asked to come and meet you. His name is Caleb Asherton."

For a moment, the thought flashed through Darla's mind that her friend had suddenly decided to play the role of matchmaker.

"He's a lawyer," Sue Ellen said. "He's over at the bank now."

A tall, slender man with friendly eyes and a distinguished manner, Asherton got to his feet when Darla entered the bank president's office. Cradled in one arm was a large sheaf of documents. "Ma'am," he said, "it's a pleasure to meet you."

Jessup Stanley, the bank president, stood behind his desk, nodding. Darla knew who he was though she could never remember being introduced to the man who ran her husband's bank.

Both waited for her to move to a nearby chair.

"Mrs. Ringewald . . ." Asherton said.

"Darla will be fine," she said.

"I understand. Darla, it is. As you've probably already been told, I'm here at the request of my friend Luke Bradley. He and his wife, who I've only recently met, care a great deal about you and thought I might be of some assistance."

The lawyer placed the documents on the edge of the desk and got straight to the point. "Ma'am, you are now a wealthy woman. A very, very wealthy woman, and there are matters that you will soon need to address."

He was, she realized, there to bring to light matters that she had been avoiding, keeping them pushed far to the back of her mind.

For the next hour, he carefully detailed her inheritance from her late husband's estate. Never informed of his business matters during their marriage, she was taken aback by the magnitude of the captain's wealth. And though she knew few details, she was aware that much of his fortune had come from dealings that would not have met with her approval. In a sense, she knew, she was a rich woman partially because of other people's suffering.

Stanley, who had presided over the bank

even before the captain bought it, explained the balance in her husband's account. It alone was a staggering figure. There were also stocks and bonds whose value he had not completely tallied. He had papers ready for her to sign, transferring accounts into her name. Then he turned the presentation back to Asherton.

"In addition to the ranch and all of the livestock," he said, "you are now the owner of the saloon and café and, of course, this very institution where you're now sitting. And there are various other small properties scattered throughout the county. For now, everything seems to be running as it did before Mr. Ringewald's untimely death. But in time you will need to assume responsibility."

He explained that Stanley had agreed to remain as bank president and would make no operational changes without her approval. Bill Claxton, a longtime employee of her husband, was serving as ranch foreman at the request of Sheriff Barnes and was ready to assume the responsibility on a permanent basis. Bernie Leftwitch, the bartender, would continue to manage the daily operations of the saloon and café. "Everyone who was on your husband's payroll has said they will stay if it pleases you," he said, "but it is now your responsibility to see that they receive their monthly wages, determine who is retained or let go, and decide on any new hires you wish to make. Unless you are an experienced businesswoman, I would suggest at some point you will need help to administer all this, but of course, that will be your decision. The bottom line, Mrs. Ring— Darla . . . is that you are now the boss."

She was overwhelmed, her stomach suddenly in knots and the palms of her hands moist.

"I realize it will take some time for you to digest all this," Asherton said. "I'm leaving for San Antonio on tomorrow morning's stage. If there is anything I can do to further assist you, please feel free to contact me. In the meantime, I offer you my sincere best wishes."

As she stood to leave, Stanley rushed to open the door for her. "I have taken the liberty of preparing you an office here in the bank," he said. "At your leisure, feel free to come in and make any changes you might like."

Darla's legs felt rubbery as she walked into the lobby, where Sue Ellen and Little Luke were waiting. As they made their way toward the Blessed Redeemer, she briefly outlined the life-altering conversation that had just taken place.

Sue Ellen was thrilled. "Not bad for someone who's been living in a one-room hideaway and wearing borrowed dresses," she said. Sensing his mother's delight, Little Luke began to giggle.

"What am I going to do?" Darla said.

"You'll figure it out."

Sleep was impossible as she lay in the darkness, contemplating the magnitude of the responsibility that had suddenly fallen to her. She had never aspired to be a rich person, yet suddenly she was one and frightened by the prospect. Her life, she knew, had forever changed.

It was just after dawn when Lewis and Dolly arrived at the livery. Darla was sitting on Ezzie's bench, waiting.

"I need to talk," she said.

Seeing that she hadn't slept, Lewis offered another suggestion. "First, you need some coffee," he said.

While they waited for it to brew, she told him of her meeting with the lawyer and of the list of new responsibilities she was assuming. Even Lewis was amazed at the vastness of the inheritance she described.

"I know my husband was not a good

man," she said, "and much of what they say is now mine was taken from decent, hard-working people he ran from their land after paying them only a fraction of the worth. He was stealing. Even I knew that. All you had to do was listen to what others were saying about the way he did business. There were a few times when I overheard him bragging about it. And I did nothing, said nothing, and it shames me."

"What could you have done? The things he did were not your fault."

"But they're now my responsibility, Lewis. I've inherited the blame."

"You can't change things that happened in the past. Believe me, I know."

"Maybe you're wrong." She told him that she would soon have an office in the bank. "Once I get my bearings," she said, "I hope to find a way. In the meantime, do you and your daddy, maybe the sheriff, know the names of those who were forced by my husband to give up their farms?"

The answer to that question launched her life as a wealthy businesswoman.

She visited the mercantile and ordered a few new dresses from its catalog, and began airing out the long-vacant house where her father had lived and died. It was strange at first, returning to the place where she had grown up, the musty rooms reviving wonderful memories. Meanwhile, it also brought back painful thoughts of losing her father and the pain he had suffered before he died. Putting the feelings aside, she was determined to make the house a home again.

Thanking Reverend Daniels for his kindness and friendship, she made a sizable donation to the church in her late father's name before leaving.

Those Sheriff Barnes had assigned to keep watch on her found their job increasingly demanding.

At her insistence, she traveled alone to San Antonio for a meeting with Caleb Asherton and made arrangements for him to serve as her legal counsel and financial adviser. He agreed to spend three days a week in Gila Bend, working out of the office above the mercantile, which had once been occupied by Ridley Merriwether. Darla suggested he could either sleep on a cot in the office or bunk with the ranch hands out at the Rocking R.

His job, she explained, would require occasional travel. Soon, he was involved in the most unusual work he had experienced during his legal career.

With the help of the sheriff, he located

the seven farmers whose land had been bullied from them by Ringewald and his men. At each stop, he arrived with a deed that restored their old property to them at no cost. They could also keep whatever paltry amount they had been paid by the captain.

He explained to each farmer he visited that the foreman of the Rocking R had already been instructed to cut a dozen young Longhorns from the herd. Upon their arrival home, the cattle would be driven to their farm, and the hands would assist in building whatever new fences were necessary to prevent the animals from straying.

Six of the seven readily agreed to the generous offer. One, a particularly stubborn old man named Troy Dunfeld, initially ordered the attorney off his property at gunpoint, insisting he never wanted to see Gila Bend or his old place again. However, when Asherton upped the number of Longhorns he would be given to twenty, the farmer signed the agreement and invited him to stay for supper.

The two spinsters who had co-owned the women's dress and notions shop before it was burned were approached and asked if they would come out of retirement if Darla agreed to fund the rebuilding of their store and became a silent partner. Construction was begun almost immediately.

Asherton visited Sheriff Barnes's office and presented him a check that was to pay for the salaries of two additional deputies.

Jessup Stanley met with Darla in her new office and was told that he was to continue operating the bank efficiently but show a bit more patience with those who might occasionally be late with their mortgage payments. Never comfortable with her late husband's strong arm tactics, he welcomed the idea.

"If I didn't know you better," Lewis said as she was giving him a tour of her home, "I'd think you've been doing a lot of heavy drinking lately, the way you've been spending money. Want to buy a run-down old livery?"

"And have Ezzie Zale screaming at me from his grave? I think not."

A feeling of revitalization swept through Gila Bend. Old residents were warmly welcomed home, and a new sense of well-being was in evidence everywhere. Rainbow's End was doing such a flourishing business that Daisy reached out to her niece in Kansas City, asking if she would considerer coming to help with the baking and running the store. B. J. wasn't of much use, she explained in her letter, since his mama pig had produced a new litter and needed his attention.

Lewis Taylor was even getting more proficient at shoeing horses.

Only he and Sheriff Barnes continued to talk of El Diablo, and then only in private discussions. They knew he was still out there, a threat that would eventually have to be dealt with.

For now, though, all seemed well, much to the credit of the town's new benefactor.

Chapter Twenty-Nine

Her friends were delighted to see Darla's enthusiastic involvement in the community. There was new energy in her step, and she had a smile for all who passed her way. Her only discomfort came when people attempted to express their gratitude for things she was doing. She begged Luke Bradley not to mention her name in the *Sentinel,* and he begrudgingly agreed. Simply put, she didn't want the attention. Nor did she like being identified as Mrs. Ringewald. She had asked Caleb Asherton to handle whatever paperwork necessary to restore her maiden name so that she might again be known as Darla Winslow.

"That, too, will soon change," Sue Ellen told her husband one evening as they prepared for bed. "Just watch."

"And you know this how?"

"Trust me. Women know these things. She'll not be a rich widow for too long. And

I'm not talking about some smooth-talking gold digger riding into town and sweeping her off her feet. It will be a good, trustworthy man who wins her hand."

Luke smiled. "Without mentioning any names," he said, "I'll bet you one of Daisy's pear pies I can guess who you're talking about." He knew she was referring to his friend, the new livery owner.

"Just remember to act surprised when it happens," she said. "Good night."

Lewis Taylor was unsure of how to react to the new Darla — rich, single, and no longer in hiding. That they had renewed their friendship upon his return home pleased him greatly. But since she had been married, however unhappily, he had tried to dismiss thoughts that their relationship might ever return to what it had been before he went to prison. Still, it was not easy.

Now things had become even more complicated by her financial windfall. Despite Ezzie's gift of the livery, he was hardly a man of means. And unless their motives were unsavory and self-serving, poor men did not court women who were rich. It was, he assumed, one of society's unwritten rules.

And there was the lingering matter of El Diablo. Though Lewis had become increasingly convinced that he wanted only to settle matters with him, he worried that Darla might still be in harm's way simply because of their friendship.

So he reluctantly kept his distance, seldom going out of his way to be in her company. Still, he watched with great admiration as she quietly went about helping the community and delighted in seeing her vitality renewed. Though the sheriff continued to insist that she have a protective escort, Lewis volunteered for the duty less and less, comfortable in the knowledge that others would do the job.

He was resigned to the belief that only time would provide him the answers to questions he was asking himself.

Others in Gila Bend were not reluctant to predict a renewed romance between Darla and Lewis Taylor. It wasn't just Sue Ellen and Luke. Reverend Daniels patiently waited for Darla to stop by the Blessed Redeemer and seek his advice, and Sheriff Barnes had gone so far as to tell Lewis that it was high time for him to "get off your hind legs and admit your feelings."

Lewis's father joined in and was even more blunt. "If it were me," Axel said one evening as they groomed the horses, "I'd hitch up the wagon and be asking her out on a picnic. I'll gladly cook you a brisket and make some potato salad. Fill a jug with sweet tea. You could pick up one of Daisy's pies. Son, everybody who knows you and Darla is aware that you two have feelings for one another. It's no secret you need to be hiding. Why not just admit it and be done?"

Before Lewis could make an argument, his father continued.

"I don't care if she's got more money than God Himself. You can't pile it high enough to keep from being lonesome. She's got nobody. And I've seen you walking around here, all hangdog and lovesick. It doesn't take a genius to know it's her you're thinking about. You ask me, a man's not supposed to live his life without the companionship of a good woman."

"You've been doing it for quite some time now," Lewis said.

"Yep, but I had my time. My days with your ma were the best a man could ever hope for. I came awake every morning, looking forward to seeing her smiling face. Even when she got sick, she was the most beautiful sight I've ever seen, a true joy to behold. I'd like you to experience that one of these days."

It fell to the Bradleys to give things a

gentle nudge. Luke, making his weekly delivery of the *Sentinel,* stopped in at the livery to invite Lewis to supper on the weekend. "Sue Ellen wants to celebrate the opening of the dress shop and has invited the two old maids over. Darla's coming also. I'll need someone to sneak out in the yard and have a cigar with when I've had my fill of women's talk."

All Lewis really heard was that Darla had also been invited. Before he could devise a satisfactory excuse, Luke was on his way out the door. "Sue Ellen says you're to bring a pie," he said. "Little Luke prefers Mrs. Dixon's buttermilk."

The elderly guests of honor were thrilled by the attention being paid to them. Like two schoolgirls, they giggled and clapped their hands as they praised the aromas coming from Sue Ellen's kitchen, repeatedly told Little Luke what a fine-looking young man he was, and kept hugging Darla, thanking her for putting them back in business.

After the meal was finished, the men along with Little Luke excused themselves to the backyard and their cigars. The evenings were growing cooler, and Luke amused his son by blowing lazy smoke rings into the air as they enjoyed being away from talk of a new line of dresses that had been ordered from some Chicago manufacturer.

Lewis was watching Little Luke's attention turn to chasing fireflies when he felt a hand on his shoulder.

"I think you were roped into being here," Darla said. "I'm sorry."

"No apology needed," he said. "I was looking forward to seeing you."

Luke excused himself, saying it was time he got his son ready for bed.

"I'm glad you're getting out and about," Lewis said. "Everybody in town's talking about you and all the good things you're doing. You're a busy lady."

She asked how things were going at the livery and what Axel had been doing lately. "Seems I only see you from a distance these days," she said.

Both realized the conversation was forced and uncomfortable. Darla reached out for his hand. "You know, I'm no different from the person you came to rescue down in that dreadful cabin. Except that I'm no longer married."

"And as I hear it, mighty rich."

"I didn't ask for it, Lewis." She leaned forward and kissed his cheek. "I think it would be good for us to have a talk . . . whenever you're ready."

She turned back to the house, leaving him alone in the darkness, his heart pounding against his chest. Fireflies continued to float among the trees, and the breeze seemed somehow gentler. He stood alone for some time, feeling better than he had in longer than he could remember.

From inside, he heard a child's voice call out. "G'night, Mr. Taylor," Little Luke said.

CHAPTER THIRTY

During the almost two months El Diablo had been in Hell's Half Acre, he had grown weary of drinking alone, being amused by the fights that routinely broke out in the saloons, and paying occasional visits to the gambling houses. Poker bored him, probably because he was no good at it. He was getting impatient, and Captain Ringewald's money was running low.

One evening, as he was leaving his hotel, he met an out-of-work cowboy named Austin Wansley. He was sitting on the edge of the sidewalk, nursing a badly swollen eye and a bleeding lip.

"Looks like a horse ran over you," El Diablo said.

"I'd have whipped him good if I hadn't been so drunk. If you're looking for a fight, I suggest you just move on. I'm about fought out for the time being."

El Diablo sat down beside him and extended his hand. "Name's Dain Hayes," he said. "I bet you could use another drink."

"You buying?"

They drank late into the night as El Diablo listened to the talkative young man brag about his travels and expertise at breaking horses. He made no mention of why he was currently without a job.

"I once even worked for an outfit that rustled stock from small farms and ranches, then sold them to the big trail bosses," Wansley said. "They would keep them separate from the other cattle they were moving, then sell them again once they got to market. Ever hear of anything like that?"

"Not a bad idea," El Diablo said. For several nights, he continued to buy the drinks.

"I've got some work you might be interested in," he finally said one evening before Wansley got too drunk. "It won't take but a few days, there's no risk involved, and I'll pay you well."

"It's not like I don't have time to spare."

"You got a horse?"

Wansley, already getting tipsy, grinned. "Shouldn't be a problem," he said, "considering there are horses everywhere you look in this town."

"We'll talk more about it tomorrow," El

Diablo said. He wanted Wansley sober when he outlined what he had in mind.

Instead of drinking, they had supper the following evening. As Wansley eagerly devoured his steak and potatoes, El Diablo showed him a map he had drawn. It was directions to a town down south called Gila Bend.

"What is it you want me to do once I get there?" Wansley said as he cut away another large bite of his T-bone.

"Just spend a couple of days there learning what's going on. Visit the saloon and talk with folks. Stop in at the feedstore. There's a man who runs the livery you might look in on. It would also be good to know the location of his farm. If anyone asks why you're there, tell them you're looking for work and heard that the big ranch outside of town is hiring."

The assignment seemed strange to Wansley, but the pay that was mentioned eased his concern. "And I'm not to shoot or rob anybody?" He was only half joking.

"All I want is for you to return and give me an idea of what the mood of the town is. Do things appear calm and normal? Are a lot of people carrying guns? I want to know what folks are talking about."

Wansley knew that asking Hayes's reason

for wanting to know such things would get him no answer. "When do you want me to leave?"

El Diablo slid a small bag of gold coins across the table. "As soon as you can steal yourself a decent horse," he said. Both men had a good laugh; then Dain Hayes ordered a bottle of tequila.

Wansley liked the little town. People he passed on the street seemed friendly, the saloon was lively, and the café served the best pie he'd ever tasted. At the feedstore, spit-and-whittlers discussed the need for more rain and readily volunteered the location of the livery owner's farm. All Wansley had to do was mention that he and the farmer had served together for the Confederacy.

He had seen more men carrying sidearms in a single block of the Half Acre than he did in the entire town of Gila Bend.

The man who ran the livery had seemed a bit guarded at first, but when Wansley explained that he was hoping to find work at the Rocking R, he warmed and said he was welcome to bed down with his horse for the night. The following morning he gave the stranger a cup of coffee and directions to the ranch. "The fellow you'll want to see," Taylor said, "is a man named Bill Claxton. He's the foreman."

While mingling with the saloon patrons, Wansley got the impression that there had been an unsettling event a couple of months earlier — the former owner of the ranch he said he was planning to visit had been killed — but apparently things were now more peaceful than ever.

He came to the quick conclusion that if a man was inclined to settle down and raise a family, Gila Bend would do nicely. After two days, he had learned all he could.

On his way back to Fort Worth, he was thinking to himself that it was the easiest job he'd ever had. For a fleeting moment, he was even sorry he'd not actually gone out to the ranch to see what wages it was paying.

His report, brief though it was, seemed to please Dain Hayes. "Truth is, there's just not much going on there," Wansley said.

"Did you happen to see the sheriff?"

"You wouldn't have known there even was one. It didn't appear to me he's got much to do."

"And the man at the livery?"

"A nice enough fellow, but I can't recall his name."

"Taylor," Dain said. "Lewis Taylor."

Leaving Wansley to drink himself into a stupor or find another fight, whichever came first, El Diablo returned to his hotel room. It would, he had already decided, be his last night there.

It was time.

He made the ride leisurely, stopping often to allow his horse to rest and drink. When he found a camping spot that appealed to him, he built a small fire and warmed a can of beans or cooked a rabbit he had shot along the way. He drank sparingly from the bottle of tequila he'd brought. Under the stars, breathing the fresh night air, he slept far better than he had in the Hell's Half Acre hotel room.

Though he was pacing himself, his every waking moment was focused on the purpose of his trip. He repeatedly tried to picture Lewis Taylor in his mind and was frustrated that he could only retrieve a hazy image. It had been too long. There were moments when he even struggled to recall the origin of his hatred, but then he would remember that Taylor was the reason he had been lured into the Rocking R nightmare. He had called him a coward in the local paper. And there was the scene he found near the Guadalupe River where his two men were dead and the woman they had held hostage was gone. He had plenty of reason to seek revenge.

On the third day, he rode well past sunset since he knew he was getting close. Finally, not wishing his horse to step into a gopher hole and be injured in the moonless dark, he camped. Tired but feeling the growing excitement for what lay ahead, he had no appetite, so he didn't even bother to lay a fire. Instead, he took a deep swallow from his tequila bottle and was soon asleep.

It was still dark when he woke to the sweet aroma of something baking. At first, he thought he was dreaming, but as he got to his feet, the smell grew stronger. Curious, he saddled his horse and slowly rode toward what he realized was a small farm. A lantern lit one of the cabin windows, and there was the faint squealing of what sounded like piglets insisting to their mother that it was feeding time.

He waited for the first predawn light, then pulled his spyglass from his saddlebag. He watched as a vaguely familiar figure hitched up a strange-looking buggy; then he saw a woman making trips in and out of the cabin to place her sweet-smelling baked goods onto small shelves. Soon, she was riding away, and the young man, moving about on a crutch, turned his attention to the pigpen.

It was the crutch that triggered El Diablo's memory. He had once seen the man in the company of Lewis Taylor. He slapped his horse's flank and rode toward him.

"Fine-looking litter," he said.

B. J. had not heard him ride up, and he was momentarily startled. He thought he had seen the man somewhere before, but was unable to put a name to the face.

"Just passing through?"

El Diablo smiled. "I've got business in Gila Bend," he said.

"Do I know you?"

"Could be." And with that brief exchange he turned to leave, his purpose accomplished. It wouldn't take long, he knew, for word to reach town that he was on the way.

It wasn't until later in the morning, after his helper had arrived and they were replacing hinges on the gate to the chicken coop, that it dawned on B. J. who his earlier visitor was. He cursed and asked for help to saddle his horse. "I've got to get to town," he said, a sudden urgency in his voice.

Lewis had not been at the livery long when Bill Claxton arrived, wanting to schedule a time to bring several of the Rocking R cow ponies in for shoeing.

They chatted briefly about his new role as a ranch foreman. "I've got to say, things are a lot better these days," he said. "Mrs. Ringewald's a breath of fresh air, content to leave things to my judgment. She's never even come out to the place since the captain passed. She did send her lawyer out to tell me that instead of rebuilding the bunk-house, she had decided to just turn the big house over to us. He said she never wants to set foot in the place again. So these days I'm doing my work out of the captain's old office."

"You take on that new fellow?"

It was obvious Claxton had no idea what he was talking about.

"He was in town just a few days ago," Lewis said. "Stayed the night here. He asked a lot of questions and said he was looking for work. I gave him your name and directions to the ranch."

"Never saw him. Wish I had. We're in need of a few more good hands."

Long after Claxton had left, Taylor thought about their conversation. As the day went on, he began to have an uneasy feeling about the visit from the out-of-work cowboy.

He better understood after B. J. arrived and breathlessly announced that he had been visited by someone he had recognized.

"He looked a little different, but I'm sure it was him, that El Diablo fellow. He didn't say much, except that he had business in town," Dixon said. "I figure he was making reference to you."

The cowboy, Taylor realized, had been sent on a scouting mission.

From his ridge hideaway, El Diablo was watching.

Chapter Thirty-One

Lewis stood in front of the livery, watching as the town came alive. People were leaving the café after having breakfast, and two wagons were already parked in front of the feedstore. He saw Luke Bradley standing in the doorway of the dress shop, no doubt trying to sell the old maids an ad in the *Sentinel.* A couple of young boys were running down the street, late for school. Darla, he assumed, was in her office over at the bank.

During the trying months when the threat of a showdown with El Diablo lingered, Taylor had considered a range of scenarios. The best he had come up with was to be certain it played out in a place he was familiar with. There was only one notion he totally disregarded. The last thing he wanted was for there to be gunfire in town, putting the lives of innocent people in danger.

For that reason, he had asked B. J. to go

to the farm and have Axel come to town immediately. "Tell him whatever you have to, that there's some kind of emergency at the livery," Lewis said. "Just get him here as quickly as you can."

"Will Mama be safe at her shop?" Dixon said as he glanced toward Rainbow's End.

Taylor nodded. "I'm counting on town being the safest place to be. You might tell her to stay open late today. It would be a good idea for you to be here with her."

B. J. agreed. "Are you going to alert the sheriff?"

"Nope. Nobody but you and I need to know about this."

When the elder Taylor arrived, his face was pale, and he was out of breath. "How bad is it?" he said as he hurried into the barn.

"How bad is what?" Lewis said.

"B. J. said you burned yourself real bad while firing up the forge."

"No, I'm okay. I told him to fudge the truth a little if that was what it took to get you here. I just need your help while I go tend to something. As soon as I'm gone, I need you to lock up and go over to the bank and keep an eye on Darla until I get back."

"Isn't somebody already doing that?"

"I'd feel more comfortable if it was you today."

The tone of his son's voice worried Axel. "What's going on, Lewis? Is it what I'm thinking?"

"Please, Pa, just do what I'm asking."

A bank of dark clouds was forming to the south as Lewis rode toward the farm. Several times Dolly flinched at the sound of distant thunder as she traveled her well-known route. Lewis was going home, the place he knew better than any other, and he would wait for El Diablo to come there.

After putting his horse in the barn, he went into the cabin and pulled Axel's Winchester from the wall. He made sure it was loaded and stuffed a handful of extra shells into the pocket of his britches. He lifted his pistol from its holster to make sure it, too, was ready. He then took a chair from the kitchen and moved it onto the porch. There he would wait. He didn't expect it to be long.

El Diablo had watched Taylor leave the livery and, figuring he knew where he was headed, followed at a distance. Earlier, he had thought about first visiting the farm and setting fire to the cabin and barn just for pleasure. Now, however, that would have to wait until he was done with his killing.

The directions Wansley had given him were good, and when he neared the Taylor farm, El Diablo tethered his horse in a small grove and slowly began his approach from the back side of the property. He had initially been disappointed that Lewis had decided to leave town, robbing him of a public display of his revenge. But he had warmed to the logic of a more private confrontation. This way, once his job was done, he could quickly be gone, headed back to the border before anyone could give chase.

As the sky darkened even more and a gentle rain began to fall, Taylor knew his adversary was nearby. He could feel him. His eyes constantly roamed, looking for movement near the barn or the smokehouse. Even the chickens had suddenly disappeared, deserting their constant pecking in the yard in favor of the dry interior of their roost. Only the leaves of a pecan tree, brushing against the cabin roof, and Whisper, glad to have his master nearby, interrupted the stillness. Resting at Taylor's feet, his head between his paws, the dog would only be roused by the occasional flash of distant lightning or a rumbling clap of thunder.

Slipping along a tree line bordering a meadow, El Diablo stopped and pointed his spyglass toward the porch. That it was getting dark would work to his advantage. The rain was coming harder, and now a stiff wind whipped at his face. The spyglass became useless, and he tossed it away.

"I'm not the only storm that's coming," he whispered.

When the rain began to blow onto the porch, Whisper reluctantly moved inside. Taylor, however, stayed in place, watching, his finger never leaving the trigger of his rifle.

Covered in mud and with rainwater dripping from the brim of his hat, El Diablo crawled to the back side of the smokehouse, careful to keep his rifle off the soggy ground. There was a stack of firewood piled against the wall, and he used it to climb onto the roof. Lying on his belly, he brushed water from his eyes and tried to get a fix on his target.

It was not the shot he wanted — too far away — but he had grown impatient with the elements and wanted to kill Taylor and be gone. Aiming in the direction of the shadowy figure he could barely see, he fired. The shot mixed with a loud clap of thunder and buried itself into the eave of the roof.

"Here we go," Lewis said to himself. In one quick motion, he left his chair and was on one knee, returning a shot toward the smokehouse. He then jumped from the porch and crouched behind a rain barrel that had already begun to overflow.

"If we keep this up," he yelled, "we'll both soon be out of bullets with nothing to show for it. Come out in the open so we can get this over and done with."

El Diablo's response was two more wild shots. "I'm not leaving until you're dead," he said. Inside the cabin, Whisper cowered under Axel Taylor's bed as the rain began to pound even harder against the tin roof.

Lewis considered his options. He could retreat into the cabin and make a stand from there, but once inside, he would be trapped. He mentally measured the distance to the barn and decided there was too much open ground to cover. The rain barrel he was hiding behind was hardly adequate cover.

Since he knew the lay of the land much better than El Diablo, maybe he could make his way through the nearby underbrush and come up behind him.

His boots were caked with mud as he crouched and ran toward the corner of the cabin, surprised that no shots came. Discarding his soggy hat, he got down on hands and knees and slowly made his way into the mass of weeds and vines. Behind him, he heard more shots fired in the direction of the rain barrel.

El Diablo waited for return fire, and when none came, he wondered if perhaps a lucky shot had found its mark. He called Taylor's name several times but got no answer. Finally, he made his way down from the smokehouse roof, cursed the rain under his breath, and looked for a safe route that would get him closer to the cabin.

In town, the lobby of the bank was empty except for the man pacing near the entrance. Outside, the windblown rain had filled the street, making it look as if a small river was running through Gila Bend.

Axel Taylor was silently watching the downpour when Darla emerged from her office. "I guess the farmers are going to be happy, if they don't get washed away," she said.

The look she saw on the elder Taylor's face quickly told her he was not interested in discussing the weather.

"What's wrong?" she said.

"My boy just asked that I come and see that you're doing okay."

Her voice was firmer when she asked a second time, "What's wrong, Axel?"

He stared into the rain for several seconds in an attempt to avoid facing her. "The fellow who kidnapped you, he's come back . . . and I think Lewis has gone to settle things with him."

Darla clutched a fist to her mouth, then moved it to her side. "Where?"

"He wouldn't say, but I'm guessing he's gone out to the farm."

"Alone?" Before he could reply, she was out the front door and into the rain, running toward the sheriff's office. Axel pulled his hat tight onto his head and followed.

Milton Barnes was surprised to see them sloshing through the water, nearing his door. He met Darla on the sidewalk and handed her his slicker. Then he reached out to help Axel up the steps. As he hurried them inside, he said, "If somebody's robbing the bank, there's no need to worry. They'll drown before they can get out of town."

"It's Lewis," she said. "He went looking for . . ."

Sheriff Barnes finished her sentence. "El Diablo."

Axel nodded. "I think he's out at the farm."

"He went alone," Darla said. "You've got to get out there."

Barnes went to the window and saw that the rain was coming down even harder and the wind had ripped part of the roof off the saloon. A wagon had toppled on its side in front of the feedstore. Gila Bend looked like a ghost town.

"There's no way to go anywhere until this storm eases," he said. Darla was fighting back tears.

Lewis slowly made his way toward the creek, hoping to position himself in back of El Diablo. The banks were already overflowing, and tree limbs and other debris floated past in the rushing water. Though he had stood in this very spot hundreds of times as a boy, hunting squirrels or fishing for carp, he could only guess that he had reached the spot he wanted. His boyhood "climbing tree" should have been nearby and would provide an ideal perch from which to locate El Diablo.

Even after he made his way up his old rope ladder and onto one of the higher limbs, he could see little. The rain had formed a dense curtain that blocked out everything.

El Diablo had also been on the move,

carefully advancing toward the cabin. If Lewis Taylor was inside, waiting, he was perfectly willing to engage in an exchange of gunfire. All patience had been washed away by the unrelenting storm. If he never saw rain again, El Diablo thought, he would die a happy man.

Once on the porch, he listened for a moment and thought he could hear a faint noise, almost a whining sound. Pistol cocked and pointed, he kicked open the front door and fired a shot aimed into the darkness. Standing in the middle of the room was a dog, teeth bared and no longer whining. Otherwise, the cabin was empty.

El Diablo tossed one of Axel's boots at Whisper, sending the dog back to his hiding place. Then he took advantage of being out of the rain to find something to dry himself. He kept watch from the front door as he used a kitchen towel to wipe his face and get the mud from his boots. Hanging on a peg near the door were an old rain slicker and a dry hat, and he put them on.

Still near the creek, Lewis heard the shot and assumed El Diablo was now close to the cabin.

Moving quickly to the ground, he found shelter beneath an oak tree on the edge of the garden. He had a decent view of the cabin, just twenty yards away, and aimed his rifle at the doorway. The thought flashed through his mind that Whisper was inside, and he needed to be careful that a stray shot didn't hit him.

Lewis aimed toward the roof and fired a warning shot. "Might as well show yourself," he called out. "There's only one way out."

A flash of lightning suddenly lit the yard, and he could see El Diablo running toward the barn, his pistol drawn. He fired a rapid series of shots in the direction of Lewis's voice. One buried itself into the trunk of the tree. The others kicked up small sprays of water in the garden.

Taylor knew if El Diablo reached the barn he would gain the advantage, and he was sorry he had left the door open after putting Dolly inside.

The standoff was about to begin.

Climbing the ladder into the loft, El Diablo moved to the small door that was already ajar. He was glad to again be out of the downpour and to have a vantage point that allowed him to look out on the entire yard. Despite the rain, he had a decent view of the tree Taylor was kneeling behind.

For the next half hour, they exchanged gunfire, doing no damage. Neither man, it seemed, knew what to do next.

Drenched and cold, trapped in his hiding place, Lewis tried to think of a plan. If he could get to the barn, there was ample cover inside. It would even things up, leaving the final result to the better shot. He decided it was a risky idea. Though the rain might provide some cover, he was looking at too much open ground to successfully make the run.

Finally, after several more harmless exchanges, Mother Nature played an unexpected role. A jagged bolt of lightning struck the roof of the barn just above where El Diablo was seated. Smoldering boards fell around him onto a bed of loose hay. Soon, there was smoke, then fire.

El Diablo removed his slicker and began frantically swatting at the flames but only succeeded in scattering embers throughout the loft. Lewis, meanwhile, peppered the open window with shots as smoke began to boil from the upper level of the old building. El Diablo deserted the loft and hurried down the ladder, the flames close behind him.

The rain did little to halt the blaze being spread by the howling wind. Coughing and blinded by smoke, El Diablo was suddenly knocked to the ground. Dolly, having broken out of her stall, was racing to the open doorway. Lewis was pleased to see her emerge safely, shaking her head vigorously as the rain pelted her. Soon, he knew, El Diablo would follow if he didn't want to be burned to death.

He ventured from behind the tree and began slowly walking toward the barn. Leaving his rifle behind, he had his pistol drawn and pointed toward the blaze. An eerie glow now brightened the storm-darkened yard.

Taylor was close enough to feel the fire's heat when he saw El Diablo stumble through the door. One leg of his britches was smoldering, and the smoke was making him cough violently. He had his pistol pointed toward Lewis.

Neither said anything before they began to shoot.

Lewis felt a burning pain in his shoulder as El Diablo's first shot connected. Yet before El Diablo could cock and fire again, Lewis's return shot thudded into the other man's chest. A second one hit him high in the leg, knocking him to the ground. Lewis continued to shoot as he moved forward, watching El Diablo's body jerk grotesquely as each bullet hit its mark.

El Diablo was facedown in a large puddle, the only sign of life the slight trembling of the hand that had once held his pistol.

Lewis stepped closer and placed his boot against the back of El Diablo's neck, forcing his face deeper into the muddy water.

Finally, it was over, he thought.

As he lifted his face skyward into the cool rain, Lewis didn't see the dying El Diablo reach into his boot and draw the same knife that had killed Captain Ringewald and his guards. Shakily, El Diablo rose to his knees and began swinging the blade wildly. Failing to reach Lewis's throat, he managed only to open a lengthy gash on Taylor's already wounded shoulder. As he began to lose consciousness and fall away, he plunged the blade deep into Lewis's thigh.

Enraged, Taylor fired his last shot into El Diablo's face from point-blank range. With a final shudder, the knife slipped from El Diablo's hand. He was dead. Now it was over.

Lewis attempted to pull the knife away but suddenly lacked the strength. He felt sick to his stomach, and everything around him began to spin wildly. His eyes rolled back, and he went to his knees, then fell across El Diablo's body.

It was late afternoon before the storm passed, and Sheriff Barnes and Axel were able to travel to the farm. As they neared, they could see smoke drifting into the now clear sky and hurried their horses along.

It was Axel who first saw the bodies lying near the smoldering remains of the barn. Dolly and Whisper, both wet and mud spattered, waited nearby as if standing guard. "Oh, my God," the elder Taylor said as he quickly dismounted.

The first thing he saw was the great amount of blood, diluted by the rain and mud. Kneeling next to the bodies, he gently rolled his son over and put an ear close to his face. After several seconds, he thought he heard Lewis expel a faint breath. Then another that was a bit stronger. And finally, a low groan.

"He's alive," Axel said. "He's in bad shape, but he's alive." He looked at the knife that still protruded from Lewis's thigh and worried that if he attempted to remove it he might cause further bleeding.

"Let's let Doc Johnson make that decision," the sheriff said. "Best we can do for him now is get him inside, where it's dry and warm." He looked toward the barn and saw that Axel's wagon had been destroyed by the fire. "There's no way we can get him to town on horseback. You stay here, and I'll go fetch the doc."

Dolly and Whisper followed along as the

men gently carried Lewis to the cabin.

When they reached the porch, Barnes turned to look back at El Diablo's lifeless body. "Finally," he said. "I just wish it could have been me who put you down."

It was almost a week before Lewis regained full consciousness. For a time he slept restlessly, mumbling words that were mostly nonsense. He kept calling for B. J., insisting that the pigs needed to be fed, and instructed someone he called Billy Wayne to saddle Dolly so he could take a ride. He kept asking if the rain had stopped, and on one occasion, Darla thought she heard him say her name.

Whisper dutifully stayed at the foot of the bed, pleased to hear his voice no matter what he was saying.

Upon his arrival at the Taylor farm, Doc Johnson had removed the knife after applying a tourniquet to control the bleeding. He then cleansed both knife wounds, applied a generous amount of sulfur powder, and stitched them. The good news, he said, was that there appeared to be no serious muscle or artery damage. There was no bullet to remove from the shoulder since it had cleanly exited just below Lewis's collarbone. The wound also required disinfectant and stitches.

"Most likely, he'll sleep for quite a while," the doctor said, "but should he wake up, I'd prescribe a couple of good shots of whiskey. He's going to be in considerable pain."

Darla, who had insisted on accompanying the doctor, applied cool towels to Lewis's brow in an effort to bring down his fever. When the doctor said it would be unwise to move him for a few days, she informed Axel he would be having a houseguest.

Sheriff Barnes put an arm across Axel's shoulders. "I know you're worried," he said, "but looks like he's going to be fine. Probably won't be any blacksmithing for a while, and he might need to take lessons from B. J. about getting around on a crutch, but soon enough he'll be good as new." He looked into the eyes of the worried father. "What your boy just did will make him a hero in the eyes of a lot of folks. The world just became a better place with the killing of El Diablo."

"Amen to that," Darla said from her bedside post.

When Barnes returned to town, he instructed a couple of his deputies to go to the farm and remove El Diablo's body. He sent a telegram to the Eagle Pass sheriff, telling him of the famed bandito's death and asking what he wanted him to do about the body.

A few days later, two young men arrived and took El Diablo away. Barnes didn't bother explaining how he had died. Nor did he understand everything they were saying in their broken English, but it had something to do with a *muy grande* cockfight that would soon be held in the deceased's honor.

The first thing Lewis saw when he finally opened his eyes was Darla smiling at him. She leaned forward and kissed his forehead. "How are you feeling?" she said.

"I hurt all over."

"I can't imagine why," she said. "You only got shot and stabbed."

Lewis had only a vague recollection of how the gun battle had ended. "Is he dead?"

"Yes, he's dead. It's finally over, just as you promised it would be, though I must say it took you long enough."

Lewis attempted a laugh, but when he did, the pain in his shoulder forced him to grit his teeth instead. He then asked again if the rain had finally stopped.

"The sky is blue, and the sun is shining brightly," Darla said.

Through the nearby window, he could hear voices and the sounds of hammering.

"What's going on out there?" he said.

"You're missing out on the raising of a new barn," she said. "Everybody in Gila Bend is here."

He leaned his head back on the pillow, closed his eyes, and smiled.

It felt good to be home.

Chapter Thirty-Two

In the days that followed, business was brisk at the livery. Lewis, still unable to fully use his left arm and getting around with the aid of a crutch, watched as his father took care of his customers. Meanwhile, he tried with little success to maintain a low profile. It wasn't easy after the story Luke Bradley wrote for the *Sentinel.* "The Storm Is Over," the headline read, and with Sheriff Barnes's full cooperation, he detailed the tangled history of El Diablo, Captain Ringewald, Taylor, and the community of Gila Bend. Grudgingly, Lewis shared what he could recall from when El Diablo died during the heaviest rainfall in the county's history. It was the most dramatic story Bradley had ever written. It took up all of the space in his paper and, unlike those written by big-city reporters, was as true as he could make it.

Townspeople who rarely had reason to

visit the livery stopped in just to shake Lewis's hand. The sheriff passed along a letter of commendation that had been sent by the governor.

Needing to stay close to Doc Johnson while he healed, Lewis settled in Ezzie's old sleeping room despite Darla's suggestion that he move into her father's bedroom at her house. Instead, she stopped in several times a day to check on him. Daisy Dixon brought him a slice of pie every morning.

Reverend Daniels came by to invite him to attend Sunday's service at the Blessed Redeemer. He said he was preparing a special sermon about a courageous man who led his flock from the wilderness.

Even some hands from the Rocking R rode in to see how he was doing, though Lewis suspected their main purpose was to make sure repairs on the saloon roof were nearing completion.

Sheriff Barnes came only once more, to let him know that he had decided to announce his retirement. "Things have gotten too quiet," he said. "And I've gotten too old."

One early evening, as they sat on the bench out front enjoying the sunset, Lewis asked a favor of his father.

"Do you think sometime soon you might

cook up that brisket and make some potato salad? Maybe a jar of sweet tea?"

Axel looked at his son and smiled.

"I think it's time I go on that picnic."

ACKNOWLEDGMENTS

A heartfelt thanks to Berkley editor Jennifer Snyder for her patient guidance and encouragement. Having friends like Spur Award winner Jeff Guinn, A. C. Greene Award recipient James Ward Lee, and the lady of the house, Pat Stowers, reading along kept the project moving. And, as always, agent Jim Donovan was there when called upon.

Ralph Compton, I'm honored to follow in your footsteps.

ABOUT THE AUTHORS

Ralph Compton stood six foot eight without his boots. He worked as a musician, a radio announcer, a songwriter, and a newspaper columnist. His first novel, *The Goodnight Trail,* was a finalist for the Western Writers of America Medicine Pipe Bearer Award for best debut novel. He was the *USA Today* bestselling author of the Trail of the Gunfighter series, the Border Empire series, the Sundown Riders series, and the Trail Drive series, among others.

Carlton Stowers is an award-winning journalist and the author of more than two dozen books, including *Comanche Trail,* which was named a finalist for both the Western Fictioneers and the Texas Institute of Letters best first novel awards. He lives in Cedar Hill, Texas.

The employees of Thorndike Press hope you have enjoyed this Large Print book. All our Thorndike, Wheeler, and Kennebec Large Print titles are designed for easy reading, and all our books are made to last. Other Thorndike Press Large Print books are available at your library, through selected bookstores, or directly from us.

For information about titles, please call:
(800) 223-1244

or visit our website at:
gale.com/thorndike

To share your comments, please write:
Publisher
Thorndike Press
10 Water St., Suite 310
Waterville, ME 04901